MW01087501

Also by Kate Parker

The Victorian Bookshop Mysteries

The Vanishing Thief

The Counterfeit Lady

The Royal Assassin

The Conspiring Woman

The Detecting Duchess

The Milliner Mysteries

The Killing at Kaldaire House

Murder at the Marlowe Club

The Deadly Series

Deadly Scandal

Deadly Wedding

Deadly Fashion

Deadly Deception

The Mystery at Chadwick House

MURDER AT THE MARLOWE CLUB

Kate Parker

JDP Press

Murder at the Marlowe Club copyright © 2020 by Kate Parker

ISBN: 978-1-7332294-0-1 {ebook}

ISBN: 978-1-7332294-1-8 {print}

Published by JDP Press

Cover design by Lyndsey Lewellen of Lewellen Designs

Dedication:

To my Mom, still the queen of the one-line zingers at 97.
To my children, who light up my life.
To John, forever.

London, 1905

Chapter One

I shivered in the damp early morning chill and plodded on to the park gate. The park was private, but I knew if I squeezed around the gate at the corner of the square and cut diagonally across, I could save myself a three-minute walk. It was too early for anyone but servants to be out. No one would catch me trespassing.

I looked both ways. No bobbies. No one at all. Only a cat hiding under the cover of a wheelbarrow. Everyone was wisely indoors, where I would be if I didn't have a hat to deliver to a fussy baronet's wife. And collect my fee from her unwilling fingers.

Once inside the dripping gate, soaking one glove in the process, I hurried past the cat and the wheelbarrow, the formal flower beds with their tiny plants, and the benches soaked with rain. I kept my gaze firmly fixed in the direction of the gazebo in the center of the park where the paths met. I hoped I looked like I belonged here.

Only householders on this square in Mayfair had keys to this park. The rest of us, middle class included, were expected to walk around the edges of the square, outside the wrought-iron fence.

A gust of wind nearly took my umbrella into a clump of bushes, pelting my face with raindrops. Grumbling, I marched on.

Why did Lady Meacham insist on having her new hat delivered this morning of all mornings? I doubted she'd wear it today. I was having enough trouble keeping the box dry under my umbrella. Even the protection of a carriage would not guarantee the hat's survival if she chose to wear it in this steady rain.

No committee meeting or good deed session could possibly warrant my trip through this foul weather. Worse, the new hat would have to be adjusted to her hairdo once I arrived at her home. Did she think that demanding I go out in this weather to fit her hat was a good way to get me to forget the money she owed me? Did she think in the Year of our Lord 1905 that tradesmen in a cosmopolitan city like London would wait for their fee as if they were medieval serfs?

Fuming, I had nearly reached the gazebo when I spotted what at first appeared to be a bundle of brightly colored rags. Then I saw a pale hand and arm sticking out from the garish garments.

Lady Meacham vanished from my mind as I hurried to the round bench in the center of the shelter. A woman, her hair in disarray, lay sprawled on the bench. Rust-colored blood streaked outward from under the pink scarf that encircled her neck.

She was dressed in a red-striped satin and white lace garment that was little more than a corset. Under and around her was wrapped a pale green satin cape that covered her limbs except for the hand and arm I'd noticed and her bare feet. The woman, whoever she was, wore neither shoes nor stockings.

Poor wretch. She looked to be in her mid-twenties. My age. I knew how dangerous London could be for any young woman, no matter how careful and respectable.

I suspected she was a lady of the night, although why would she be out on the streets barefoot? And what was she doing in this private park? Even high-class kept women wouldn't be allowed in this park. They wouldn't dress the way this woman was dressed, either.

I reached out to take her hand to see if there was life in the body. It was as cold as the morning, but dry. Her cape was also dry.

My curiosity would count for nothing if I were caught with this murder victim. My reputation would dissolve in tatters, and my business, Duquesne's, milliner to the aristocracy, would fail.

I went in search of a bobby.

I retraced my steps, past the cat and the wheelbarrow, and out the gate. I saw a bobby at a distance and hurried toward him, my umbrella pulled this way and that by the wind. At the next corner, I nearly collided with Betsy, a maid who worked for Lady Kaldaire.

She fumbled her shopping basket and came close to dumping the day's bread on the ground. I grabbed the basket to keep it from falling while holding on to the hatbox and clutching my umbrella. Betsy rescued the loaves of bread.

"Miss Gates, where are you going in such a rush?" Betsy asked as she caught the bread and her breath.

"To find a bobby. There's a dead woman in the park." A shiver wracked my body as a stream of water from her umbrella hit my shoe. The words came out before I thought.

By the look in her widened eyes, I realized I should have kept that knowledge to myself. "Oh, my goodness," she exclaimed as she ran toward Lady Kaldaire's. Once again, the basket threatened to tip over as it swung with each step.

The bobby reached me as I dashed toward him into the street. "Good morning, miss. Watch out for traffic."

"There's a body in the middle of the park."

"A body? You mean, a dead body?" he asked. He appeared both young and astounded, but with enough presence of mind to turn so the rain stopped striking his reddened face. "Who is it, miss?"

"I don't know who she is. It's a woman, and she's— well, you need to see her yourself."

"Come along with me, miss," the bobby said, now sounding gruff and in command. The wide eyes in his young face ruined any impression he might have tried to make.

I hurried down the block to the gate, the constable right behind me. When I wiggled through the metal bars, he stopped me.

"Did you enter here illegally?" he asked, now trying to sound stern.

"Of course not," I said with the haughtiness I'd learned

from my clients. "The body is in the gazebo."

He gave me a skeptical look, but he maneuvered his larger frame through the gate and followed me. When we reached the edge of the pavilion, he stopped, getting dripped on. I stepped onto the paving under the gazebo for cover from the rain and set my umbrella to the side.

"You shouldn't do that, miss. Nobody should get too close until my sergeant says you can," the bobby said.

"I've already been closer than this when I first found her. I'd hoped to find warmth or a pulse on her wrist, but she was as cold as the grave." I glanced at the leaden sky. "Besides, I don't like getting rained on." Already, my shoes and the hem of my skirt were soggy. At least the hat box was still dry.

"What happened to her?" he asked as he stared at the woman, twisting his hands and breathing shallowly. I suspected he'd never seen a dead body before that wasn't decently coffined. "Did she freeze to death with her feet bare?"

"That looks like a gash and blood coming from under the scarf around her neck," I told him.

The bobby leaned closer to peer at the streaks. He blanched before saying, "Don't touch anything while I call for help." Then he ran back the way we'd come, blowing his whistle in short bursts.

It wasn't long before he returned with two other bobbies and Lady Kaldaire, who was carrying a large ring of keys in her hand. At my surprise on seeing her, she said, "Someone had to open the gate to let them in. What is this about a dead woman?" She stepped closer. "And why is she dressed like that?"

"I don't know." That was for certain.

Lady Kaldaire shook her head and clucked her tongue. "Poor creature. How did she die?"

"I think perhaps her neck was sliced and the wound covered with the scarf," I told her. "That's a great deal of dried blood on the scarf. Perhaps she was murdered elsewhere and then her body moved. There's no blood on the paving under the bench," I pointed out.

Lady Kaldaire turned to the closest bobby. "You should inform Detective Inspector Russell of Scotland Yard to come and investigate this crime. Tell him Lady Kaldaire specifically requests his presence."

"My lady, I don't—"

"Did you not hear me? Go."

The bobbies looked at each other and then the one Lady Kaldaire had spoken to left. Meanwhile, I was glad no one was looking at me. Inspector Russell, James when we were alone, had taken a few dinners with my family since we caught the man who killed Lord Kaldaire.

Then James was sent to Manchester for two weeks, and I hadn't seen him since.

I could tell by the heat on my face while the rest of me was chilled that I must be blushing.

Lady Kaldaire joined me under the roof of the gazebo. She furled her umbrella and leaned on it before she looked me square in the eye and said, "It's early to be paying calls. Who is the hat for?"

I knew better than to avoid answering. "Lady Meacham."

With a disapproving sniff, Lady Kaldaire said, "That woman is getting above herself. She's only a baronet's wife. And this woman…"

Lady Kaldaire took a closer look at the dead woman and became so still and pale I was afraid she would faint.

"My lady, are you unwell?" I asked.

"I'm perfectly fine, thank you." She appeared to study the bare branches of a nearby bush, her chest sharply rising and falling despite her corset, but I felt I could hear gears spinning to life inside her gray-and-brown-haired head. Others might think of her as an insignificant widow dressed completely in black and veils, but I knew better.

"What is it?" I murmured.

"What is what?"

"What is bothering you? Do you know her?"

Lady Kaldaire looked down her long nose at me. "Why would you ask if I know a common trollop?"

"She's not a common trollop. Look at her hands. Perhaps someone stole her clothes."

The bobbies heard me and came over to stand by the body. The younger one, who'd come into the park with me, examined both her hands. "No calluses. She's never worked a day in her life."

"It's her back that should be calloused," the other bobby said with a smirk. Then he glanced at Lady Kaldaire, who was glaring arrows at him, and turned beet red. Taking a step back as he was dripped on by a tree branch, he said, "Beggin' your pardon, my lady."

"I'm middle class and I have calluses," I told the bobby who'd examined the woman's hands. "My nails aren't cut and buffed as beautifully as hers. The only women with hands like that are in the aristocracy." Then I turned and looked at Lady Kaldaire. "Do you recognize her?"

"What a monstrous thing to say." She turned away, her chin elevated.

"I'm sure her family is searching for her. They must be worried sick." The dead woman was too old to be a debutante, but aristocrats of all ages attended the numerous balls held in London every spring. This was the beginning of the mating season for aristocrats, as single women presented at court searched for a suitable husband.

The beginning of the Season, when aristocrats who'd been at their country estates since last August returned to London and required new wardrobes. My thoughts slid off in a new direction. New wardrobes necessitated new hats. Milliners like me were kept busy and thankful.

I glanced at Lady Kaldaire and the bobbies. I was wasting valuable time. I had hats to design back at my shop.

"I'm sure her family is not searching for her," Lady Kaldaire snapped at me.

That sounded odd, but she seemed sure. "How can you be certain?"

Her arms folded over her chest, Lady Kaldaire stared once more at the body. "Because I know the family. It's Lady Theodore Hughes. The notorious Roxanne."

Now the bobbies and I stared open-mouthed. They must have read the same gossip I had in the penny press. All London had heard of the notorious Lady Theodore

Hughes, or the notorious Lady Roxanne, as the scandal rags called her.

Chapter Two

I'd read in the papers that Roxanne Starley had a reputation for daring, for being unconventional, before she'd married Lord Theodore Hughes, second son of the Duke of Wallingford. He'd had a reputation for being a rogue before the wedding. Together they'd become the center of scandal. No wonder Lady Kaldaire wasn't eager to acknowledge her acquaintance.

I'd heard it said theirs was a match made in a gin-soaked brothel. Personally, I didn't believe that piece of gossip. No lady of the night would pass the inspection of a duke's family before the wedding. And no duke's son would marry without the family's approval, not if he wanted to keep his allowance.

Roxanne, now Lady Theodore Hughes, the daughter of a now-deceased wealthy brewer, barely made the cut for a younger son.

The gossip, murmured behind the hands of my customers before the wedding, had grown since that date nearly two years before. Drunken carriage races through the streets. Rumors of group sex, drug usage, and huge debts. Tales of massive family rows.

The scandalmonger newspapers had happy days covering the rumors. Then a month ago, Lord Theodore died. The proper newspapers reported his death as due to an accident. The scandal rags suggested poison. Drugs. Dark secrets.

Within a day, Scotland Yard declared there was no reason for an investigation. No autopsy was performed. The lower-class penny newspapers suggested, keeping just this side of the law, that Scotland Yard had been bought off.

All London read the stories with self-righteous glee.

"I've never seen her except for some terrible photographs in the newspapers. Had you ever met her?" I asked Lady Kaldaire.

"Yes."

Her tone was so bitter that I couldn't help but ask, "What happened?"

She gave me a scathing look. "What didn't happen? I'm an old friend of Theo's mother, Lulu. She has rapidly aged as the family name has been dragged through the mud by these—horrid events. Then Theo died and she has taken to her bed. She's devastated."

"Now there will be the publicity of a murder in the family. Poor woman." I felt truly sorry for Lord Theodore's mother. To be made a victim of curiosity and ridicule in the press as well as to lose a son.

"Can we not disguise her cause of death?" Lady Kaldaire asked me as well as the constables.

The bobbies and I said "No" in unison. Someone had tried to disguise the cut across her neck with a scarf, but it wasn't sufficient to hide the wound or the blood stains.

"Please, do not give the newspapers a reason to look

into this death," Lady Kaldaire asked.

"Too late," I murmured. Bobbies came into the park with a camera and supplies to cordon off the gazebo, followed by some men in regular wear and carrying umbrellas. I focused on one of them. Detective Inspector James Russell.

I felt my heart flutter. I dared not call out to him, as much as I wanted to. Lady Kaldaire had no such restraint. "Good. Inspector Russell, I'm glad you're here. This needs to be kept quiet. The Duchess of Wallingford has suffered enough." She used the same tone of voice the old queen, Victoria, must have used on her dimmer servants.

Russell said something to the men he was with and then came over to us under the gazebo roof. "My lady, Miss Gates, you shouldn't be here. This is the scene of a crime."

"Emily found the body. And I have identified the woman."

Russell looked at the clothing on the victim and said, "Really?" in an amazed tone.

"She's Lady Theodore Hughes, widow of the second son of the Duke of Wallingford. Also called the notorious Lady Roxanne." Lady Kaldaire spoke as if the words were foul tasting in her mouth.

He looked closer. "You're joking."

"Rest assured, Inspector, I do not joke about such matters." Lady Kaldaire gave him a withering glare.

Russell seemed immune to such looks. "Thank you for your information. Now, if you ladies will go about your day out of the rain, we will take care of this unfortunate business. I will interview both of you at your residences later. Ladies." He tipped his bowler to us and then handed us down from the gazebo.

The step was only a few inches. I suspected he did that to send Lady Kaldaire on her way. In my case, he gave my hand a squeeze and whispered, "Later."

We locked gazes for a moment, and then Inspector Russell turned to his men and started issuing orders as he moved forward to examine the body.

I looked away with a sigh.

As I turned toward the far gate, the hat box kept safely under my umbrella, Lady Kaldaire said, "Emily, I want you to come with me to Wallingford House. It would be unkind to let strangers descend on Lulu without her being prepared for the shock."

"I have to deliver this hat first." I didn't want to risk it getting soaked and ruined. I didn't want to waste my time making it twice.

"Lady Meacham is not as important as the Duchess of Wallingford," she said, keeping up with me on the path.

"I have some idea of the order of precedence and how the wife of a younger son of a duke should be addressed. However, neither the Duchess nor Lady Theodore—can I call her Roxanne between the two of us?"

"No." Lady Kaldaire sounded horrified.

"Neither woman owes me money for this hat and a couple of others," I said in a snippy tone.

"Emily, you're being very middle class."

"I am middle class. And I have next semester's fees to pay for Matthew at the Doncaster School for the Deaf." My little brother had been deafened at the age of eight by the same fever that carried away our mother. Now that he was fourteen, I had finally raised the funds to send him away for a better education than he could get locally.

"If you're quite determined to go to Lady Meacham's first, I'll go with you. Then we can go together to break the news to Lulu about her son's wife." Lady Kaldaire used her lady-of-the-manor tone as she unlocked the gate for me.

I didn't want two of us to show up on Lady Meacham's front steps, our skirts and shoes soaked, but disagreement was futile. I'd dealt with Lady Kaldaire long enough to know when to save my breath.

Lady Meacham looked horrified as she faced the two of us dripping in her front hallway. Nevertheless, she greeted Lady Kaldaire effusively, sent her girl for tea and, with the aid of another maid, arranged her small yellow and blue morning room with a large looking glass so I could properly set her hat on her hairdo.

"Lady Kaldaire, what brings you out so early on such a dismal day?" Lady Meacham asked as she studied her reflection in a second looking glass that the maid held. "I think the hat needs to be at more of an angle to the left. Thank goodness you kept the hat dry."

My feet were soaked, but I knew what mattered to these ladies, and it wasn't my health.

As I adjusted the wide-brimmed, pink-flowered and feathered afternoon hat suitable for a summer picnic, Lady Kaldaire said, "Emily found herself in difficulty while bringing you the hat. My maid saw her and told me, and I went out to assist her."

I saw Lady Meacham's reflection in the glass watching

me with skepticism. "What sort of bother?"

"I found a body and was searching for a constable."

"A body? A dead body? In our neighborhood?" came out in a screech. Lady Meacham turned in the chair, nearly knocking her hat off. "Who was it?"

"I don't know. I'd never seen the woman before."

I saw Lady Kaldaire frown as I answered.

The tea tray arrived and I waited until my customer had poured and we'd had a chance to enjoy a sip before I went back to work. Then Lady Meacham continued to question me. "A woman? Not a respectable woman, I gather."

That was a harder question to answer without giving away the woman's identity. And from the look Lady Kaldaire was giving me, that was not a question I should reply to. "I don't know."

"Now, don't keep me in suspense. Surely you could tell from her dress." Lady Meacham used her usual demanding tone.

"Her clothing was partially missing. She was barefoot, for one thing, and no woman would ever go out like that. Particularly in this weather." I had been questioned enough. "That looks excellent."

Lady Meacham studied her reflection from different angles. "Yes, it does."

"The hat is one pound eight, please." It was expensive, but she'd wanted a great quantity of flowers and feathers perched on her head.

I wanted to ask her for her past-due payment as well, but I didn't think embarrassing her in front of Lady

Kaldaire would accomplish any good.

Lady Meacham looked as if she wanted to debate the price of her hat. She reddened under Lady Kaldaire's gaze as she walked to a lovely credenza and fished out money to put in my hand.

I checked to make sure it was the correct amount before dropping it into my bag. "Thank you. Now, I really must get back to the shop. Are you walking with me, Lady Kaldaire?"

"Yes. I'm sure Lady Meacham has things to do wearing that beautiful hat. Good day." With a regal tilt to her head, Lady Kaldaire set down her fragile teacup and saucer and walked out of the cheery room. I caught up to her in time to retrieve my outerwear and umbrella and ready myself to escape into the rain.

"Now, Lady Kaldaire, you will let me know if you hear any more about the tragedy in our neighborhood," Lady Meacham said from behind us as we hurried out the front door.

"Of course," and we were down the pavement before Lady Kaldaire added, "that is not at all likely." Then she turned to me. "We're going to the Duke of Wallingford's house. Someone has to soften the blow for poor Lulu."

"How can I help? I don't know the duchess." She wasn't a customer of mine, and I was unlikely to know her any other way.

"You found her son's widow's body. You can answer her questions. I learned how desperately I needed answers when you found Horace's body." She linked her arm in mine. "Come along, Emily."

I decided it wouldn't take long to satisfy the woman's curiosity and then I would be free to go back to work.

The Wallingford London house was on a corner across from the park where Lady Theodore's body was found. As we approached it, I noted the mews opening and the carriage house behind the back garden, the wide Georgian frontage of four stories, with an attic and basement no doubt reserved for the servants. A house worthy of a duke.

"Are you certain I should go with you?" I asked again as we crossed the street, hoping she had changed her mind.

"Yes." Lady Kaldaire marched up the stairs and rang the bell. When I lingered on the pavement, huddled under my umbrella, she added, "Come along, Emily."

I had reached the porch when the door was opened by a formally dressed butler.

"Lady Kaldaire, would you care to wait in the morning room out of the rain? The Duchess of Wallingford has not yet risen," he told her as he peered out at the street.

"She needs to. She's about to be given a nasty shock," Lady Kaldaire said as she stepped forward, forcing the butler out of her way. "Come along, Emily."

I followed her into the house, nodding to the butler.

"If your lady's maid would like to accompany me..."

"Miss Gates is not a lady's maid, and she is the one who discovered the body." Lady Kaldaire handed off her umbrella and headed up the stairs. "You may want to call for Her Grace's maid," she called over her shoulder.

"A body?" the butler asked, his face still an unflappable mask as he stood in place in the front hall. His eyes, however, showed his confusion.

I gave the butler my soaked umbrella and followed Lady Kaldaire. At that point, it felt like the best of a wealth of unpopular choices. She reached the first floor and headed down the hall while I rushed to catch up. She knocked on the last door and opened it.

As she walked forward, I lingered in the doorway. Heavy curtains covered the windows and the room was in a twilight darkness. "Lulu, you must get up. Emily, open the curtains."

When I didn't hear any disagreement from the person who was no more than a lump under the covers, I walked across the room and pulled the purple draperies open. The soft light of a rainy day filtered in through the lace curtains still covering the window glass.

A head lifted from the pillows. "Robbie, you are the most annoying, the most infuriating—"

"Get dressed. The police are on their way." Lady Kaldaire used a tone often employed on her servants or tradesmen. I stopped and stared at her when she had used it on me. The technique partially worked, as I wasn't addressed with that tone very often.

The woman sat up then, unfazed at being spoken to as if she were a scullery maid. She appeared to be Lady Kaldaire's age, with a thin face above her flannel nightgown. "The police? Why?"

"Roxanne is dead. Murdered."

Swinging her legs over the side of the bed, the woman said, "It's about time. Call my maid."

Chapter Three

"Lulu, don't say that to the police." Lady Kaldaire looked worried. I guessed Lulu, the Duchess of Wallingford, would make a good murder suspect with that attitude.

"I'm not that addled. Hemmings, get me dressed and then have tea and toast brought to the morning room." As the somberly dressed lady's maid entered the room and began laying out her clothes, the duchess said, "You remember where that is, Robbie?"

"Of course. It hasn't been that long since you stopped seeing all your old friends. Come along, Emily."

"Who are you?" the woman demanded, glaring at me as she noticed me for the first time. I could see now that her whole body was nothing but skin and bones.

"Emily Gates. I found the body."

"I'll speak to you shortly. Robbie, take her to the morning room."

We left the room and I saw Lady Kaldaire wore a smile on her face. As we walked downstairs, she said, "It's good to see Lulu rising from her bed and sounding more like the woman I know."

I'd never heard anyone call Lady Kaldaire "Robbie" before. It seemed so unlikely a nickname for the elegant older woman that I couldn't resist. "I'm glad to hear that, Robbie."

"You are not to repeat that ridiculous name. I am Roberta, Lady Kaldaire, and don't you forget it." She stomped ahead of me and opened a door on the right of a short hallway, nearly knocking aside a footman who reached out to turn the doorknob.

Lady Kaldaire and I had a strange relationship. From the moment we met over her husband's dying body, we had learned private things about each other. She had been known to tell me things in confidence, and she would listen to my advice, unlike any other relationship I'd heard of between aristocrat and shop owner. Still, there were certain things I could not do, even in jest. Calling her "Robbie" was added to the list of never-dos.

I followed her into a chilly room done in greens and blues. Her ladyship immediately sat near the cold, clean fireplace. A maid appeared a moment later, opening the curtains before laying a fire. When she left, I took a seat across from Lady Kaldaire, hoping the room would soon heat.

I decided I would allow myself a cup of tea while I told the duchess what I knew about the corpse, and then I would hurry back to the shop. I had customers to wait on and a living to earn.

That should be enough to satisfy Lady Kaldaire.

The duchess arrived before the room was warm, looking tired and wan but acting every inch an aristocrat. She sat in a chair by Lady Kaldaire. "We'll have tea and toast in a moment, but please, tell me what happened."

Lady Kaldaire nodded for me to begin.

"I was on an early delivery when—"

"Delivery?" the duchess asked.

"I'm a milliner. Duquesne's Millinery. I was asked by Lady Meacham to bring her new hat to her home and fit it to the hairstyle she planned to wear today."

"Lady Meacham." The Duchess of Wallingford gave a little snort and rolled her eyes. "Continue."

"I cut through the park—"

"Our private park?"

I nodded.

"Why?" She demanded. "You have no right to walk through there."

"It was raining and I was in a hurry." I spoke quietly, not wanting to start an argument I couldn't win. Lady Kaldaire reached out and touched her hand. The duchess nodded for me to continue. "I saw the woman I've learned was Lady Theodore Hughes lying on the bench in the gazebo in the center of the park. I couldn't do anything for her, so I found a constable."

"Presumably Scotland Yard is now involved." The Duchess of Wallingford slid a ring up and down a finger. I suspected it had fit at one time but now was too loose due to weight loss.

"Lady Kaldaire had a bobby summon the inspector who investigated her husband's murder," I told her.

She turned to Lady Kaldaire. "Can I trust this inspector's discretion?"

"He's the best of the bunch. And you can trust Emily's discretion, too."

The duchess held my gaze for a moment before she nodded. "So how did Roxanne die?"

"Her neck was sliced and whoever did it did a poor job covering the wound with a scarf," I said. My words hung in the silence.

"And then there is the matter of how she was dressed," Lady Kaldaire added.

When the Duchess of Wallingford looked puzzled, I described her costume. I ended with, "Was this something she sometimes wore?"

"Oh, I hope not. But barefoot? I never knew her to go out of her room without her shoes and stockings. She felt her limbs didn't look their best without at least a two-inch heeled shoe. She was quite vain about her appearance."

"Was she short?" I asked.

"A little taller than average, I suppose, but she wanted to be taller. Taller, more full-figured, blonder. Never did she indicate that she wanted to be a better person. A kinder, gentler, less selfish person."

"You've been through a trial," Lady Kaldaire said, taking one of the duchess's hands.

"But it's over. Someone has delivered me." The woman smiled.

"And they'll hang for it," I said to myself.

The duchess looked at me, and I knew I'd spoken too loudly. "They won't hang if I can help it. Killing her is like killing vermin." She looked as if she'd tasted a lemon.

Lady Kaldaire said, "If you want to keep this person from hanging, Emily and I will need to find out who it is so you can protect him."

Whoever this person was, he'd hang if I found out his identity. My mother had instilled in me an unshakable belief in obeying the law. She considered it protection against my father's family's lawlessness.

Somehow, I didn't think I'd better announce that here.

Both women would probably think of me as vermin after I asked this question, but I needed to know. "Why do you think Lady Theodore was murdered?"

The Duchess of Wallingford gazed on me with cold blue eyes as she said, "Because she killed Theo. Roxanne murdered my son and now she has paid."

I stared back. "His death was reported as an accident."

"We convinced the doctors no good would come of reporting his death as murder." She leaned forward and pointed a skeletal finger at my face. "Just as I wish you hadn't interfered and called for Scotland Yard. You could have told us, and we would have brought her back here and had our doctors sign her death certificate."

I had long suspected that with a title and money, people could get away with anything, including hiding the cause of death. Could they get away with murder?

There was a quiet thud and then a maid wheeled in the tea trolley. We sat in what I found was an uncomfortable silence while the duchess poured and offered us toast and jam.

"This is very good of you, Louisa. I've not yet eaten today," Lady Kaldaire said.

"Thank you very much, Your Grace," I murmured. Lady Kaldaire might think I was clever at solving murders after I found her husband's killer, but I didn't want to repeat the experience. Both Lady Kaldaire and I had nearly died trying to unmask Lord Kaldaire's murderer.

We ate in silence for a minute or two before Lady Kaldaire said, "What other questions do you have, Emily?"

I shook my head and swallowed a bite of toast. "None."

"Emily, we will be investigating this crime." There was steel in Lady Kaldaire's tone.

"The police have no interest in me for this crime. I don't see how I can add anything to the investigation. I can only offer my sympathy to the Duchess of Wallingford and step aside to let the police do their work."

"You don't need to worry about the police, Emily. You need to worry about your business." Lady Kaldaire stared at me.

I understood Lady Kaldaire's threat. She'd learned about my father's disreputable family. They were con men, thieves, burglars, swindlers. It didn't matter how good I was at making hats. No respectable woman would wear my designs if my family connections were whispered about. I would be out of business in a fortnight if Lady Kaldaire were to tell her friends and acquaintances.

It was a very effective threat. But why was she forcing me into this investigation? It made no sense. Glancing at the duchess, I said, "How was your son murdered, if his death wasn't due to an accident?"

"He was bashed on the back of the head by some unknown object while he walked along one of our upstairs hallways. I'm sure of it." Her voice was barely above a whisper.

It seemed an odd way to kill someone. "What time was

this?"

"It was in the middle of the night."

"Where did he live?"

"He and Roxanne lived under our roof. Had since they married. We thought it might settle down their excesses. Wretched woman."

"Do you have any evidence of who might have killed him?"

"Roxanne, obviously." Her tone was stronger now as she accused her son's wife.

"Did anyone witness this? Do you have any evidence? Or is your accusation due merely to your dislike of her?" I hoped if I forced her to examine her motives, she'd decide she didn't want my help and I would be free to get back to work without infuriating Lady Kaldaire.

The duchess glared at me. "You're impertinent."

"Do you really want to know who killed your son and his wife, or are you content to cast blame without any facts?" I was sailing close to being thrown out of the house, but I didn't care. The duchess wasn't a customer. And I didn't want to investigate another murder.

The duchess pointed at the door. "Leave. Now."

"Yes, Your Grace." I set down my cup and saucer and rose from my seat.

"No. Wait. Lulu. Wouldn't you feel better if you knew?" Lady Kaldaire said.

The duchess turned her ire on Lady Kaldaire. "It won't bring Theo back."

"It didn't bring Horace back, either, but I sleep better at night." Lady Kaldaire wanted to investigate this murder, but I had no idea why. To do this, she was willing to placate the duchess. And that meant she had to find a way to turn the duchess's temper away from anger and sorrow.

"Roxanne killed Theo. No one else would dream of doing such a thing to my sweet boy."

I doubted anyone who was struck over the head in a houseful of family was a "sweet boy."

I reached the door and glanced back. The two women were glaring at each other. I was forgotten. I opened the door and walked away.

The butler had my coat and umbrella for me and opened the front door. I stepped out into the path of Detective Inspector James Russell and a uniformed sergeant before I could get my umbrella open. I ducked under the protection of James's.

James tipped his hat. "Miss Gates, you've beaten me to the people I wish to speak to. Again." He didn't sound pleased.

I nodded to him, I hoped graciously. "Lady Kaldaire wished me to speak to the duchess and prepare her for the shock awaiting her."

"And where is Lady Kaldaire now?"

I opened my mouth to answer, but what I really wanted to do was ask when he could next have dinner above the hat shop with me and my family. "She's in the morning room with the Duchess of Wallingford."

James looked at the butler, standing in the open doorway. "Is the duke at home?" he asked as he showed his badge.

"The duke is in his study."

James gave an audible sigh of relief. "Could you please take us to him?" He again tipped his hat as he gave me a smile. Then he and the sergeant entered the house and the door was firmly shut against me.

I put up my umbrella, but not in time to save me from a moment of drowning.

Chapter Four

I spent most of the rest of the day in my shop, fitting and designing hats for my wealthy clients. Despite the damp, chilly weather, they kept arriving, wanting the latest in summery fashions. I even sold two hats from my inventory to a shop assistant and a clerk. My tired feet and I were looking forward to closing time when I heard a carriage pull up in front.

The bell over the door jingled. Both Jane, my shop assistant, and I looked toward the door of my finally empty shop. A mother and her daughter, who appeared to be about six years old, walked in. Their clothes proclaimed that the mother had good taste and the income to buy the best. With a shock, I recognized the mother's hat as having been created by the famous French milliner Caroline Reboux.

My surprise must have shown on my face, because the mother said, "Yes. I suspect you recognize a fellow designer's work."

"Oh, my. It's lovely." I hoped jealousy didn't show in my tone. "I'm Miss Emily Gates, designer for Duquesne's Millinery. How may I help you?"

"My daughter, Lady Juliet, needs a hat to wear to a birthday party for a little friend. I've brought a swatch of the material the dress is made of."

I nodded to the mother and said to the young girl, "Lady Juliet, if you would care to sit over here, we will be happy to measure your head and then we can look at some ideas for your hat. Will you be wearing your hair the way it is styled today?"

I seldom had customers this young, but when I did, they were almost all ladies. Therefore, her father must be at least an earl.

The child looked at her mother with a puzzled face and clutched her doll closer to her.

The mother said, "Yes, I think your hair looks good in braids."

The child faced me then and nodded. She climbed into the chair and Jane began the measurements around her crown, down to her ears, and from the top to under her chin. I had just turned to the mother to ask about styles when Annie, our eight-year-old apprentice, burst in from the storeroom behind the shop.

Seeing customers, she froze. Then she saw Lady Juliet and smiled. Lady Juliet, seeing her in the mirror, smiled in return.

"Lady Juliet, this is my apprentice, Annie." Annie took a half step backward as if preparing to flee. "Annie, would you go into the storeroom and bring me the smallest size of the flat crown bonnet, the ribbon back bonnet, and the empire lace bonnet?"

Annie nodded and hurried away.

"These are just plain examples of the three most popular styles for young ladies. We can do any of them in any color and with any trim," I told the mother.

"I've spoken to Lady Kaldaire," the mother replied in a soft voice.

My stomach dropped. I couldn't afford to turn away customers, particularly if they paid on time, but I didn't appreciate gaining customers simply because they were interested in having the best gossip in their social circle.

Before I could say anything, she continued, "Lady Kaldaire knows that before I married, I was involved in investigations of a criminal nature."

My jaw dropped and my eyes widened before I forced my expression into a calm mask. "I'm afraid I don't even know your name, Your Ladyship."

The woman gave her daughter a reassuring smile before she turned to face me. She was about average height and had the same reddish hair that I possess. Not what I'd expect of the higher ranks of the aristocracy, who all seemed to me to be blond and washed-out. "Before I became the Duchess of Blackford, I was Miss Georgia Fenchurch of Fenchurch's Books. I was a member of the Archivist Society."

"Does the Archivist Society want to assist Lady Kaldaire with her investigation?" I could see hope for avoiding this insanity.

"I'm afraid the Archivist Society disbanded after I, and then the cofounder, Sir Broderick, married, and I became a mother. Our lives changed. We're just friends now. None of us have carried out an investigation in six years."

I had no idea who these people were, but my hope vanished into the damp spring air. There was no longer an

Archivist Society to aid Lady Kaldaire and get her off my back.

There was no enthusiasm in my tone when I said, "What can I do for you, Your Grace?"

"I was thinking I could be of some assistance to you. I ran my bookshop for many years until I married. I know how much time an investigation takes up. I don't think Lady Kaldaire appreciates your sacrifice."

I was saved from responding as Annie came back into the shop carrying the three models. At my nod, she set them out on the big central table.

The duchess walked over to them, and then glanced at Lady Juliet. When Jane told the girl she could get down, she hopped down and rushed to her mother.

They quickly agreed on the flat crown bonnet. "I want bows and flowers," Lady Juliet said.

Her mother glanced at me.

"This is a style that welcomes bows and flowers. Just how much depends on the fabric chosen and how much your mother intends to spend."

The duchess had brought with her a swatch of fine wool, soft as a baby's blanket. Using the piece of deep green material, we matched the color to velvet and silk ribbons. This was becoming an expensive hat. When I mentioned a price, the duchess blanched before she glanced at her daughter, who wore a hopeful expression, and nodded.

As I started to sketch my idea for the duchess, Annie inched a little nearer to Lady Juliet. "Your dolly is beautiful."

"This is Mrs. Peeples," Lady Juliet said in a serious tone. "She's dressed like my governess."

Indeed, the doll's clothes and hat were made in exquisite detail. She must have cost five times what the child's hat would cost her mother.

"May I show her Eliza?" Annie asked in a whisper.

"Of course."

Annie ran off, and I looked at Lady Juliet's doll again. What would my customers think of Annie's dirty, torn, much-loved toy?

I had resumed drawing the hat I was imagining when Annie returned from our flat over the shop. She showed Eliza to Lady Juliet and said proudly, "I made her hat."

Lady Juliet's eyes widened and she bounced on her toes. "That is wonderful. Isn't it, Mama? May we play?"

"Of course, dear."

The girls moved to a corner of the shop and sat on the floor with their dolls in their laps. Lady Juliet was wearing a yellow velvet dress. I winced and said, "I'm not certain how clean the floor is."

"They can worry about that when they're older," the duchess said.

"Is she your only child?" I asked, curious about the Duchess of Blackford. She wasn't how I pictured a duchess would act or speak, particularly after meeting the Duchess of Wallingford.

"No, she has two younger brothers. The Marquess of Axford, his father's heir, whom I still call Jamie, is four, and Lord William—Wills—is two."

"I remember my brother when he was little getting

dirty at every opportunity." I gave her a smile.

"All three are constantly busy, and dirty," she said, not sounding at all worried about any possible mess, before pointing to a detail in my sketch and asking about adding another ribbon flower.

I sketched it in and made a couple of other suggestions, gesturing to where they would go on the model of a flat crown bonnet. Then I mentioned another price with everything we'd discussed.

She told me the price she was willing to pay for the hat and asked how many ribbon flowers that would purchase.

I showed her on my sketch and added, "I can tell you've had experience running a business. You make both of our tasks easier by being direct."

"I don't hesitate to mention price where many of my more gently raised contemporaries have been schooled to avoid any reference to money," the duchess said. "Yes, that looks nice. Now, while the girls are playing, tell me what your connection is to Lady Theodore Hughes."

"I didn't know her in life. She wasn't a customer. Had you met her?" I hoped the duchess would be able to help.

"Yes. Wallingford House is across the street from Blackford House. Roxanne was the wife of the younger son of the Duke of Wallingford. She and Theodore made a handsome couple." She shook her head. "What a tragedy."

As long as Lady Kaldaire was determined to throw me headlong into another murder investigation, I decided I'd ask questions of the Duchess of Blackford. It was a rare day when I saw two duchesses, much less spoke to them. "Do you subscribe to the Duchess of Wallingford's theory that Lady Theodore killed her husband?"

The duchess raised her eyebrows. "She told you that?"

"Yes, and she is determined that whoever killed Lady Theodore should escape hanging." I watched her to see her reaction.

I didn't need to study her features. Her words told me everything. "If the duchess had paid attention to her son, she would have known what an evil, rotten—"

"Mama, may I go upstairs to Annie's room?" a small voice broke in.

The duchess gave a little jump. "That depends on whether it is all right with Miss Gates."

I gave a quick thought to the neatness of our flat above the shop. The cleaner had made a pass through that morning. "Annie, can you two behave upstairs?"

"Yes'm."

"Then you may."

They left in a flurry of dashing feet.

The duchess and I looked at each other with expressions that said, *They can't get into too much trouble.*

"Lord Theodore was evil?" This duchess was a contrast to the Duchess of Wallingford.

She nodded. "Most people thought Lady Theodore was the wilder of the pair, but I thought Lord Theodore was a terrible little heathen when I first met him seven years ago. At the time, he was torturing a cat."

"Good heavens." The Duchess of Wallingford thought her cat-torturing son was an angel? How deluded could she be?

"The duke—the Duke of Blackford, that is—separated

Theo and the cat. After that, I tried to avoid Theo. Many of us hoped Roxanne, Roxanne Starley as she was before her marriage, would tone down Theo's baser tendencies."

"Did she?" It was as if I was listening to a frightening tale. Ghastly, but I wanted to hear more.

"No. He got her involved with his vicious, irresponsible cronies, and Roxanne became almost as dissolute as he was. Of course, the duchess couldn't see any of this. She believed he was still her impish little boy. As his behavior worsened, she blamed it all on the notorious Roxanne."

"So, their deaths could have been due to their involvement in something dangerous or depraved?" Lady Kaldaire wanted to investigate their ends? This was not something I wanted any part of. Leave it to Scotland Yard.

"More likely because of not paying the suppliers of their debaucheries. Rumor has it they owed everyone. Tradesmen might have to be patient," she said, and at that we exchanged a knowing smile, "but those who live on the shady side of society, cocaine dealers, gamblers, and procurers of innocents, aren't known for their patience."

I swallowed before I asked, "Does anyone know who these dealers and procurers are?"

The Duchess of Blackford stared at me. "You're going to attempt to talk to these people?"

"Not willingly." I shrugged slightly. "But I suspect Lady Kaldaire will expect me to at least try to speak to them."

Her expression turned suspicious. "That could be dangerous. Why does she have such a hold on you that you would try to question frightening people for her?"

I felt my face heat as I murmured, "She's a very persuasive woman."

I was doomed. If Lady Kaldaire pressed me into service investigating the killings, I'd have to involve my father's family. There was no way I could find the people Lord and Lady Theodore owed money to on my own.

My grandfather was staunchly against the legal but questionable trade in cocaine. He forbade anyone in the family from getting involved in owning or providing for brothels. Zachariah Gates and his descendants made a good living by stealing from the rich but wouldn't touch the miseries of drugs and prostitution. I was in for a lecture I didn't want to hear the moment I asked for their help.

And if the duchess pressed me for a reason why I'd carry out Lady Kaldaire's directions, that would mean one more person who knew my secret. One more person who could force me to carry out their instructions.

She tilted her head to one side. "Why would you do such a thing just because Lady Kaldaire asked?"

I bit my lip as I shook my head.

"Miss Gates, I'm in the habit of keeping secrets from my days with the Archivist Society. You needn't worry about my discretion." The duchess gave me a tentative smile. "I believe I'll be able to help, but I always need to know I can trust the person I'm helping. I want to trust you, but I must know the whole truth."

Chapter Five

The Duchess of Blackford made clear by her expression that I had no choice. I was going to have to trust her discretion.

"I've seen very little of my father and his family my entire life," I told her. That was certainly the truth.

I saw sympathy flash in her eyes. "Your parents weren't...?"

"Oh, they were married." I sighed. "My father's a crook."

"Oh?" The sympathy disappeared.

"His whole family are crooks. They're burglars, con artists, thieves, fraudsters, and swindlers. They've probably stolen from half my clientele. If these ladies knew, they'd never do business with me again."

I took a deep breath. "I need to keep Duquesne's Millinery running to put food on the table. My younger brother is deaf and I pay his fees to the Doncaster School for the Deaf. He's doing quite well there." There was pride in my tone.

"I see why you can be coerced by Lady Kaldaire. She is rather determined. I had no plans to come here today to buy Juliet a hat until Lady Kaldaire changed my mind." She smiled ruefully.

"I'm so sorry." The heat on my face told me I was blushing.

"Don't be. It's been a success. But now I need to gather up my daughter and head home for tea." The Duchess of Blackford patted my shoulder. She was about my height, and while she must have been ten years older, there was something youthful about her. Perhaps it was happiness. "I'll try to learn more about the Wallingfords and the two deaths, and if I succeed, I'll let you know."

"Thank you." I was going to have to talk to Lady Kaldaire sooner or later. I planned to make it later.

Once they left, I sent Jane home and closed up the shop. I was sweeping the floor when I heard a knock on the door. I peeked out around the shade on the glass pane and saw Detective Inspector James Russell.

My heart did an odd little flutter as I unlocked the door.

James slipped in and glanced around before he took me in his arms and gave me a kiss.

Once I remembered how to breathe, I said, "Mrs. McCauley left us chicken stew today. There's plenty. Are you here for dinner after your long absence?"

He grimaced. "That couldn't be avoided. The Manchester police had half a dozen cases they wanted help on, and my governor agreed. I hope they send someone else next time. I don't like Manchester." He had let me go, but he still stood, in the eyes of society, improperly close.

"Were any of the investigations interesting?" I found James's work fascinating.

"One was. I'll tell you about it after dinner. In the meantime, I need to interview you about what happened this morning."

I hoped I was right when I said Mrs. McCauley was generous with the stew. James was here and staying for dinner. I would have cheered if I'd been alone. I didn't want him to see how excited I was by his spending time with me. "Please, sit down," I said as demurely as I could manage, but I still gave a little hop.

He lowered himself into one of the hat fitting chairs. "Tell me everything that happened, in order, from the time you reached the park until I arrived."

I did.

"Whose idea was it to request my help with the investigation?"

"Lady Kaldaire. And she's been telling the Duchess of Wallingford how discreet you were when you handled her husband's murder."

"So the duchess told me. She's certain it was a thief who surprised her son's wife and then felt the need to dispose of the body." He shook his head. "This is going to be difficult, and the chief constable is demanding a quick resolution."

"Because Lady Theodore had married into a duke's family?"

"And lived in their house."

"She still lived there even after her husband had died?" Even though she was hated by the duchess.

He nodded. "Strange, since I received the impression the two women didn't get along."

I decided to pass on the information the Duchess of Blackford had given me.

When I finished, James winced. "The last places I expected to go with this investigation were clubs where cocaine sellers do their business and houses of ill repute."

"I imagine those places are dangerous. No wonder both the husband and wife were murdered, if they were frequenting such places and were not paying their bills." I shuddered.

"There are a lot of places they could have been taking their pleasures that we don't have reason to enter. Those places are the ones I don't want you to visit. I can't come in to rescue you." He looked at me, worry lines etched on his forehead.

"What places?" I was curious.

He glared at me, and when I stared back, he relented. "A lot of gambling goes on in private clubs around the edges of Mayfair. And in a few of these places, more than just gambling."

"James, spell it out." Really, I wished he trusted me with information that he'd share with my grandfather.

He looked at the ceiling and exhaled heavily. Then he looked at me. "Twenty years ago, cocaine was considered good for giving people energy. Even Doctor Freud said how good it was. It wasn't until people became addicted, or died from it, that the medical community realized how dangerous cocaine is. It's still legal, but I wish it wasn't."

"In a few private clubs they gamble and do drugs. Anything else?" So far, I hadn't heard anything too shocking.

He made a face as if he'd tasted something rotten. "It's rumored in at least one place they give brandy and drugs to young ladies and then take them upstairs and do scandalous things to them."

With a herd of cousins, I'd learned things long before the adults found out I knew. "You mean sex."

"Yes." He reached out and took my hands. "I see the victims of these places. There is nothing we can do. We can't find the people who did these things to them, and we can't obtain justice."

"I'm sorry your position with the Yard forces you to visit such horrors." James was such a dear, honest, kind person. Going into these places had to have hurt him deeply.

"At least I don't have to go in alone," he said and smiled. "I always try to take the biggest sergeants with me on a raid. I'm glad Lady Kaldaire isn't involved because I don't want to rescue you, and her, from these places."

I let out a deep breath. "Lady Kaldaire is an old friend of the Duchess of Wallingford. She's already trying to get me involved. That's why the Duchess of Blackford was here this afternoon telling me what she knew of this couple."

His smile slid off his face. "Emily, if you and Lady Kaldaire want to spend time in drawing rooms sipping tea and asking questions, I'll not say no. You have a way of finding out bits of information that are important. But stay away from places where you have no business going."

"I hope Lady Kaldaire agrees with you." Somehow, I knew she wouldn't.

He made a noise between a growl and a groan. "Promise me you won't go anywhere you shouldn't. Remember, Lady Theodore was murdered when someone sliced through her neck with a knife. The scarf was added to try to hide the murder wound. Not terribly effectively, since the blood managed to seep from under the scarf."

I shuddered.

He took my hand. "We're dealing with someone strong, violent, and crafty. Promise me you won't get involved. And you won't go to any of these so-called private clubs."

When I didn't speak, he said, "Promise."

"If you can convince Lady Kaldaire, I gladly promise."

"Oh, I'll convince Lady Kaldaire if I have to threaten her with jail."

James didn't sound as if he were joking.

We went upstairs to a wonderful dinner with my little apprentice, Annie, and Noah, my mother's cousin and my business partner, and James entertained us with tales from his stay in Manchester. I didn't give Lady Kaldaire another thought.

* * *

Lady Kaldaire came into my shop the next morning, sat down on one of my fitting chairs as if she owned the place, and took off her hat.

"How may I help your ladyship?" I asked loud enough that the customer Jane was helping on the other side of the partition, a barrister's wife, could hear me.

"I need a new hat. Black, obviously, but something a little more spring-like."

"Spring-like?" She was in the first phase of mourning for her husband. Society didn't allow her much variation in her dress, and none at all in her wearing black from head to toe.

"Yes. Something not so weighty."

"Get rid of the veils? Add some ribbon trim?"

"Exactly."

I lowered my voice. "Has Inspector Russell spoken to you?"

"Yes. Silly man. He thinks he can frighten me."

Oh, dear. "He doesn't want either of us visiting…certain locations," I said, nodding in the direction of the woman in the next chair, "but we are free to ask any questions we want in any drawing room in London."

Lady Kaldaire glanced in the woman's direction and said, "I'd like you to accompany me to Wallingford House this afternoon to speak to the ladies there. And then we may need to visit some out of the way places."

I knew exactly what she meant by "out of the way places." They were the locations James didn't want us to visit. "Can't you take the duchess or somebody else with you?" I figured it was worth a try.

"Not if you don't want the story of your relatives to shock your customers." She kept her voice lowered.

"You wouldn't." I glared at her while whispering.

"I can, and if you cross me on this, I will." I could read her determination in her eyes.

"It's not fair."

She gave my pouting face a bored stare. "Things seldom are. Directly after you close the shop."

Matthew was doing so well at his school. He was making deaf friends. I had to keep paying his school fees. *Blast.* "No. Not until you give me a good reason why I should endanger my reputation and my life in the hunt for a killer."

She thought for a moment. "There's a tea shop down the street. Let's go there."

"Why can't you tell me here?"

"And have all your customers listen to my business? No."

"Jane?" I said in a normal voice as I popped my head around the divider.

She saw the expression on my face. "I'll take care of the shop."

"Thank you." I stared at Lady Kaldaire, ignoring the look of surprise on the face of the barrister's wife. "Let's go."

The morning was bright, so we carried our umbrellas furled and enjoyed the sunshine as we walked down the pavement. The hour was still early and delivery wagons crowded the street, moving slowly or blocking the pavement while being unloaded. Lady Kaldaire could squeeze past boxes and still look aristocratic. I just looked clumsy.

The teashop hadn't been open long and wasn't busy. We chose a table in a corner and ordered tea and muffins.

"Lady Kaldaire, let's discuss this quickly. I have a business to run."

"And I have an old and dear friend to protect." We exchanged a hard stare before she added, "I don't want to harm your business, but I would throw you into the Thames to protect Lulu."

I jerked back in my chair. I had never had a friend I felt that strongly about, and at that moment I would have gladly thrown Lady Kaldaire into the river. Still, I had to ask. "Why? As long as I make your hats and do your bidding, I'm allowed to carry on. But if I disagree with you, you're willing to destroy my business? You're willing to drown me?"

She shook her head. "You tried to save Horace's life, and for that I thank you. But Lulu actually did save my life. When we were young, traveling around Europe on our grand tour, she saved me before I died from strangulation."

Chapter Six

My curiosity overcame my desire to get back to the shop as I waited for her to begin her tale.

"We were in Italy." She shook her head. "Always a breeding ground for anarchists. We'd been to see Michelangelo's David, magnificent creature, and some other statues under the watchful gaze of our governesses. Lulu's wasn't too bad, but mine was useless in a crisis. She couldn't make a pot of tea or find a lost trunk, much less deal with what we were about to face."

I tried to remember my history. Italy hadn't been a country when Lady Kaldaire would have been a young miss. At that time, Germany and Italy were just collections of little states governed by local princes.

"We were warned by the police that due to political unrest we were to go back to our hotel and stay there. It was a large, sprawling building and our rooms were on the first floor. Each room opened onto a balcony that overlooked a garden."

The tea was brought to our table and Lady Kaldaire poured. I picked up one of the muffins, gooey with butter, waiting to hear the tale. I was hungry, and I'm afraid I gobbled down two of the muffins before the tea was ready.

Finally, she took a sip of her tea and said, "We could hear a mob coming closer and shouting in Italian. It's a language made for rioting. None of us could make out their grievance. Then the shouting seemed to come from all around the hotel and up and down every street. My governess was huddled in a corner sobbing loudly and regretting that she'd ever left England."

I could picture the earth shaking with stomping feet and echoing with a million voices. Having never heard Italian, my imagination served up a rumbling sound.

"Lulu and her governess came into my room. Lulu and I talked her governess into dealing with mine while we leaned over the balcony railing and listened to the danger that seemed to surround us. It was exciting, hearing the mob but not being able to see them. We thought we were safe."

She shook her head. "Suddenly, there were about twenty or thirty men in the garden. Each one carried a torch, and their faces in the torchlight looked menacing. Evil.

"One of them looked up and saw us. He called out and several of them began to climb the ivy that grew on the stone walls. We had no weapons to repel them. No cricket bats. No tennis rackets. No swords.

"And our dresses. All flounces and bustles and useless material. We ran inside and shut the French doors to the balcony, but a half-dozen men broke through. Lulu and I screamed. My governess fainted dead away, landing on Lulu's governess and pinning her down. At least that's what she claimed later.

"One of the men saw the jewelry I was wearing and grabbed for my necklace. My father had a particularly strong cord run through it so it couldn't be easily snatched from my neck. He said the jewels were too expensive to chance a theft. What he didn't realize was it now was being used to strangle me.

"I was on my knees, choking, thinking I was about to die as the world went black. Lulu told me she picked up a chamber pot and bashed the man over the head. I was so grateful when I could again draw breath through my painful throat. She then grabbed a small replica of David and hit another man in the face with it. Blood went everywhere. For a moment I thought she'd killed him."

Lady Kaldaire took a sip of tea and fell silent.

I'd met the Duchess of Wallingford. She seemed so frail I couldn't imagine her acting so forcefully. "It's hard to picture."

"Do you doubt my words?" Lady Kaldaire demanded.

"No." I'd found Lady Kaldaire to be truthful.

"Lulu saved my life. No one else was in a position to act. She was incredible, and I lived to tell everyone about her courage. I am in her debt," Lady Kaldaire said.

"What happened then?"

"One of them grabbed my jewelry box. I picked up a paperweight and hurled it at him. Hit him in the head and dropped him like a pheasant. Then the police showed up and arrested some of them while the rest escaped empty-handed."

She smiled. "My parents were not happy."

I imagined them being hundreds of miles away from

their daughter, trying to travel to reach her. "What did they do?"

"What could they do? The trip was already half over. I suggested they come out and join me, since I was continuing on. In the end, they agreed that I should continue with my useless governess since they had no desire to travel to these barbaric places where they didn't speak English." Lady Kaldaire smiled at something only she could see. "Lulu and I had a frightfully good time after that."

I looked at her over my teacup. "I understand better now why you feel the need to repay her by protecting her life."

"And I need your help to make sure no one harms her. I will do anything, anything at all, to ensure she stays safe. That includes destroying your business if anyone attempts to hurt her and you don't help me." She held my gaze.

That raised a bigger question in my mind. "If despite our best efforts, someone hurts her, will you destroy my business?"

She shook her head. "All you can do is your best. Your best is quite formidable." She gave me a weak smile. "I won't punish you for failing. Only for not trying."

I finished my tea and rose. "I have to get back to work. I'll see you later."

"And I have a hat to order."

We returned to the millinery to find Jane was the only person there. Lady Kaldaire sat down again and looked at me expectantly.

"I can give you an hour this afternoon to visit

Wallingford House if it would suit your ladyship," I told her, "but that will be the only place I can visit away from my shop today. What time would you like me there?"

"Meet me at my home at three. We'll go together. No sense in your arriving ahead of me."

I nodded. "Do you want me to work up some sketches or do you trust my imagination for your new hat?"

"Do a quick sketch so I know we're imagining the same hat."

As it turned out, I was correct about the shape, her favorite mushroom style. I was off on everything else. In place of a veil, she wanted a small bunch of ribbon roses on one side attached to a wide ribbon band around the base of the crown. I finally convinced her that I should add a bit of netting across the front of the brim to appear as if she had pushed the veil up.

"Since it will be in black, it will hardly be spring-like, but it is certainly better than having all those heavy veils Lady Montague is wearing," Lady Kaldaire said. "And Lord Montague was such a philanderer. Not worth the effort." She made a *tsking* noise.

Lady Montague was a customer of mine. I had created the hat Lady Kaldaire mentioned according to Lady Montague's wishes. Quickly changing the subject, I said, "So this is what you have in mind, despite the color?"

"Yes," she grumbled.

I suspected she was counting down the days until she could get into second mourning and add lilac and gray to her outfits. "I'll get to work on this for you. And we're working on the replacement for your first mourning hat.

You must have really liked it to wear it out so quickly."

"I blame it on the heavy rains we've had lately. Positively destroys hats."

Inwardly, I cheered for heavy rains. Then I mentioned the price of her new hat.

"Fine. Fine," she told me as she waved off the price with one hand. "I will see you at three." It wasn't a question.

"Yes, my lady." I hoped I sounded more willing than I felt. I suspected I sounded annoyed.

* * *

Things were quiet in the shop. I crossed the alley to the factory and told Noah and Annie I'd be late for dinner and to eat without me. Annie took my announcement in stride, but Noah's eyes narrowed dangerously. He gestured to the door and we stepped into the alley, away from our employees. "What does that woman have you doing now?"

Noah was not only my business partner, he was my mother's cousin and had known me all my life. He was protective of both me and our business, and not kindly disposed toward either my father's family or Lady Kaldaire and her demands. There was no good way to put this. "Lady Kaldaire and I are going to track down who killed her friend's son and daughter-in-law."

"Why are you doing this?"

"The man who was killed died in the house of Lady Kaldaire's good friend. This friend may be in danger."

He shook his head. "That's why she's doing it. Why are you doing this?"

"Because if I don't, she'll ruin us. She'll tell everyone about my father's family."

"I don't think you'd lose as many customers as you think."

I wished Noah was right. He stayed in the workshop making hats while I worked in the shop with the customers. He didn't have to deal with aristocrats. "You don't know these women the way I do. They seek out gossip and then shun anyone who falls short of their standards. Their lofty standards. And every other milliner in London would like to steal my clients. They would all use my father's criminal record against me."

He patted my arm. "It can't be that bad."

"Oh, yes, it can. Please, say a prayer we find out something useful and I can walk away from this." I stared into his eyes until he nodded.

"How late will you be?"

"Not late. I'll do this as fast as I can."

"Good luck."

I returned through the back door of the shop to find we had another customer.

* * *

At two in the afternoon, I left Jane with the shop, cleaned up, and then dressed in my nicest suit, a lightweight navy wool paired with a new white shirtwaist and a red and blue patterned bow at my neck. My hat was a wide-brimmed, low-crowned affair in navy with red trim and roses. I took my stout black umbrella, refusing to ruin my new suit and hat in a spring downpour.

It was a look middle-class teachers and shop owners

were wearing that season, copied from the Americans. I might as well make obvious my different status from the ladies present.

I rang the bell at Lady Kaldaire's as the first fat drops hit the pavement and jumped inside as the butler, Lyle, opened the door.

"Good afternoon, Miss Gates," Lyle said, showing no surprise that I'd nearly run him over.

"Hello, Lyle. Is Lady Kaldaire ready?" I hated wasting time I could be at work on those few occasions when she was quite late.

"She should welcome you in just a moment," Lyle said. He would have told me that no matter how long she kept me there unemployed. "Would you care to wait in the morning room?"

"Yes." I walked into what I knew was the sunniest room on the ground floor, expecting to sit there for a long time.

As it turned out, Lady Kaldaire sailed by me in the front hall two minutes later, calling out, "Don't dawdle, Emily." I hurried after her as she marched out the front door, down to the pavement, and toward Wallingford House. "Both her daughter and daughter-in-law will be there with the duchess," she told me as I caught up.

"Will they be able to tell us anything the duchess can't?" I asked, hearing large drops hit the top of my umbrella.

"I hope so, although I couldn't convince Lulu not to join us." Lady Kaldaire held her umbrella at that aristocratic angle that dared the raindrops to strike. I could never quite copy that pose.

"If the Wallingfords stick together, how will we learn anything about either of these deaths?" I felt certain the two deaths were related.

"We can't ask about Theo's death. That's too painful for his mother." Lady Kaldaire used her haughty tone.

Annoyed because I had hats to design and create that had to wait due to Lady Kaldaire's ill-timed investigation, I was not about to be quieted by her haughty attitude. "Then we need to get the daughter and the son's wife away from the duchess and question them."

I expected her to fight me. Instead, she remained quiet for the rest of our short walk.

When we arrived, the Wallingford butler showed us in and, after taking our umbrellas, escorted us to the front drawing room that faced the park. A moment later, a pretty blonde in a black day dress with an overabundance of black lace and frills followed us in.

Lady Kaldaire walked up to her and said, "Dorothy, how are you coping?"

Tears sprang to her blue eyes. "He is such a dear little baby. How could anyone do something so vile?" She pulled a white linen handkerchief from her sleeve and covered her face.

I was completely lost. I doubted she would refer to Lord Theodore as a baby. Was there another victim in this house?

"What happened?" I asked, glancing from one woman to the other.

"Lord Alfred was attacked one night," Dorothy got out

between sobs. "When we found him, he was on the floor, bloody and whimpering. The doctors don't know how much of the damage from his injuries will stay with him."

"Where was the night nurse?" All these big houses had twenty- four-hour nurses for their children.

"She'd also been thrown to the floor and was unconscious."

"Your house has been visited by great tragedy. Your baby injured, your brother- and sister-in-law—" I began.

She turned red-rimmed but furious eyes toward me. "They were nothing. Silly, selfish creatures. Lord Alfred is heir to the dukedom. And he is mine. *My* precious baby." Her glare seemed to burn through my skin.

I'd heard the Duchess of Wallingford's opinion of Lord Theo and his wife, Lady Theodore. Here was their sister-in-law, who found them both beneath notice. Didn't anyone like anyone else in this house?

Chapter Seven

"I beg your pardon. You must be terribly worried about your little boy," I began. This woman seemed distraught over her baby's condition. "His injuries aren't serious, I hope." Perhaps she was overreacting to the accident.

"He did nothing but sleep for days after the attack. We could barely get him to eat. The doctor was very concerned. And he's been fussy and listless since then." Tears flowed down Dorothy's cheeks.

"I'm so sorry. I wish I could do something useful. Your mother-in-law seems very upset about Lord Theo." I didn't want to rile someone who might have the answers we needed to find a killer. The sooner, the better as far as I was concerned.

"She doesn't realize how evil Theo was. And the family won't let me tell her. They don't believe me," Dorothy said, simultaneously sniffing and glowering.

"Of course, we believe you, Dorothy," said a woman's voice behind me, "but it doesn't help to tell Mama and upset her now that Theo's gone."

I turned to find a dark-haired, rather plain woman in an elegant walking suit of dull black behind me. Lady Kaldaire stepped forward to embrace her. "Tragedy seems to follow your family, Margaret."

"There are tragedies and there are tragedies," Margaret replied from over Lady Kaldaire's shoulder as she stared at Dorothy. I read her expression to mean *Keep your mouth shut.*

I decided to try to question Dorothy on my own.

Lady Kaldaire introduced me to the ladies, referring to me as her private secretary. I wondered if they were aware of how often Lady Kaldaire embellished the truth.

It turned out Dorothy was the Marchioness of Frethorton, the future duchess, and Margaret was Lady Ellingham, the current duchess's daughter, who was married to a peer.

I had work to do, and neither of these ladies was a customer of mine. I asked, "Do either of you have any idea how these terrible events occurred?"

Dorothy vigorously shook her head.

Margaret said, "Of course not. And if we did, we'd tell Scotland Yard." *Not you,* echoed silently.

"Lady Kaldaire has an idea that we might be of more use than Scotland Yard. We can speak to people who may not be willing to talk to the police, precisely because we're not officials. My ladies," I added belatedly. I didn't want to spend my working hours talking to them any more than they wanted to talk to me.

Dorothy shook her head again.

Margaret glared at me. "What good will it do to find the killer?"

"Don't you think your brother's killer should be punished?" Lady Kaldaire demanded.

"My mother thinks Theo's killer is dead." Margaret transferred her glare to Lady Kaldaire.

"And if he's not, you think he should get away with it?" Lady Kaldaire demanded. The two women were toe to toe now, growing red in the face with their fury.

"Robbie. Margaret. Stop it." The Duchess of Wallingford walked up to the pair. I could see now that she was naturally thin, but the trauma she'd been through this last month had taken its toll. However, since I'd seen her the day before, she'd been dressed, coiffed, and fed, and now looked and sounded like an aristocrat.

"Yes, Mother."

"Of course, Lulu." Both women stepped back. With a last glare, they walked to different areas of the room.

"Would you please be seated?" the duchess asked as she rang the bell.

When a maid appeared, the duchess ordered tea. Then she sat in a high-backed armchair and said, "Robbie doesn't think Roxanne killed Theo."

"Why?" Margaret demanded.

"If Roxanne killed Theo, who killed Roxanne?" Lady Kaldaire said.

"Do we care?"

I could resist no longer. "Other than the fact that murder is illegal in this country and it is the duty of every law-abiding citizen to follow the hue and cry?" When I glanced at the two ladies, they looked down. "It would have taken two people to undress Roxanne if she were dead or incapacitated. It may have taken two people to move her body to where I found it in the park. If these two people broke into your parents' house to kill her, how do you know they won't come back and attack your mother or father? Or attack Lady Frethorton's baby again?"

Dorothy gasped and burst into tears.

Her reaction earned me a glare from Margaret and the duchess. "My parents aren't involved in gaming, or using cocaine, or procuring helpless people for sex slaves," Margaret snapped.

"Indeed, we are not," her mother agreed. The duchess, with her mourning dress of black and her silvery hair, was a study in rectitude where all the color had been drained away.

"Do you know how these gamblers and cocaine peddlers entered the house and escaped again, not once, but twice?" If I was given a good answer to that question, I was pretty certain I could convince Lady Kaldaire to let Scotland Yard investigate without our interference.

"Maybe...," Dorothy said and then made a helpless gesture.

"While avoiding a houseful of servants and locks on the doors and windows? No, we have no idea how anyone could enter from outside," Margaret said. She gave me a defiant look. "Ask Scotland Yard. They should be able to figure it out."

"Not if you won't tell them anything," Lady Kaldaire said in a dry tone.

A maid brought in a tea tray loaded with little sandwiches and cakes as well as small plates, cups, and saucers in delicate bone china with a tiny yellow rose pattern. Lady Kaldaire and Lady Ellingham fell silent, making their point with glares. The duchess invited us to help ourselves while she removed the cozy from the teapot.

I waited, understanding my role here was not *honored guest*. Dorothy took two tiny watercress sandwiches and a tea cake. Margaret glanced at her sister-in-law's plate and smiled before giving her mother a pointed look.

"I'm glad to see your appetite has improved," the duchess said.

"Yes. I'm feeling more myself today," Dorothy said and sat before accepting a cup of tea.

"These sandwiches look good," Lady Kaldaire said, helping herself to a tea cake and then taking a cup of tea. "I think if you hadn't seen anything out of the ordinary at the time of these two deaths, a servant may have. May we question them?"

"Do you think we haven't already?" Margaret said, taking a dainty sandwich.

"Miss Gates?" the duchess said.

I looked at her, wondering how I was supposed to convince her to let us question her servants.

"Would you like a sandwich?"

Oh. "Yes, Your Grace, they look delicious." I took one and watched Dorothy take a third one before I managed a single bite. I finished mine with a second bite, had a sip of tea, and said, "Your Grace, may Lady Kaldaire and I question your staff? Perhaps something will jog someone's memory."

"You think it might be helpful, Robbie?" the duchess asked.

"If I didn't think so, I wouldn't ask, Lulu. I know how trying the last month has been for you."

The Duchess of Wallingford sat completely still for a moment and then reached for the bell pull. A moment later, the butler appeared.

"Set up a schedule of times for Lady Kaldaire and her assistant to question the staff about anything untoward at the time of the deaths of Lord Theo and Lady Theodore." The duchess turned to Lady Kaldaire. "Is that satisfactory?"

"Thank you, Lulu."

"Let us know when it is ready, Mathers."

He bowed deeply. "Yes, Your Grace." Backing up two steps, he left the room.

"Anyone for more tea?" the duchess asked.

I sat quietly, keeping one eye on the clock, while Margaret, the duchess, and Lady Kaldaire carried on a boring conversation concerning weather, flowers, and upcoming weddings. I made a mental note on the weddings, hoping it meant more business for my shop. Dorothy downed three more sandwiches and two tea cakes.

Mathers returned in under ten minutes with a full schedule written up in a neat hand. He handed it to his employer with a bow, who passed it to Lady Kaldaire, who handed it to me. Out of the corner of my eye, I saw Dorothy give a quizzical look to Margaret, who shook her head.

I stared at the butler. "You aren't on here, Mathers."

"I doubt I could add anything of value," he said in his deep, somber voice.

"Oh, I doubt that," I said. I was raised to believe butlers knew everything that happened in a household.

"Shall I speak to you now?" he asked.

I rose. "Please. Lead the way."

"Thank you, Lulu," Lady Kaldaire said as she rose to follow me out of the room.

We walked single file to the butler's office in the cellar amid the warren of storerooms and sculleries. I could hear the din from the kitchen as dinner was being prepared. Once we were seated with Mathers staring anxiously at the bell by his doorway, I asked, "Are their graces having a dinner party tonight?"

"Just a small one. Family and close friends."

"The attack on Lady Frethorton's baby, when was that?"

"The night Lord Theo died."

"Was the attack reported to the police?"

"His Grace forbade it. The doctor had his hands full with three patients—"

"Three?"

"Lady Frethorton was shattered by the events and had to be put to bed with a sedative. And of course Lord Alfred was injured."

"And the third?" I pressed.

"The night nurse. His Grace fired her for shirking her duties, which meant one of the maids had to take over. The nurse left in the morning, bewailing her mistreatment." The butler's face said what he thought of her actions.

"Could Lord Theo have crossed paths with the baby's attacker?"

"It is possible."

"I'd like the night nurse's name and address, please." She might have information that Scotland Yard didn't possess.

"I don't see—"

"Would you rather I had to disturb the duchess for the nurse's details, reminding her of that tragic night?" Lady Kaldaire asked.

The butler immediately jumped up to find and copy the information.

"Who is responsible for seeing to the locking up of the house each night?" I asked.

"It is my duty as butler." He sounded huffy.

"Including the night the baby was attacked and the night Lady Theodore was murdered?"

"Yes."

"Then how did these evil people get into this house?" I hoped he'd admit to failing his duty, although looking at his stiff-backed posture, I wouldn't believe it.

He shook his head. "I don't know. I locked everything up. The servants know better than to unlock a door at night without me being present."

The servants knew better, but... "And the family?"

"They have their own keys for when I've locked up for the night."

"Has a key gone missing lately?"

"Scotland Yard already asked that." His back appeared to grow stiffer.

"If you mean your employers well, you won't mind answering a simple question again." I kept my voice low and calm.

Suddenly, Mathers seemed to slump into himself. "Lord Theo misplaced a front-door key a few days before he died." He glanced at me and added, "I informed His Grace. He wasn't concerned. He believed the key was left in the boy's room or had fallen down a sewer."

Lord Theo was hardly a boy in my mind. "Do you know where Lord Theo went the day he lost the key?"

"He lost it at night, and I prefer not to know the details of where the young master went or with whom." The butler shuddered.

The rest of the staff denied knowing anything about the events of those two nights until awakened from their beds. No one knew anything about Lord Theo's missing key or had seen anyone suspicious lurking about.

I glanced at Lady Kaldaire after we'd interviewed the last maid. "The only thing we've learned is Lord Theo lost a key. It could be that someone he owed money to saw him drop it and used it to try to collect what was due. In the process, both the man and later his wife were murdered. That would explain how the killers entered the house undetected. But it doesn't explain why the man was murdered but not his wife at that time, and then she was killed a month later and in a more public way."

Lady Kaldaire eyed me closely. "So, you think it was two different killers with different motives?"

"Yes." I couldn't think of a single reason that would account for two separate murders on different nights by a solitary killer.

Lady Kaldaire rose and said, "Then we need to find

these killers." She strode out of the small butler's office so fast I had to hurry to keep up. I followed her upstairs, back to the drawing room. I could see from the doorway that the women hadn't moved since we left.

Lady Kaldaire sat across from the duchess once again and took her hand. "You know that Theo lost his front-door key a few days before he died?"

Lady Wallingford's eyes widened. "You think that's how the killer entered the house?"

"Yes."

"It's not true."

"Lulu…"

"I knew how careless he was. When we found him—" she sniffed, "the first thing I checked was his key ring. They were all there."

Lady Kaldaire sat even straighter than usual. "Then why did Mathers lie to us?"

"Out of loyalty. He doesn't want you bothering me. No one does." Lady Wallingford gave a weak smile.

"For pity's sake, Lulu, someone entered this house on two separate occasions and killed your son and his wife. Doesn't that make you just a teeny bit anxious?"

"And my baby boy was attacked," came from a small voice behind me. I turned to see Dorothy seated in a high-backed chair in the corner. She clutched a handkerchief in one hand.

Here was my chance to hear something honest in this house. "Lady Frethorton, would you like to tell me about it?" I said in my calmest voice.

She rose and, as she walked out of the room, looked

back at me with a sorrowful expression and said, "Come along."

Chapter Eight

Lady Dorothy Frethorton led the way up two flights of stairs and then down a hall. She knocked on a door and then opened it. Inside I saw a children's nurse holding a baby on her lap. She was trying to interest the baby in a brightly painted toy, but the baby only batted at it without much interest.

"This is my baby, Lord Alfred," Dorothy told me with an enraptured smile on her face.

"He seems like a happy child," I said. "Very handsome. How old is he?"

"Almost ten months. But I wish you'd seen him before the attack. He was so much brighter. He's stopped crawling and standing."

"That's because he cries if he's put down," the nurse said in a stern tone. "He can't develop his muscles if he's held all the time. He's been coddled too much. My lady, if we—"

"He's been through a terrible ordeal," Dorothy said, sounding close to tears. She snatched the boy from the nurse's arms and hugged him closely, nuzzling his little ear. "Oh, poor little Alfred."

"Tell me about the night your baby was attacked," I said before the nurse had a chance to begin the lecture she seemed poised to deliver. I should have said "my lady," but I kept thinking of her as Dorothy and not the Marchioness of Frethorton.

"I'm a light sleeper. I was awakened by the commotion. I came up here to the nursery and found my precious boy on the wooden floor of the night nursery. He was crying. The nurse was also on the floor, blood pouring from under her head."

The poor night nurse. "Oh, dear. Was anyone else around?"

The nurse seemed to have heard the story multiple times. She turned a disinterested face toward the fire and took up a poker to prod the flames to give off a little more warmth. As was true in most homes, the nursery received cast-offs. The shovel was dented and the poker slightly bent.

"Yes. Theo was in the hall. He tried pulling me back, away from my baby." Dorothy's eyes took on a feral gleam as she held the baby tighter. The baby started to fuss and tried to squirm away.

Had Theo seen the person who attacked the baby and the nurse? What was he afraid of, that he held Dorothy back from her baby? "Anyone else?"

"Not until later. I had to get to my baby. He was whining so piteously. I had to help him. Don't you see?" Dorothy's voice rose in a wail.

"Of course she does, Dorothy. Let's go back downstairs." Margaret, Lady Ellingham, hurried up to her and gently separated the young mother from her son. Once the nurse was in possession of the child again,

Margaret linked arms with Dorothy and walked into the hall. Dorothy kept staring over her shoulder at her son. Margaret turned and threw an angry glance at me.

I followed close enough behind to hear Margaret say, "You need to protect this baby, too."

So the baby's mother was again in an interesting condition. Was she when her first child was injured? Probably. It had only been a month ago.

No one was willing to tell Lady Kaldaire or me about that night except Lady Frethorton. And she didn't seem like the most stable of witnesses.

Who else had been in the house that night? Could Lord Theo have let him in? But why would Lord Theo have been upstairs near the nursery if he had a guest?

I followed the two ladies back to the drawing room, despite Margaret's apparent desire to order the door slammed in my face. I kept thinking of her as Margaret and not Lady Ellingham, probably because she was making her dislike of me so obvious.

Both the duchess and Lady Kaldaire stared at me when I walked in.

"I'm leaving now, my lady, if you want to walk with me," I said.

"Of course, Emily. Lulu, I'll see you later. Thank you for letting us speak to your servants," Lady Kaldaire said as she rose.

"I said it would be to no purpose," the duchess told her.

"It was worth a try if we could discover how the killers came into your home. If we could, you'd be able to sleep more securely in your beds." Lady Kaldaire gave her a pat on the shoulder and a sympathetic expression. Not an expression I often saw on her face.

The duchess leaned over and clutched Lady Kaldaire's hands. "Oh, Robbie, I appreciate your efforts. I know you mean well. But we'll be all right. You'll see."

We went back out into a drizzle as we followed the pavement around the park to Lady Kaldaire's home. "I wonder who was telling us the truth, the duchess or her butler." I was inclined to believe Mathers, the butler.

"I would suspect Mathers was saying whatever the duke told him to say," Lady Kaldaire said.

"Then we're no further along." And I'd wasted half the afternoon when I could have been working in my shop, I didn't add.

"Not at all. We need to find out which gamblers and cocaine dealers Theo and Roxanne owed money to, and then whether they had a key to the house and whether they killed the couple." Lady Kaldaire strode along, sounding as if this were as simple as planning a tea party.

"How do you think we're going to do that?" I all but snapped at her.

"I have no idea, but you'll think of something," she said as we reached her front walk. "I'll talk to you tomorrow, Emily."

She walked into her house, leaving me standing in the drizzle under my umbrella, shaking my head. What I wanted to do was scream.

I knew that meant she was going to force me to find a way to get the answers she wanted under threat of telling my clients about my father's disreputable family. With a deep sigh, I headed to the East End, where my father's entire clan, or gang, or herd, lived.

It made no sense to go back to the shop before I learned if the Gates gang could help me.

I knew which alleys were dead ends and which led to my grandfather's house, the headquarters of the family enterprise. I made my way there, my pace quickened by cold puddles splashing on my shoes and skirt hem, until I reached the family home behind the livery stables my grandmother managed.

My grandmother answered the door. "He's not here."

At least I was under cover on the porch. Before she could shut the door in my face, I said, "How are you, Gran?"

"All right, I guess."

"Matthew sends his love."

"Oh, how is he? Is school going all right?" Her voice softened at the mention of Matthew's name. As much as she had disliked my father's late wife, she had recently developed a love for my younger brother. She was learning to tolerate me.

"Being around other deaf students and being taught by teachers who can communicate with him is making a great deal of difference for him. He seems to be happy there, and he's learning so much. But he can't wait for a holiday to come home to eat more of your cooking." As long as she treated Matthew well, I was willing to try to get along with her.

"Hello, Emily. What brings you over here?"

I turned around to see my uncle Thomas climb the

porch steps. A younger version of my grandfather, today he was dressed in a conservative black suit with a gray vest and what could pass as a school tie. I didn't want to imagine what confidence trick Uncle Thomas was playing.

"I found a body yesterday morning, the body of an aristocrat."

"You didn't break in to anyone's house again, did you?" Uncle Thomas was grinning. That was how I'd found Lord Kaldaire, in his study in the middle of the night, dying, when I tried a burglary scheme to collect the money owed me for Lady Kaldaire's hats.

"No. I was cutting through a private park."

"That's so much better." He was broadly smiling now.

"It was raining." I glared at him before I continued. "It was Lady Theodore Hughes, known in the papers as the notorious Lady Roxanne. Her mother-in-law is the Duchess of Wallingford, a childhood friend of Lady Kaldaire."

He whistled before his expression hardened. "Don't tell me that woman wants you to investigate another murder."

I nodded sadly. "Lady Theodore and her husband lived with the duke and duchess and apparently owed gamblers and cocaine peddlers money. Her husband, the late Lord Theo, might have lost a front-door key shortly before he was killed. Lady Kaldaire wants me to find out who these shady people are and whether they have a key to Wallingford house. She doesn't want the duke and duchess murdered."

My uncle said what he thought of aristocrats in

colorful language, ending with "Wait until your grandfather hears about this."

"Hears about what? Hello, Pet. How's my favorite granddaughter?"

I smiled. I was his only granddaughter among his well over a dozen grandchildren. My grandfather was dressed as an aging aristocrat in an ancient morning suit and top hat. I suspected he had been sitting in one of the big West End political or social clubs learning what he could to his advantage.

He once told me he never knew what piece of information could turn into a valuable "enterprise."

He swept us all into the house, kissed my grandmother on the cheek, and had us sit at the dining room table where councils of war were held.

After I told him all, he sat silently for a very long time. I knew I was in trouble.

Uncle Thomas broke in first. "I tried to tell her we don't get involved in selling drugs, and gaming is a fool's business if it's not rigged. Those hells are a totally different business. They are rigged. We may leave people poorer, but we don't destroy them and take their lives."

I knew my question would not be popular with my father's family. "Do you know who Lord and Lady Theodore Hughes owed for their pleasures? Anyone who is known for killing those who don't pay up?"

My grandfather continued to stare at me. Finally, he said, "We hear rumors about who is involved in the rough end of loaning to aristocrats, and we stay away from them. Now, I don't mind you doing a little surreptitious entry or safe cracking or working a con to keep on the right side of that widow, but these people you're talking about can be dangerous. Deadly dangerous. Don't try to con them. You stay away from them and let Inspector Russell do his job."

"I'd love to. Inspector Russell would be able to find the killers if the Duke of Wallingford and his family would just cooperate." I hoped I hadn't blushed when I said James's name.

"He's very capable," my grandfather said as he patted my hand.

I didn't imagine there could be too many people who could gain from the deaths of Lord Theo or the notorious Lady Roxanne. Or would kill them for not paying up. "Are there a lot of people taking bets from wild young aristocrats in London who use drugs and do scandalous things and don't pay their debts?"

"Yes, but most of those who work the West End, supplying the wild children of the aristocracy, work for one man. Lucky Marlowe."

I nearly laughed at my grandfather's words. "Is that really a name?"

"That's not his first name, but that's what everyone calls him. Gives him a bit of anonymity from the coppers," my uncle said.

"Although he really doesn't need it. He keeps his connection to the drugs and prostitution at arm's length, and the coppers can't find any reason to bother him," my grandfather added.

"He must have his gaming club around here." I might as well learn what I could. It might help me convince Lady

Kaldaire not to get involved later.

"To fleece aristocrats? No, he's set up as a private club in the West End. It looks respectable from the outside, but inside there is every sort of debauchery. Things I don't want my granddaughter to ever learn about." My grandfather shook his white head.

"Everything there is available for a price," my uncle added. "But there's nothing there that you should spend your money on."

"And you don't want anyone there spending their money on you," my grandfather added. "So stay away. Tell Lady Kaldaire this is a step too far."

I shook my head. So far, I'd heard nothing that would help. "I have to protect my business, and that means convincing her she doesn't want to go there."

"Doesn't she have the sense to stay away from evil without anyone having to tell her?" my grandfather asked in a rising tone, giving vent to his exasperation.

"Can't you just tell her no?" my uncle asked.

"She'll tell my customers that my father is a criminal, and then I won't have any customers. And no money to pay for Matthew's schooling."

My grandfather looked at me sadly. "I'll pay for that, pet."

"No." I lifted my chin and thinned my lips. "My brother. My responsibility."

"Stubborn. Just like your mother," my uncle grumbled.

"She knew her own mind. That's why you didn't like her, isn't it?" It was an accusation I'd long believed.

"No, it's because she treated my brother so badly."

Uncle Thomas and I stared at each other, anger washing over both of us.

My grandfather was having none of it. "Stop this right now. Tom, you can't know the inside of your brother's marriage. Pet, we aren't as ghastly as your mother made us seem."

I shook my head. "I've never thought of you as terrible, although you've taught me many skills I can never admit to in polite society." I gave him a smile. "I love you all. You're family."

Uncle Thomas reached over and patted my hand. "We love you, too, even if you are the stubbornest..."

"Tom," Grandfather used his warning voice.

"Uncle Thomas, I don't tell you how to run your business. Don't tell me how to run mine. And as long as Lady Kaldaire can blackmail me with my father's career, I have to go along with her crazy schemes."

I knew, somehow, Lady Kaldaire would find a way to have the two of us confront Lucky Marlowe. I just hoped the two of us would get away unscathed.

Chapter Nine

I didn't have to wait long the next day before Lady Kaldaire came into my shop. She settled gracefully on the chair in one of the booths and took off her hat. "My maid is doing something different with my hair, so you may want to change the measurements for my new hat."

Her hair looked the same to me, but I obediently began to measure her head.

"Have you gotten any further with who might have killed Lord and Lady Theodore?" she murmured.

I was grateful we didn't have any other customers present. "I asked certain people, and they said if you wanted to look for excitement in the style of Theo and Roxanne—"

"Emily, they are properly addressed as Lord Theodore and Lady Theodore."

"I bet their killers didn't call them that," I responded. "For excitement, they would most likely go to a man called Lucky Marlowe who has a club in the West End somewhere. And then I was warned not to look for such debauchery." I tried to sound as stern as my grandfather had.

"Why?"

"I'm told the debauchery is beyond my imagination."

"Emily, I suspect your imagination isn't as experienced as mine."

I decided not to argue the point. She had been married. I hadn't. "Still, we shouldn't go looking for trouble."

"Oh, we won't go looking for it," Lady Kaldaire told me as she turned around, messing up my current measurement. "I'll ask Lulu where Lord Theo and Lady Theo gambled. Be ready to go over there with me when you close the shop today."

"Today?" I was not prepared to see debauchery directly after work. I had no desire to deal with debauchery ever. I wasn't even sure what it was, specifically, but it sounded terrible.

"Today. Now, please finish with the measurements so you can construct my new hat correctly."

I finished and wrote down the figures on the card I kept for her in a box with all my customers' measurements. Since they changed hairstyles often, the cards were more a hindrance than a help. "I don't want to go to this place, wherever it is."

Lady Kaldaire rose from her chair and said, "If we go early, we should be out of there before anything happens to bring a blush to your maidenly cheeks. Come to my house immediately after you close the shop tonight."

* * *

At closing time, I put on a violet wide-brimmed hat that matched the trim on my purplish-rose day dress, grabbed my umbrella in case of more showers, and went to Lady Kaldaire's.

I was surprised to see she was ready. She hurried me out her front door and down the pavement. "We have a stop to make before we can go to the club and find out what they know."

"Why do we have to stop somewhere?" I had invited James to dinner and I didn't want to be made late by extra visits. I hoped I could visit the club quickly and run home so no one would know where I'd been.

"Lulu doesn't know where Lord and Lady Theo went to gamble. But she says the Duke of Blackford does."

"And he's just going to tell us?" I was amazed at the things Lady Kaldaire would ask people. I didn't believe he'd answer.

"He investigated crimes with his wife before they married. You've met the duchess. You know that she'll understand what we are doing and why." Her tone said she didn't understand why I found this so surprising.

I went with her, expecting to be thrown out of Blackford House. The duke was reported in the newspapers to be an immensely rich aristocrat with business interests around the world. It was rumored he undertook special negotiations for the British government. Why would he make time for us?

Blackford House was directly across a side street from Wallingford House and was even larger than the house where the Duke and Duchess of Wallingford lived with their two sons and their families. As I stood on the pavement, my knees knocked. I'd never before been thrown out of anywhere.

Lady Kaldaire, cloaked in aristocratic privilege,

marched up to the door and rang the bell while I lingered behind her. She presented her card as she asked for the duchess and we were shown into a small parlor off the front hall.

The duchess appeared a few minutes later in an emerald green gown that must have cost a semester's fees for Matthew's school. She smiled when she saw us and said, "I received your note, Lady Kaldaire. While Lady Juliet is excited about her new hat, I'm sure that's not why you're here, Miss Gates."

She was pleasant. She was serene. But there was a steel about her that made her both more attractive and more of a commoner. I definitely liked Georgia, Duchess of Blackford.

Lady Kaldaire explained what we needed to learn as the duchess went pale. "You'd have to ask the duke, but I'm not sure you're going to like his answer. It's not the sort of place a respectable woman would go."

"I don't want to go," I told the duchess. "I don't want to ask your husband for the name of this club. But Lady Kaldaire is determined to ask whoever is in charge what he might know about the deaths of Lord and Lady Theodore Hughes, and I can't let her go alone." Actually, I'd like to, but it wouldn't work out well for either of us.

She stared at both of us with her violet eyes. Finally, she said, "Let's go ask him."

The duchess led the way, Lady Kaldaire on her heels. I trudged along after them, half-hoping the duke would say no. The duchess stopped and tapped on a door, waited a moment, and then walked in.

I was the last one in, momentarily stunned by the paneled study with leather upholstered chairs and a huge mahogany desk. Two huge windows looked out over the private park where I'd found the body. A large globe, the British Empire in pink, sat in its frame in a corner.

The number of leather-bound books on the large bookshelves was a wonder in its own right. I wondered if the duchess, a former bookshop owner, had a hand in the selection, or if these were all the property of the duke.

The duke looked lean and fit, with gray at the temples of his dark hair. His impeccably tailored jacket and vest may have come from any of a number of bespoke tailors, but his were so unblemished they appeared to have been ironed while he wore them.

He looked at his wife, surprised but not upset that she had interrupted him from reviewing a stack of papers.

"These two ladies want to visit the club that Lord and Lady Theo Hughes frequented," she told him.

"Why?" His voice was dangerously quiet as he looked us over.

Lady Kaldaire looked at me. I swallowed and said, "No one knows how the killers entered Wallingford House, unless they found the key Lord Theo supposedly lost. If whoever killed Lord and Lady Theo isn't finished yet, the rest of the household may be in danger."

He stared at me with his piercing dark eyes and I felt my heart pound. He was a powerful man and his expression left no doubt that he was in charge and he was not amused. As he continued to gaze at me, I felt Lady Kaldaire, who was standing next to me, start to squirm. It took a lot to make that lady uncomfortable.

"Come back tomorrow after five in the afternoon."

"Tomorrow?" I asked.

"If you want my help, you'll wait." With that, he turned his attention back to his papers.

The duchess escorted us out of the study. Once we were in the hallway heading toward the front door, Lady Kaldaire said, "What can possibly be gained by waiting a day?"

"I don't know, but I have my suspicions. You'd do well to take his advice," the duchess told us.

"We'll return tomorrow after five," I said as the butler opened the door to show us out. The last thing I wanted to do was repeat this the next day and waste more time.

"We'll see you then," the duchess said with a smile.

"Thank you so much, Duchess." Lady Kaldaire kissed her on the cheek and followed me out.

We walked in silence until we reached Lady Kaldaire's steps. "Be here at a quarter after," she said.

"Do I have a choice?" I asked.

"No."

From one perspective, I didn't mind. I wanted to see what a duke would do when dealing with a frightening gaming club and two respectable women who wanted to invade this dangerous world.

But this was also the night I had invited James Russell to dinner. I hurried home to find Jane had shut the shop on time and gone home. Then I found James had arrived early for once and was talking to Noah in our tiny drawing room.

Both men rose when they saw me, but neither

expression was welcoming. "Noah tells me you left early to meet Lady Kaldaire," James said in his Scotland Yard detective inspector tone.

"Yes." What else could I say?

"Where were the two of you going?"

"The Duchess of Blackford's house." It was the truth. And I could tell it shocked James.

"Emily," Noah said, "I don't want you getting hurt. Everything that woman does is dangerous."

"No, it isn't. Strange, perhaps, or surprising. But not dangerous." I decided to change the subject before their queries led to my activities the next day. "Shall I dish up dinner?"

They were both willing to leave me alone so they could get fed. At least until James and I were alone in the kitchen doing dishes.

"Emily, you and Lady Kaldaire aren't planning on doing anything dangerous, are you?" he asked.

"Why would you think that?"

"Because you're being evasive." He crossed his arms, a tea towel in one hand.

"You said you didn't mind us asking questions in drawing rooms. I suspect there'll be a great deal of that."

"And nothing else?"

"Nothing else." I grinned at him. "Those dishes won't dry themselves."

He got to work on the dishes, leaving me to feel guilty about lying.

* * *

The next afternoon, Lady Kaldaire and I reached

Blackford House precisely at twenty-five after five. The butler showed us into the front drawing room again, and this time we were joined by not only the duke and duchess, but two other men. The older, squatter man of the two was introduced as retired Metropolitan Police Sergeant Adam Fogarty. The younger, about the age of the duke, was introduced as Mr. John Sumner. He had the powerful look of a man handy with any sort of combat and the ramrod backbone of a military man.

"These two men will accompany you to the gaming club and will see you safely away from there." There was a note of finality in the duke's voice.

"Thank you, Your Grace," I said with a curtsy before Lady Kaldaire had a chance to object.

"Is this really necessary?" she asked.

"Yes." The duke seemed to favor one-word replies.

The four of us set off. As I reached the pavement, I looked back to see the duke and duchess framed by the doorway. He had an arm around her waist. She was leaning against him as he looked at her devotedly.

It made me feel warm to see them. Perhaps, someday, with James…

We walked down Regent Street and veered off on a side street. Sergeant Fogarty stopped in front of a large three-story-and- basement brick building with a brass plate located discreetly by the front door. *The Marlowe Club, please ring bell* it read.

Mr. Sumner held up a hand and walked up the steps to ring the bell. We followed closely, Sergeant Fogarty bringing up the rear as he glanced this way and that along the busy street.

An older man opened the door a few inches. "We're closed."

Mr. Sumner shoved the door open before it could be closed in his face. "Good. Then Lucky Marlowe will have time to talk to us."

I stepped into the entry way on Mr. Sumner's heels. Right behind the former soldier seemed the safest place to be. Lady Kaldaire stepped daintily onto the wood floor as if trying to avoid horse manure. Sergeant Fogarty came in last, his plodding steps echoing in the building.

The older man, who was dressed in black tails, tried to get in front of us, but Mr. Sumner strode ahead of him down the hall and then through drawing rooms furnished with chairs arranged around tables and chest-high serving cabinets with different- sized glasses on top. All of the draperies, upholstery, and carpeting was bright red. Whether silk, damask, or velvet, the shade of red was exactly the same.

Sumner headed directly to a door off to one side. He twisted the doorknob without knocking and walked in. Still on his heels, I went in right behind him, with the older man trying to shove me aside.

"I'm sorry, Mr. Marlowe. I tried to stop them," the old man said in a begging tone from over my shoulder.

I peeked around Mr. Sumner to see a man with dark hair and eyes seated behind a desk littered with papers and account books. He glared at me through the eyes of Satan, and I understood why everyone was afraid of him.

I also knew that women would be fascinated by this

handsome devil.

Chapter Ten

"This is a private club. Leave immediately or I'll have you ejected," the devil said with a sneer.

Lady Kaldaire crowded in next to me, brushing the older man aside. "I'm Lady Kaldaire, and I want to know if you had Lord and Lady Theodore Hughes killed."

I couldn't believe she had just burst into this man's business and was now accusing him of murder. It was typical of her, but I still couldn't believe she was that foolhardy.

The man burst into laughter, but his eyes stayed hard. "Why would I kill Theo and Roxanne?"

"Because they owed you money."

"If I killed everyone who owed me money, half the aristocracy would be dead."

That silenced Lady Kaldaire.

Two thugs larger than Mr. Sumner stood in the doorway and pinned the four of us plus the old man into the office with Lucky. Silence descended on the room like a pall as we glanced at each other, not looking anyone directly in the eye.

"But if you killed the people who owed you the most money, perhaps the others would pay up," I suggested. I'd been taught early that if you're in a tight spot, keep them talking.

"Make an example of them." The man behind the desk nailed me in place with his stare. "It sounds like a good idea in theory, but I didn't kill Theo and Roxanne. I make it a point not to kill my customers."

Lady Kaldaire harrumphed.

"I've heard you saw more of them than their family did. Do you have any idea who would want to kill them? Other members of the club? You can't be the only person here that they owed money to," I said.

So far, it felt like I was the only one talking. We were still in a tight spot, with more footsteps and murmuring voices outside the office. I didn't take my eyes off Lucky Marlowe. And still I hadn't discovered a thing.

"I'm sure they owed others, and not just in currency. But I make it my business not to know the private business of members." He stared at me with a half-smile that frightened me, but I wasn't certain why.

"What would they have owed if not money?" I was confused.

"You have the look of someone. What is your name?"

"Miss Gates. Miss Emily Gates."

He found that quite amusing. When he finally stopped chuckling, he said, "Miss Gates, I am not going to shock the sensibilities of an innocent. I'll just say aristocrats in Theo and Roxanne's circle paid off bets in a variety of ways."

"Do you know anyone in particular they owed more to than most?"

"I might."

"Mr. Marlowe, I don't want to take up any more of

your time than necessary, unless you had Lord and Lady Theodore Hughes murdered." I held up a hand when he sat forward as if to rise. "You say you didn't, and I believe you. But I also believe you might know about the missing front-door key to Wallingford House and the names of people we should be talking to. Who were their friends? Who did they come here with, and who did they talk to?"

He raised one dark, narrow eyebrow, giving him a quizzical expression not unlike a puzzled demon. "Missing key?"

"Emily, do you really think you should—bargain with this individual?" Lady Kaldaire asked. So far, both Mr. Sumner and Sergeant Fogarty had kept silent but watchful.

I saw Lucky Marlowe's eyes narrow, and I had a sense of a man who didn't like being dismissed by aristocrats as just another common little man. "Yes, I do. Mr. Marlowe is a busy man who appreciates honest dealing. Now, Lord Theo may have lost a front-door key shortly before he died. A key that may have given his attacker a way in, to kill Lord Theo and badly injure a young child and his nurse. Say what you will about Lord and Lady Theo, the idea of injuring an innocent baby is appalling."

He spread out his hands, displaying long, tapered fingers. The hands of a card player. Or a strangler. "I don't have the key. I didn't kill anyone. I can't help you."

"Very well, Mr. Marlowe. Thank you for your time." I took out one of my cards for Duquesne's Millinery and set it on his desk. "If you remember something that might help, please contact me." Then I turned toward the door.

The two henchmen stepped aside and Sergeant Fogarty and Lady Kaldaire stepped out of the small study. I was in the doorway when I heard, "Miss Gates."

I turned to face the man behind the desk.

He held my gaze with his dark eyes. "If I discover something about the key, I will contact you. Despite what you might think, I don't approve of hurting children or servants."

"Thank you, Mr. Marlowe." I turned then and fled the building.

When we regrouped on the pavement, Mr. Sumner said, "Do you think you accomplished anything, Miss Gates?"

"I won't know until I hear from him."

"Oh, Emily, no. You don't want to hear from that man," Lady Kaldaire said.

"Why not? Don't you want him to contact me? That's why we're here." It wasn't like Lady Kaldaire to show fear.

"I'm afraid he'll hurt you."

She so seldom expressed concern for me that I was momentarily shocked into silence. Finally I said, "If he contacts me, it will tell me he had no interest in whether Lord and Lady Theo lived or died, which would mean he had no hand in their death." I locked gazes with Lady Kaldaire. "In that case, who might have killed them?"

"You might want to consider why Lord Theo was killed a month before his wife," Mr. Sumner said.

I looked up at him, surprised. "How did you know when he was killed?"

"I'm a frequent visitor at Blackford House, and two

odd deaths one month apart at the neighbors' is bound to be commented on." The smile he gave me would have frightened Marlowe. It certainly frightened me.

"My only thought was that they were killed by different people for different reasons." My mind traveled down a new path. "Unless Lady Theo wasn't present the night her husband was killed. How would we find out?"

"I'll find out," Lady Kaldaire said with a sigh. "Thank you, gentlemen, for accompanying us."

As she began to walk up the street, Sergeant Fogarty said, "You head home, Sumner. Lady Kaldaire, may I escort you?"

"Why thank you, Sergeant." The two gray heads headed toward Lady Kaldaire's part of Mayfair.

"Do you need escorting?" Mr. Sumner asked me.

"Goodness, no. It's still daylight out. Thank you for going with us to visit the Marlowe Club. That isn't a place I'd want to go into on my own, or with only Lady Kaldaire."

"That man would just as soon eat you alive as look at you." Spoken by a man with a nasty scar down the side of his face and powerful-looking muscles inside his well-tailored jacket, his words weren't a good reference for Mr. Marlowe. "If he gets back in contact with you, don't return on your own. Ask the duchess to get in touch with me, and I'll travel there with you."

"Have you known the Duchess of Blackford long?"

"Since the duke first met her. I had been in his employ a year at that time."

"Do you still work for him?"

"Only on special assignments. Good day, Miss Gates."

He tipped his bowler to me and strode off.

Traffic was almost at a stop due to a delivery wagon blocking a hansom cab. The two drivers were shouting obscenities and shaking their fists at each other. Only one lane could pass them and those drivers were proceeding slowly.

I took several steps into the street, only to discover the hansom cab had moved on and now a carriage raced toward me. I took a step or two backward, but the carriage seemed aimed directly at me as it veered to my side of the road.

The horses' hooves hammered a staccato beat as they bore down on me, the driver cracking a whip over them. Time seemed to stand still. I couldn't get my legs to move.

A tug on my sleeve sent me tumbling backward into a solid figure. He pulled me onto the pavement. Wind blew up my skirt as the carriage rumbled past as it brushed by. With a gasp, I watched the plain carriage disappear around a corner and then looked up into the concerned face of Mr. Sumner.

"He came out of nowhere," I said, my heart pounding and my breath coming in gasps.

"I think I'd better escort you home," he said.

"I don't live around here. Perhaps you could go with me to catch the omnibus?" I was starting to tremble as I realized how close I had come to injury.

"First, I'll rescue your shoe." He bent over and snatched it from the gutter.

I pulled it on before I said, "Thank you, Mr. Sumner. Please, would you escort me to the omnibus?"

Mr. Sumner took my arm before he walked me across the street and down two blocks to where I could catch the bus. I made it home in time to serve dinner.

Noah gave me a speculative glance and I nodded. He knew about Lady Kaldaire and her crusades. I saw no point to tell him about my close call. It must have been a careless or impatient driver. Road accidents were common on London streets.

Annie seemed unaware of the tension at the table as she chatted on about the letter she had received from Matthew. Our little apprentice seemed to be opening up, going to school willingly and making friends with the children in the neighborhood. However, any question about her family sent her back into her shell like a turtle and no one would hear another word from her for two days.

Before, her silence had lasted a week.

Annie and I finished the dishes, and while she read, I sketched out an idea for a hat for a very tall industrialist's daughter. A knock on the door made us all look up. When Noah slowly rose to answer, I waved him back. "You've been on your feet all day. I'll get it."

I hurried downstairs and looked out. It was my cousin Petey. "What do you want?"

"Gran said you'd talk to me like that." He started to turn away before he added, "Grandpa wants to see you." Then he disappeared into the night.

I trudged upstairs. "My grandfather wants me to come 'round. I won't be gone long."

"You shouldn't go out on your own, Emmy."

"I'll find a hansom cab. I'll be fine." I certainly wouldn't tell him now about my near accident. I put on my hat, cloak, and gloves, grabbed an umbrella, and set off.

I didn't bother with the cab, but I did take the bus until I reached the warren of lanes around my grandfather's house in the East End. All the time I worried. Had something happened to one of my cousins? An aunt or uncle? Gran?

When I knocked on the door, Uncle Thomas answered with "Petey returned ages ago."

"He said Grandfather wanted to see me and ran off. I had to put on my hat and cloak before I could come over. What's wrong?"

Uncle Thomas walked down the hall bellowing, "Petey!" I followed him in to where my grandparents, uncles, and cousins sat around the drawing room. Petey sat pressed up to my grandmother's skirts.

"Leave the poor lad alone," she was saying. When she saw me, she said, "What do you hear from your brother?"

"Annie got a letter from him today. He told her about his classes and the friends he's made. His teachers are pleased with his work." I looked around. "You all look well. Why did Petey tell me to come?"

"I said she'd say it was my fault," Petey said to my grandmother rather than Uncle Wilbur, his father. Uncle Wilbur wasn't any more likely to put up with Petey's whining than any of the other male members of the family.

"You were supposed to escort her back here. She's a young lady and shouldn't be out alone after dark," my grandmother said. That was the nicest thing she'd ever said about me.

That should have warned Petey not to continue, but he'd always been the slow one. "Young lady, ha! She's just one of us."

Rather than kick him as I would have as a child, I said quietly, "I think, Petey, Gran wants you to show me the same manners as you would show her. You'd escort Gran home after dark, wouldn't you?"

Petey looked from me to our grandmother and said, "Oh."

My grandfather rose, a smile on his face, and said, "Let's go into the dining room, Pet."

Uncle Thomas and I followed him in and sat at one end of the table. I was surprised when Uncle Thomas began. "I had a visitor at the pub. Jeb Marlowe."

I watched him closely. A number of people went to Uncle Thomas's pub. Some of them went strictly for legitimate purposes. I suspected Marlowe went there primarily to get me into trouble.

Grandfather explained, "Jeb Marlowe is better known as Lucky Marlowe."

Oh. I knew with that tone I was in trouble.

"He wanted to know what your interest is in a couple of his customers. Imagine his surprise when I didn't know as much about your visit as he did," Uncle Thomas told me.

"And he came to see you because he guessed with my last name, that I'm part of the family and he wanted to know what kind of a con I was playing on him." It seemed like a good guess.

Uncle Thomas nodded. "That and he said you look like

a Gates. Who was the big bloke with the scar down the side of his face? Jeb asked me, and I told him I didn't know him."

"His name's John Sumner. He works for the Duke of Blackford, who knew where to find Lucky Marlowe's club. The duke didn't want Lady Kaldaire and me to go there alone, so he sent Mr. Sumner and a retired police sergeant named Adam Fogarty with us."

"I remember Fogarty," my uncle said.

"We may yet need to make Mr. Sumner's acquaintance," my grandfather said, giving Uncle Thomas an unreadable look. "You'd better tell us what this is about, Pet." He wasn't smiling.

I told them why I had gone to the Marlowe Club and what little I had learned so far about the two deaths. When I finished, both men shook their heads.

"Helping Lady Kaldaire will lead to nothing but trouble, Pet."

"If my customers find out that I'm related to the notorious Gates gang, they'll go to other milliners. It's not like I'm the only one in London." I was hurt and frustrated, and my anguish poured out with my words.

"But you're the best," Uncle Thomas said. He had no idea if I was or not, but it was sweet of him to say so.

"Do you want us to nose around and see what we can find out?" my grandfather asked.

"No. This is my problem, and I need to find the solution." Then I looked at Uncle Thomas. "Did Jeb Marlowe say anything that might help? Mention any friends of Lord and Lady Theodore Hughes? Mention anyone angry with them?"

"He said one strange thing. He said, 'Instead of asking me, why doesn't she talk to the Archers or Lady Beatrix and her nameless friend?'"

Chapter Eleven

Uncle Thomas couldn't tell me any other details, and it was getting late. At least I still had a business that required me to be ready to face customers in the morning. So far, Lady Kaldaire hadn't found a reason to carry out her threat.

This time, Cousin Garrett saw me home. We discussed family news while carefully never straying into my investigation or their illegal activities.

I worked hard the next morning, designing hats and convincing customers that we had the perfect hats for their new spring outfits. At lunchtime, I left Jane minding the shop while I hurried to Mayfair to see Lady Kaldaire.

Passing Lyle, her butler, as soon as he opened the door, I walked in and looked around the main hallway as I said, "Is Lady Kaldaire here?"

"Yes, Emily," she called out. A minute later, she came down the stairs. "Have you learned something?"

"Do you know who the Archers are or Lady Beatrix and her nameless friend?"

Lady Kaldaire stared at me for a moment. "Should I be acquainted with them?"

"I hope so. Lucky Marlowe went to see one of my uncles after we left to ask what we were doing there. He told my uncle that Lord and Lady Hughes's friends, so far as he knew, were these people."

"I've never heard of them, but still, well done, Emily. Come over at tea time and we'll see what the gossips know."

"I must get back to work. I'll close the shop at five and come back here afterward."

She looked up at me, her brows raised. "That won't leave us much time."

"That's the best I can do."

She rose. "Very well. Let me walk out with you. It'll be shorter for you to go across the park. Then maybe you'll return earlier."

Lady Kaldaire could be generous when she tried. And it suited her.

She unlocked the gate and we walked along the path toward the gazebo. This was the first time I'd seen it since that awful morning when I found the woman referred to as the notorious Lady Roxanne. Now there were children climbing over and under the bench and jumping off the base onto the grass.

With a start, I realized I recognized Lady Juliet among the children.

Then, coming down another path, I saw the Duchess of Blackford and another lady. Lady Kaldaire led the way toward them.

The duchess did the introductions while I stood, amazed. The blonde with the duchess was without doubt the most beautiful woman I'd even seen. She was a few years older than me, with blue eyes, flawless features, and creamy skin. I felt every blemish down to my toes.

I would love to design hats for someone as lovely as this woman. She'd make any hat look brilliant.

I expected her to be another duchess.

Suddenly, I realized where I'd heard her name before. "Mrs. Emma Sumner? Are you married to Mr. John Sumner?" He was scarred. Dangerous looking. And she was as beautiful as a stained-glass window.

It was as if the sun had lit up her face. "You've met John? Oh, of course you have if you've met the duke."

"Emma was my shop assistant before she married John," the duchess told me, "but we've been friends for longer than that."

"What sort of work does Mr. Sumner do?" I wondered if he was the butler.

"He's a writer. He writes novels." Mrs. Sumner and the duchess looked at each other and grinned. "Gothic novels. He writes under the name of Mrs. Hepplewhite."

I blinked, silenced by shock. Then my enthusiasm won out. "I love her books. Well, his books, I guess."

Anything else that might have been said was lost as a very young boy toddled over at high speed toward us, his nursemaid right behind him. The child crashed into the duchess, who picked him up. "It's fine," she told the nursemaid before she said to us, "this is my youngest, Will. Say hello to the ladies, Will."

He buried his face in her bodice.

"And the other children?" I asked.

"You've met Juliet. Miss Gates is the milliner I was telling you is making Juliet's hat for the party."

Mrs. Sumner nodded.

"The very dirty boy in the blue short pants is the future Duke of Blackford, called Jamie. You can't tell by looking at him now, can you?"

"That's probably for the best," I said, earning a sharp look from Lady Kaldaire. I stared back at her. "Children should enjoy their childhoods."

"The other two ruffians are my sons, Matt and Luke," Mrs. Sumner said. She didn't sound upset in the least that they were as dirty as a future duke.

"Matt? Matthew? That's my brother's name. He's fourteen," I told them.

"My Matt is only seven. Luke is four."

"They're wonderful children," I said, enjoying their enjoyment of their games.

"Is Annie your daughter?" the duchess asked.

"No—she's, well, I guess she's my apprentice. We found her the winter before last bedded down in the hay with our horse. She won't tell us who her family is, and we weren't going to send her to the poorhouse. So..." My voice drifted off. I really didn't know how to explain how hard we'd tried to find her family or how much she'd come to mean to Noah, Matthew, and me.

An odd look passed between the duchess and Mrs. Sumner.

Before I could say anything more, Lady Kaldaire reminded me that I needed to get back to work.

With a smile and more curtsies, we left. When Lady Kaldaire opened the far gate for me, I thanked her and looked back. The women were sitting in the gazebo while the children still played around them in the grass, overseen by their nurse.

* * *

I put in a busy afternoon taking orders for spring hats, working on a few new designs, and conferring with my business partner, Noah. He and our hat makers worked in the factory across the alley and did most of the work on the orders, but I never admitted that to my customers. They were aristocrats. They preferred to think I did everything especially for them.

Telling Noah what I was doing after I closed the shop for the day was my hardest task. He was livid. "It's too dangerous."

"Sitting in a drawing room sipping tea and listening to these aristocrats talk is dangerous?"

He took a few steps away from me before returning. "Why do I waste my breath? Go chase after these killers. Just be back in time for dinner."

I gave him a smile and crossed the alley to get back to work in the shop.

I'd worn a lovely dove-gray gown with dark blue accents that carried over to my hat that day, almost expecting I'd have to follow Lady Kaldaire's lead and find these unknown people in the hunt for a killer. After I saw Jane off and closed the shop, I just needed to pin on my hat, pull on my gloves, and pick up my umbrella.

I rode an omnibus to Mayfair, glad the day was pleasant and dry, and walked the last few blocks to Lady Kaldaire's. As soon as I rang the bell, Lady Kaldaire nearly knocked Lyle over in her haste to be off. "We're going to

Blackford House. I talked to the duchess after you left. She's invited us and some others she thinks may have some knowledge of Lord and Lady Theo's friends."

Lady Kaldaire marched down the block and around the corner to the massive residence, where she strode up to the front door. I trailed behind. The Duchess of Blackford was a kind person, but I still felt unequal to the task of sitting in her drawing room, drinking tea and speaking as if I belonged there.

We were escorted up the stairs to what I guessed was the main drawing room. The chairs were in gold satin, the sofas in blue, the tables in the style of Queen Anne. Still, the room had the free and uncluttered feel of modern décor rather than the crowded style favored during Queen Victoria's reign.

Half a dozen women sat facing each other. I recognized the duchess and two of my customers. Drat. They were both middle-aged and gossipy and likely to ask me difficult questions.

The duchess rose and walked up to us. "I'm so glad to see you both."

I gave her a curtsy and murmured, "Your Grace." I had no idea how to obtain the information I wanted in a gathering of aristocrats. Would they even speak to me? Suddenly, my lovely afternoon gown seemed shabby.

"Georgia, how good to see you again. Thank you for inviting us," Lady Kaldaire said.

"Come have a seat. I asked if anyone knew the Archers, and received an interesting reply. Ernestine, if you'd tell Lady Kaldaire and Miss Gates what you thought of. It's so clever." The Duchess of Blackford gestured for us to sit as she spoke to Lady Trampwell, one of my most gossipy customers.

"Are you familiar with the Ravenbrook family crest? It's a stylized version of two archers standing back to back. During the time of one of the early King Henrys, the original Ravenbrook stood with his back to Henry and shot down the king's enemies sneaking up behind with his bow. Rescued the king from a nasty situation in the middle of a battle, for which the original Ravenbrook was made a baron." Lady Trampwell smiled benevolently and then took a sip of her tea.

"And it's the current Ravenbrook and his wife who refer to themselves as the 'Archers'?" the duchess asked, prodding the lady to come to the point.

"Yes. Not socially, you understand, but when they get involved with that racy crowd at the Marlowe Club, they call each other by their chosen *nom de guerre.*"

"So, the Ravenbrooks call themselves the Archers. Who calls herself Lady Beatrix?" I asked.

"What is your interest in the Marlowe Club?" Lady Trampwell asked.

Blast. "Two suspicious deaths have occurred at Wallingford House. Lady Kaldaire, being a good friend of the duchess, is concerned something terrible may befall her friend. We hope to speak to Lord and Lady Theodore Hughes's friends to see if they can shed any light on certain details."

I thought my reply sounded good, but Lady Trampwell was having none of my fine words. "Why should they talk to you? Why not the police? Does the Duchess of Wallingford want you nosing around in what should be their family business?"

"She'd much rather deal with Emily than with the police. And she'd rather feel safe in her bed at night instead of not knowing how certain parties might have entered her house to kill her son." Lady Kaldaire stared at Lady Trampwell until the other woman was forced to look away.

"The most daring woman in London, now that the notorious Lady Roxanne is dead, is the Countess of Westkirk," the Duchess of Blackford said into the silence. "You might find out if she and Roxanne were friends."

I wondered if two women as wild as Lady Theo was reported to have been could ever be friends. I didn't want to be the one to ask.

Chapter Twelve

"Who is the Countess of Westkirk? The name isn't familiar to me." I looked around, hoping someone would tell me.

The women looked at each other out of the corners of their eyes. Finally, the Duchess of Blackford said, "She's a young woman married to the much older Earl of Westkirk." She didn't sound pleased.

"A withered old Scotsman," someone murmured.

"No wonder she's running around w—" ended with a squeak as one of the high-bred ladies kicked another in the foot.

"But her Christian name isn't Beatrix. It's Bianca," someone else quickly informed me, "so it can't be her."

"So, she wouldn't be the lady with the 'nameless friend,'" I replied.

Everyone looked away from me, and then one of them said, "I'm so glad it stopped raining. It's tiresome seeing gloomy skies day after day."

I glanced at Lady Kaldaire, who gave me a smile. I suspected she'd learn the identity of the nameless man from the duchess.

* * *

I wasn't surprised the next morning when Lady

Kaldaire walked into my shop. I asked her to please wait and did she know my current customer, Lady Smythe. Lady Kaldaire knew the viscountess and the two women proceeded to use my shop to visit as they would in a drawing room.

Lady Kaldaire flattered Lady Smythe on her choice of hat and asked me about her own hat, which was not yet ready. I refrained from adding that the hat wasn't ready because Lady Kaldaire had me chasing down a possible killer.

Once Lady Smythe left, Lady Kaldaire said, "I learned the identity of Lady Westkirk's unknown friend. It's Lord Armstrong."

"Then he isn't nameless, is he?" This made no sense. Why call him the nameless friend if everyone knew his name?

"He's been escorting her around town, but the king doesn't want anyone to mention Armstrong's name and the Marlowe Club or Lady Westkirk in the same breath."

"The king? Why?" Why would Edward the Seventh, who'd flown close to scandal before he ascended to the throne, want to protect some aristocrat? Why would he care?

"Lady Armstrong is a royal. A descendant of George the Third. She refuses to have anything to do with her husband, a fact more people will discover if he is linked to another woman and the Marlowe Club."

"Which would link royalty to the Marlowe Club in the gossip rags, which the king can't afford." Not with his reputation from his younger days. I was beginning to understand.

"Then there would be pressure put on the king to shut down the Marlowe Club, and the press would have a glorious time spelling out the worst excesses of the place and repeating the king's missteps as a lad. The king would be embarrassed and reputations would be ruined." Lady Kaldaire looked horrified by her own words.

I nodded, having heard the rumors about the king's antics while he was Prince of Wales. Having worked on hats for so many aristocrats, I guessed he was no better or worse than the rest of them.

"We need to question Lady Westkirk and Lady Ravenbrook."

"We?" I wanted none of this. I had a business to run.

"Emily, you will go with me to question them. Either at their homes or at the club."

"Are you crazy? I'm running a millinery shop. I have to work all day, every day, to put food on the table and send Matthew to school." I took a deep breath. "Please don't ask me to do this." I was begging and I didn't care who knew.

"If your days are full, we'll question them in the evening." She made it sound so simple.

I felt my eyes widen as I took a half step backward. "Not the Marlowe Club. I don't dare. I have to protect my reputation."

"I have no desire to go back there, either." Lady Kaldaire huffed out a breath. "I'll arrange something. Just be ready with your best evening gown when you get the word."

She gave me a regal smile, nodded to Jane, and walked

out the door as she greeted the next customer arriving at my shop.

Jane gave me a disbelieving look, shook her head, and then walked over to greet our newest customer.

It was nearly two hours before business slowed enough for Jane and me to have a quiet word. "So that's where you've been running off to. What is going on?" she asked.

"The son of a dear friend of Lady Kaldaire's was murdered in his mother's house. Lady Kaldaire thinks I have a talent for finding killers, and she wants me to find the murderer and keep her friend safe."

Jane folded her arms over her chest. "Just say no."

"She knows about my father's family. If it got out that I was related to a gang of con artists, no one would trust me and this business would die. And you'd be out of a job."

"And the evening gown? What is that about?"

"The murdered son and his wife spent a great deal of time with friends at the Marlowe Club. Not a respectable establishment. I found out who the friends are, and now Lady Kaldaire wants me running all over London to question them. I'm not sure where the evening gown comes into her plans, unless she plans to visit the club in the evening." I shuddered at the thought of losing my good reputation.

Jane gave me a sympathetic gaze. "All of which takes time away from the shop."

I nodded.

"What are you going to do?"

"Hope my one and only evening gown will do and

hope no one ever finds out if I have to spend time at the Marlowe Club questioning people."

Jane appeared puzzled. "What are you going to ask them? It's not as if aristocrats are excited to answer your questions." Shaking her head, she added, "I don't think this is going to be successful. Nor will it help the shop."

"Who knows? I have..." The bell over the door jingled and we went back to work.

* * *

It was late that afternoon before I found out what Lady Kaldaire had in mind. An envelope embossed with the Duke of Blackford's coat of arms was delivered by uniformed messenger. Jane and both our customers were struck silent by awe. I was probably struck bright red with embarrassment.

"Well, open it," the barrister's wife demanded.

I did and looked at the handwritten card inside. "There must be some mistake."

"What is it?"

"I've been invited to a ball in two days' time in honor of Miss Lucinda Webb. She must be one of this year's debutantes."

"She's the daughter of Sir Henry Webb, and the younger sister of Lady Ravenbrook," our other customer, a baronet's wife, told us.

That explained the invitation. I was sure Lady Kaldaire had received one as well. My one and only evening gown wouldn't survive scrutiny in such august company. I needed to start sewing today.

But first, I needed to buy fabric.

Leaving Jane to close up shop once again, I hurried down to Regent Street and found a beautiful dark blue silk before the shop closed their doors. I went home, planning to start sewing as soon as the dinner dishes were done.

I didn't know Inspector James Russell would be waiting for me by the door. I was thrilled to see him, but I didn't want him to see my purchase. Or explain it.

"Would you like to come in?" I tried to hide my parcel on my other side.

"Yes."

I unlocked the door. The fragrance of roasted chicken filled my head and made my stomach growl. "Are you staying for dinner?"

He breathed deeply. "That smells delicious, but I suspect whether I stay depends on what is in your package."

I turned just inside the door to look at him. My confusion must have been evident. "Why?"

"A small tapestry was stolen from a Greenwich gallery that would fit in a package just that size. A theft that was clever, daring, and well planned. In other words, it has all the signs of being perpetrated by the Gates gang."

"James, how dare you?" My glare should have warned him how far he'd gone wrong. He should have known by now I didn't have anything to do with my Gates relatives. Or at least my Gates relatives' criminal activities and their stolen loot.

"I wouldn't have asked except you're standing there, trying to hide a package just the right size and—"

I was so angry I could have slapped him. "Get out."

"Emily, I don't expect it to be the—"

Tears threatened to overflow my eyes. His accusation pierced my chest. "If you must know, it's fabric for a ballgown. I've been invited to attend a ball, where no one would dare ask if I were carrying stolen goods."

"Well, I hope you have a nice time." He didn't sound like he meant it.

"It'll be nice to speak to people who won't make your cruel accusations. Good night, James." I turned partly away from him, my heart aching. I cared for him so much, and all he saw was my father's daughter. A potential criminal.

He stood in the doorway, speechless, unmoving, for what felt like ages. "I'm sorry, Emily, about the accusation. I wouldn't believe it of you. But I won't apologize for my job, or the necessity of asking painful questions."

Was there any hope for a friendship, let alone a romance, between the two of us? I didn't look at him. I couldn't. "Good night, James."

After a moment, I heard him walking away. It felt like each step pounded into my heart.

I shut the door and leaned against it, sobbing. When I ran out of tears, I went upstairs. The roasted chicken no longer smelled good.

Noah was sitting in his comfortable chair, the newspaper in his lap. "Was that James?"

"Yes."

"Is he staying for dinner?"

I hated to lie to my cousin and business partner. "No. He only stopped by for a moment."

Noah nodded and turned his attention back to his

paper.

I turned my attention to dinner and, after clearing up, began work on my new evening gown. It would be simple, and needed jewelry I didn't have, but I hoped it would be as beautiful as my hat designs.

Working with the silk, I pinned the fabric out on paper and checked it twice before I cut. Working late into the evening, I was able to get some of the sewing done. Fortunately, it was a ball. I wouldn't need a hat to match.

I dragged myself out of bed in the morning, saw that Annie was ready for school, and managed tea and toast before going downstairs to open up the shop. Every time the bell rang, I looked up hoping to see James in my doorway, ready to make his apology.

He never arrived. He wouldn't get to see me in my new gown.

Somehow, that was not comforting.

Lady Kaldaire came in the afternoon to pick up the replacement for her original mourning hat. I'd made it for her shortly after Lord Kaldaire died, and she'd worn it so much in all sorts of weather that it now looked bedraggled beyond anything she would be seen in.

She tried the new copy on, I made a few adjustments, and then I boxed it up for her in one of our eight-sided boxes with "Duquesne's Millinery" printed on the side in script.

"Here you go, Emily," she said, handing me the cost of the hat. "I imagine you received your invitation."

"Yes." Without the invitation, I wouldn't have bought the fabric that had caused the row with James. In some vague way, Lady Kaldaire was at fault, and I was too angry to be fair to her.

"This way, you can question both ladies without missing any time from your shop or setting foot back in the Marlowe Club." She studied me for a moment, her head cocked to one side. "Don't look so unhappy. I met every one of your conditions for helping me. I'm sure Lady Ravenbrook will attend since the ball is for her sister, and Lady Westkirk never misses a ball."

I wasn't ready to be glad Lady Kaldaire was trying to be cooperative. "I had an argument with Inspector Russell over the fabric I bought to make a new gown for the ball. He thought it was something else. Something stolen."

"Foolish man. You're an honest young lady. If you weren't, I wouldn't ask you to help me. Now, pull that lower lip back in. Quite unflattering."

Lady Kaldaire smiled benevolently and left with her hat.

The next day and a half were a blur of working in the shop and sewing my new gown. I was still working on the tiny white ribbon flowers at my waist and around the seam of my cap sleeves when it was time to get ready.

I rushed through dressing and fixing my hair and then gazed in my looking glass. The dress was perfect. I was not.

When I paraded in front of Noah and Annie, they looked at each other. Then Noah said, "Help Emily with her hair while I get a white ribbon for her neck."

I sat in front of the looking glass as Annie helped me turn my haystack of reddish hair into a sleek knot. Annie didn't have much talent for hat-making, but she loved to play with my hair. Her efforts were quite good.

Then Noah came in with the ribbon and a brooch to hold it in place. Now the area between my face and my décolletage was cut in two, making that area of flesh look fashionable and not wanton.

This time I looked as perfect as my gown. Noah and Annie were well pleased with their handiwork, too.

I took a hansom cab to the address, my invitation in my tiny beaded bag. When I rang the bell, I could hear music from a string quartet gliding on the air. I was bowed into the entry hall by the butler who gave no sign that he'd seen me only a few days before.

Handing over my cloak and taking a few steps forward, I recognized the back of a formally dressed man. Elegant. Broad shouldered. Handsome.

Detective Inspector James Russell.

What was *he* doing there?

Chapter Thirteen

All of a sudden, James Russell seeing me in my new ballgown seemed like a good idea. I only hoped I looked as attractive as he did.

I moved forward and put a hand on the back of his evening jacket's sleeve. He turned slightly to see who was behind him and then jerked around, his mouth slightly open. His eyebrows went skyward.

"Good evening." When he didn't respond, I said, "Surely you remember me."

"Ah, um, Emily. What are you doing here?"

"Remember the package that got you into so much trouble? It was the fabric for this dress." I gave a sweeping gesture down the front of my gown.

He put his hand on the flesh of my bare upper arm above my long glove. "You need to go. Gatecrashers—"

"I have an invitation. Do you?" I jerked my arm out of his grip.

"Yes." He was maneuvering me toward the front door.

After all the work that had gone into my gown, not to mention Lady Kaldaire's work to get me invited so I wouldn't have to take more time away from my shop, I wasn't going to allow him to put me outside. I twisted so I could back into a door at the side of the hall and reached behind me to turn the knob. We both nearly fell into the room.

James shut the door behind him as I stepped away and looked around. It was the small drawing room I'd been in before. Now, only one dim light burned and there was no fire lit. With the draperies closed, it was scandalously dark. And horribly chilly.

"What are you doing here?" I asked.

"No. That's my question."

I decided part of the truth was enough for that night. "Lady Kaldaire and I want to speak to Lady Ravenbrook and Lady Westkirk without returning to the Marlowe Club."

His eyes narrowed. "Why?"

"Why not?"

He advanced on me, appearing larger and more fearsome with each step. My breath shortened. No, I decided, not fearsome. Exciting. "Because I'm here to assist the duke's staff in keeping order during this ball, and I won't let you and her ladyship cause trouble."

My chin went up. "We have no intention of causing trouble."

"No, you just manage it without any effort on your part." He shook his head. "If you want to attend this ball, you'll have to stay with me all night."

"I have no objection," I said with a smile. I was certain something would happen and while he was restoring order, I could slip away and talk to the two ladies. He probably wouldn't notice I was gone.

"Neither do I." He opened the door and held it while I

walked out. I wasn't fast enough. He had the door shut and walked beside me before I could reach the ballroom. And he didn't hold out his arm so I could take it. He gripped my glove-covered elbow in such a way that I couldn't escape.

Too bad he was with Scotland Yard. He had learned skills that I hadn't learned to combat. At least not without causing a scene.

He marched me to the ballroom where we were announced and then I curtsied to the Duke and Duchess of Blackford while James executed a smart bow. Not a flicker of amazement that we were together crossed the duke's face, but I saw a question form in the duchess's eyes.

Then we faced the ballroom and I was in awe. This was the first aristocratic ball I had seen. The jewels alone would have kept my father's family busy for several years. The dress that I was so proud of looked plain and shabby next to the gowns these women wore. The chandeliers gleamed above the gathering, bouncing light off the jewelry.

"May I have this dance?" James asked as he whisked me onto the highly polished floor.

And for a moment I felt as if I belonged waltzing around the room in James's arms. As we finished the first loop, he said, "Yes, I was right. You are the most beautiful woman here."

I looked at him, stunned. I could see he was lying. All around me were women in new gowns, glittering with sparkling bracelets, antique necklaces, and earrings worth a king's ransom, and whose maids had done their hair. "I can't compete with these people."

"Why would you? You already outshine them." He pressed me a little closer to his stiff shirt-front.

Even if he wasn't sincere, I would love him forever for his words. "Thank you. Coming from someone who belongs, that is a compliment."

"I don't belong. I learned to act as if I do at Oxford."

"I wish I'd learned that trick."

"I suspect your father's family taught you. Not only is it a skill needed by the police, it's also required by confidence men."

Confidence men. His words stung. I studied his expression. He appeared to be perfectly serious. "So, there isn't much difference between the two professions," I said, trying to wound in return.

He grinned at me. "I suppose not. Although a copper's pay is nothing like the earnings of a good confidence man. That tapestry I'm looking for is worth several years of my pay."

"You sound like you want to join my father's family business." I couldn't believe that of James.

"Can't. I was raised by a clergyman. I wouldn't be happy anywhere but on the side of law and order. I can guarantee I won't ever be wealthy." He grinned, looking as if wealth didn't matter to him. Not as much as being happy.

I smiled at him. "I won't ever be, either. Now tell me. Are you here in your official capacity or have you been hired by the duke?"

He glanced around to make sure no one could hear us over the music. Then he leaned over and whispered in my ear, "In my official capacity with the duke's blessing. There have been thefts from these balls. Small objects of great value. We want to catch the thieves."

"It's not anyone I'm related to."

"Are you certain?"

I looked him in the eye and knew I couldn't lie. I shook my head. "I don't think it is. Robbing a house while it is full of people during a ball sounds reckless. My relatives aren't reckless."

James looked around again. "It sounds more like something this crowd would do. The younger ones, at least. And they're among the only ones present during all these thefts."

I glanced around, wondering if I were dancing near this thief. Then I spotted Lady Kaldaire signaling to me with a demure wave of her fan. "Lady Kaldaire wants me to join her after this dance. It looks like I need to get to work talking to people with her."

"Why?"

"Lady Kaldaire is determined to learn who killed Lord and Lady Theodore and if her good friend the Duchess of Wallingford is in danger of being murdered next."

James was scowling now. "Why does she need you?"

"I'm more likely to catch someone in a lie. Lady Kaldaire can't believe anyone would dare lie to her."

I gave him a grin, which he returned before he turned somber. "Be careful."

"I will," I promised as the string quartet finished playing.

"You're in a house full of people, but a killer who feels cornered can strike anywhere. I don't want to lose you."

James escorted me over to Lady Kaldaire, bowed, and walked away.

"He cleans up well," she told me.

"Can you recognize either of the women we want to talk to?"

"Of course. I just saw Lady Westkirk go into the card room. And if I'm not mistaken, that is Lady Ravenbrook heading toward the supper room."

Lady Kaldaire followed Lady Ravenbrook and I trailed behind. When Lady Kaldaire and I reached the supper room, there were only two people there, a man and a woman, clustered around the punch bowl, laughing. Lady Kaldaire headed straight toward the woman while I stood blocking the doorway.

The man moved toward me saying, "Would you like some of the punch? It's very good." His voice was slimy and I shivered.

"Did you spike it?" I asked. I had heard of that before.

"Not the way you mean it, you little dove," the man said. He leaned uncomfortably close to me so I could smell strong spirits on his breath.

"What did you add?" I asked, trying to sound interested instead of repulsed.

"Never mind," the woman who was facing Lady Kaldaire said. "You," she waved a hand toward the man, "go away."

I jumped out of the way before he could rub his body against me. He passed me with a leer on his way out. I walked over to the two ladies.

"You have my attention. What do you want?" Lady

Ravenbrook said, refilling her cup from the punchbowl.

"Who killed Lord and Lady Theodore Hughes?" Lady Kaldaire asked.

"I have no idea. I hope you find out. I might be next on their list."

"You don't believe that," I said. She appeared too confident. Too indifferent.

Her answer was a shrug with a thin shoulder that nearly dropped the fabric holding up the gown on that side. I decided the ballgown was designed to appear that way. Having just made my own simply cut, ordinary gown, I was in awe of her designer, whoever that might be.

"Who do you think killed them?" I asked. "It's not anyone involved in the Marlowe Club."

Lady Ravenbrook focused her full attention on me. "What do you know about the Marlowe Club?"

"More than you do." We stared at each other. When she looked away, I added, "Who killed them?"

"It's obvious. Someone in that insane household." She drained her glass. I could smell the liquor from the cup and didn't think it was her first one that evening.

"Why would they?"

"To save them the shame of embarrassment. Theo was becoming more and more violent, to the point he was about to be thrown out of the Marlowe Club." She laughed. It was a brittle, manic sound. "That's really bad behavior, to be banned from there. Roxanne was ready to leave him and quit that house. She was afraid for her life."

"Why didn't she leave, either before or after Theo's death?"

"The duchess wouldn't allow it. The old hag said she'd cut her off without a penny, and where would Roxie be without money? She loved money, our Roxie did." Lady Ravenbrook did a twirl with her arms outstretched and nearly landed on her bottom.

Lady Kaldaire gave a small snort.

A footman came in with some game pies. I took the tray from him. "Find the Ravenbrook coachman and have him bring their carriage around. Then find another footman to help you get Lady Ravenbrook to the door."

"And Lord Ravenbrook?" the footman asked, puzzled.

"He'll have to fend for himself." I glanced at Lady Ravenbrook. She was now sprawled in a most unladylike fashion in one of the chairs lined up against the wall. "Hurry."

As the footman left, Lady Kaldaire sniffed the punch bowl. "It doesn't smell too strongly of spirits."

"From what that man said when he left, he added something to the punch, but it wasn't alcohol." I walked over to Lady Ravenbrook and held her chin with one hand. "What's in the punch?"

She looked at me and smiled, her eyes unfocused.

I heard the door open. When I turned, the Duke of Blackford and James walked in with the footman I'd ordered around earlier. James took one look at Lady Ravenbrook and sniffed the punch before dipping in a little finger and tasting.

"It's not only whiskey. See that scum along the edge? Before it's thrown out, I'll need a sample to take to the forensic chemists for analysis," James told the duke.

"I'll leave that to you. The kitchen staff will help." The duke then turned to his footman. "Send two men up to move her to the side entrance while you give the order to the Ravenbrook coachman."

As James and the footman left with their tasks and the punchbowl, the duke came over to us. "Lady Kaldaire, Miss Gates, thank you for alerting us to this difficulty."

"Had you received a warning that something would happen at tonight's ball?" I asked him. When he gave me a thin-lipped stare, I added, "There had to be some reason to call in Scotland Yard."

"Not a warning, but we acted after we considered the risk, since there have been thefts occurring at most of this season's balls." He lowered his voice even though there was no one to hear him but Lady Kaldaire and me.

"Instead, you might have had guests collapsing like Lady Ravenbrook. At her sister's ball. That would certainly damage your reputation," I told him.

He glared at a point far beyond that room. "My wife would have suffered the most from the gossip."

When I looked puzzled, Lady Kaldaire said, "The duchess, Georgia, belonged to the middle class until she married the duke. There are people who still don't like her good fortune."

"After all this time?" That was foolish. The duchess was sensible, amiable, and, I suspected, powerful.

Before I could ask for the identity of the man by the punchbowl when we arrived, another liveried footman hurried in. "Your Grace, you've been robbed."

Chapter Fourteen

"If you'll excuse me, ladies." The duke bowed and then strode off behind his footman.

Before I could stop her, Lady Kaldaire hurried after him, leaving me alone with Lady Ravenbrook.

"My lady. My lady." I shook her shoulder.

She smiled and muttered, but I couldn't make any sense of what she said.

Her small white silk bag had fallen to the floor. I picked it up and sat next to her as I opened it. She didn't object, so I began to rummage around. I found what I expected: some coins, a brush, a small mirror, and a tiny pot of rouge. It was the little gold case that contained a whitish powder that surprised me.

I slipped that into my bag to give to James.

What I didn't find surprised me even more. There was no money in there to gamble with and no sign of anything stolen or picks to open locks.

Could she be what she appeared? A guest who came to enjoy the ball and mixed too many things simultaneously? Could this be what happened to both Lord and Lady Theodore Hughes, with fatal consequences?

No. Not, as I had come to think of her, Roxanne. Her

throat had been slit and her clothes taken or changed with the aim of embarrassing her. But perhaps the moody and combative Lord Theo Hughes had succumbed to liquid or powdered refreshments. Perhaps his death was simply an accident as had been reported.

Lady Ravenbrook's head tipped forward to her chest. I lifted it and said, "My lady. Who was that man?"

Her eyes opened slits. She put her finger to her lips. "Ssh. No names." Then she went limp.

I was trying to think of what to do when two liveried footmen entered and heaved her up between them. I held the door as they took her out, her head lolling to one side.

At the same instant, a maid came in carrying the punchbowl. "Don't worry," she said with a grin. "We washed it good once that fellow put some in a bottle. He said it was poisoned." She sounded like this made the party a success in her eyes.

"Thank you." I went out the door that Lady Ravenbrook had been taken through. I hoped to find Lady Kaldaire or James or anyone who could answer questions so this night wouldn't be a complete waste of time.

I found my way to the ballroom. Except for some clients, I didn't see anyone I knew. And then I spotted the man who'd been in the room with Lady Ravenbrook and the punchbowl. I moved closer while trying to appear to move aimlessly through the crowd, hoping someone would call his name.

I'd nearly reached him when I heard a man's voice say, "Armstrong."

I looked around quickly, trying to see who would

respond, when a voice in my ear said, "Are you following me?"

It was the man who'd been in the supper room, and he had a strong hold on my arm.

"I wanted to find out who you were," I said. I wondered how much of the truth I'd have to tell to escape his grip.

"You know what curiosity did to the cat," he murmured. "Who put you up to following me?"

"No one."

His grip became painful.

Gasping, I said the only thing I could think of. "I wanted to tell you Lady Ravenbrook has been taken home."

He swore under his whiskey breath. "In her carriage?"

"Yes."

"She's becoming unreliable." He loosened his grip. "But that's not your problem." He let me go and strode away.

I looked around, but couldn't figure out which man had called out Armstrong's name. Perhaps I hadn't been speaking to Lord Armstrong. Perhaps when I looked around, he spotted me. I was frustrated that I hadn't been smart enough to get his name.

Lady Kaldaire strolled through the crowd to come up to me. "Where have you been, Emily?"

"I was with Lady Ravenbrook until they took her to her coach, and then I came down here. Who was the man in the supper room with her?"

"Lord Armstrong. I wasn't paying attention to him

because I wanted to speak to Lady Ravenbrook. And now it will have to wait until tomorrow. I wish you hadn't danced off with that handsome young man." She sounded annoyed with the one moment of the entire night that I'd enjoyed.

"I enjoyed dancing with Inspector Russell." I glared at Lady Kaldaire and she looked away. "And I just ran into Lord Armstrong here in the ballroom. He seemed upset that Lady Ravenbrook was taken home. He said she was becoming unreliable."

"Hardly a surprise," she huffed out. "I don't care what they say about cocaine giving you energy and keeping you awake like coffee, I don't believe it. That's what is making her unreliable. You mark my words. If they stopped selling the stuff to these young, rich idiots, everyone would be much better off."

I'd heard those same claims concerning cocaine, but I'd never been offered any. Probably because anyone who did such a thing would have to deal with my father's entire family, and no one wanted to face those odds.

"Emily, tomorrow afternoon we are going to call on Lady Ravenbrook."

"I need to—"

"I don't care what you need to do, Emily, this is important." Her head swiveled around to watch a lady walk quickly past us. "Lady Westkirk. I was hoping to have a word with you."

"I was just on my way out—," the young woman said, speeding up her pace.

"This will only take a minute or two," Lady Kaldaire

said, keeping up with her.

I followed them, taking the path they had cut through the sparkling crowd. I reached them in time to hear Lady Westkirk say, "I'm in a bit of a hurry. Tomorrow, perhaps."

"This will only take a minute," Lady Kaldaire said.

Lady Westkirk had already turned away from her and was making her way toward the front door. "Could you summon the Westkirk carriage?" she asked a footman before entering the retiring room to retrieve her cloak from a maid.

Lady Kaldaire blocked the doorway to the retiring room. "I must speak to you."

"Tomorrow. Come at three and bring your mousy friend." She appeared to either trip on Lady Kaldaire's foot or give her a sharp kick. "I'm terribly sorry. I hope you're all right."

As Lady Kaldaire gasped, Lady Westkirk gave me an overdone smile. She slipped past us and out the front door. From my position in the hall, I saw a carriage pull up just as she reached the street. A liveried footman jumped down and helped her inside with practiced moves. They were off in less than a minute.

"If she thinks she can get rid of me that easily, she doesn't know me very well. Be at my house at two, Emily. We'll go to see Lady Ravenbrook first." Lady Kaldaire limped away from the doorframe to stand next to me in the hall. "I think Lady Westkirk will prove more informative, but you never can tell."

"I need to be at work." I sounded childish, constantly repeating the same refrain.

"I tried to avoid your working hours, Emily, but neither woman cooperated. Now we'll have to visit them in their homes." She gave me a smile. "Unless you want to return to the Marlowe Club."

She knew that was the last thing I wanted. I asked the only thing I was curious about at that late hour. "Is Lady Westkirk younger than Lady Ravenbrook?"

"A little, perhaps. She's probably younger than you, too. I think she was barely over twenty when she married that old rogue. I see he's taught her a trick or two," Lady Kaldaire added, putting a hand on my shoulder to use me as a crutch.

We collected her cloak and I asked a footman to call for her carriage. As the footman helped her down the stairs, I considered asking for a hansom cab.

A familiar voice behind me said, "Would you like me to escort you home?"

I turned my head to give James a smile. "I'd love it, but don't you need to work?"

"I've already failed in my assignment. Besides, the damage has been done. They don't need me anymore tonight."

When I was handed my cloak, James spread it over my shoulders. I felt like a princess. When he whispered in my ear as our cab took off, "You are beautiful tonight," I easily could have collapsed into his arms. Instead, I took his hand in mine and heard a thunk as I inadvertently hit his evening jacket pocket.

I jumped. "What was that?"

"The stoppered bottles with samples from the

punchbowl and the unserved punch. After I drop you off, I'll take these over to the laboratory at Scotland Yard for analysis."

I scooted away from him on the worn leather seat in case the bottles spilled in the hopes they wouldn't ruin my new gown.

He saw what I was doing and said, "It's all right. They're not leaking."

I smiled and nodded, curious about his evening. "Something was stolen?"

"A couple pieces of the duchess's jewelry from her room, containing emeralds and diamonds. Her maid was called to help a debutante who'd had a big rip in her hem when one of the dancers stepped on her gown. She was only gone a few minutes, less than five, during the entire evening and that was when the thief struck."

"And no one was seen entering or leaving the duchess's room?"

"No."

"It would be hard to time anything that perfectly. Someone must have been watching." I knew something about timing from visits to my grandfather when I was a girl. "Do you know who stepped on the girl's gown and ripped it?"

"I don't think anyone knows. The ball had turned into a crush. I've questioned the staff, and the time the maid was absent was a busy period for all of them. No one was upstairs to see anything."

"Did you check with the duke to find out if everyone told you the truth about their assignments?" I asked. I have a naturally suspicious mind. I fear that was why Lady Kaldaire found me so helpful.

"Yes. Only the duchess's maid was supposed to be near the family sleeping quarters except for the nursery staff, and they didn't leave the nursery. They never even opened the door, so they could keep the nursery quieter."

"That doesn't sound very prudent, not to station more servants there, since you were called in because of thefts at other balls this season." I'd met the Blackfords, and they didn't seem foolish.

"I had a constable posted in the hallway standing guard, but when the young lady tore her gown at the same time Lady Ravenbrook collapsed in the supper room, 'one of the toffs,' as the constable put it, told him to report to me in the kitchens."

"Did you want him to?"

"No." He lowered his voice. "As soon as he told me why he was there, we both ran back to his post, but it was already too late. The theft occurred in those few minutes."

"Did the constable get a name or a description?"

"No name. Just a description of a man in evening dress with dark hair, my height, average weight, age between thirty-five and fifty."

"Oh, dear. That could describe half the men there." I decided to share my piece of news. "The man with Lady Ravenbrook when we first found her in the supper room was Lord Armstrong, according to Lady Kaldaire. He made a comment to me about trying out the punch while leering down my bodice, as if he knew what was in the punchbowl."

"Oh, good. That means I need to question Lord Armstrong. Who is married to a minor royal. He'll be complaining to the palace, while the duke, whom I just flubbed an assignment for, is a good friend of everyone in the government. My career is headed toward the sewers."

Not if I could help it. Anyone who said I was beautiful deserved my assistance. "Tomorrow, Lady Kaldaire and I will be questioning the women who were good friends of Lady Theodore. Of Roxanne. I suspect we'll talk to the duchess again. I'll see what we can do." I gave his hand a squeeze.

He pulled his hand away. "I don't want you to ask the Duchess of Blackford for help in saving my position at Scotland Yard when it was her jewelry I failed to protect."

We were still at an impasse when the cab stopped in front of my shop. "If I'm going to be dragged all over Mayfair tomorrow in Lady Kaldaire's hunt for a murderer, I'm going to put in a good word for you," I said as James handed me down to the street and I unlocked the door.

"Don't bother. What can the duchess do? It'll be the duke's opinion that counts," James said as he swung back into the cab and knocked on the roof for the cabbie to drive on.

James Russell had a lot to learn about women. And men. And marriage. And I was willing to teach him.

Already I was looking forward to the next afternoon, and no one better dare get in my way.

Chapter Fifteen

The next morning when Jane came in, she immediately asked about the ball. She'd seen my gown when it was nearly finished and had proclaimed it "gorgeous."

I gave her a brief rundown of all that occurred, ending with "So I need to go out this afternoon to meet with the women I didn't get to talk to last night."

"And save Inspector Russell's standing at the Yard."

"I don't think it's as dire as that, but I certainly will try to help him out. He's a very good detective." I said it with a calm demeanor, even as I remembered him calling me beautiful. The heat on my cheeks told me I was giving away my thoughts.

"I'm sure he is," Jane said before walking off, trying without success to hide her smile.

When I told Noah over lunch in our flat that I'd be absent most of the afternoon, he was not amused. "We need you here, Emily. This millinery doesn't run itself. Your wealthy clientele expects to see you when they come in for a new hat. And with springtime, and the London season, they all want new hats."

"I'll only be gone for a couple of hours—"

"That's what you always say when you're off with her

ladyship."

"And it really is important."

Noah glared at me. "To her ladyship. Not to your customers. Not to you or me."

"It is to me. I'm hoping to learn something that will help James Russell. After the ball last night, he's in trouble with his superiors." I told him the basic facts about the theft at the ball.

Shaking his head, Noah asked, "How is having the shop fail going to help James?"

"It won't fail. I'll work nights to make up the time on the designs."

"And what makes you think Inspector Russell can't solve his own problems?"

I knew he could, but I wanted to help. "I can go about learning things in a way he can't."

Noah walked away from me to find something in the kitchen to eat. "Do what you like," he said over his shoulder. "You will anyway."

I ate an apple and then went downstairs to the shop. We stayed busy and it was after two before I could leave for Lady Kaldaire's.

"I was about to give up on you," Lady Kaldaire said when I reached her house.

"I don't have much time. We're rushed off our feet in the shop today." When she still didn't move, I said, "Let's go."

Lady Kaldaire put another pin in her hat and said, "What are you waiting for?" as she sailed out the front door ahead of me.

Ravenbrook House was only a two-minute walk away, but when we rang the bell, the butler was less than welcoming. "Her ladyship is not at home," he said and started to close the door.

I hadn't left my shop to be told no.

Annoyed, frustrated, and downright angry, I shoved the door into the man and found myself in the front hall. "Lady Kaldaire and I were the ones to rescue Lady Ravenbrook last night when she was taken ill. Or poisoned."

"Poisoned?" The butler was surprised enough that Lady Kaldaire was able to gain entrance to the house without having to resort to pushing.

"Yes. Take us to her, please," Lady Kaldaire said in aristocratic tones.

The butler called a maid, who led us upstairs. When she knocked tentatively on a door, a woman's voice called out, "Go away."

No words could send Lady Kaldaire through a closed door as fast as those. She opened the door and strode in. "Lady Ravenbrook, you may have been poisoned."

The lady was stretched out on a couch, her dark hair brushed and braided into a neat plait down her back. She wore a loose pink robe and her feet were bare. Her face was devoid of color and one arm was thrown over her forehead. "Am I going to live?" she asked.

"Yes."

"Then you may leave while I recover."

Lady Kaldaire would not be put off. "Who killed Lady Theodore?"

The lady turned to look at us through big, dark eyes. "Am I a target of her killer?"

"It's possible. Tell us what you know of Lady Theodore's life before her murder," I said.

Her voice sounded stronger as she lowered her arm and stared at me. "What do you want to know?"

"Did she owe anyone money? Had she quarreled with anyone? Had she been bragging about anything?"

"Roxanne was always boasting. She'd found a way to get in and out of the duke's house through the back garden and she thought it was a lark to leave and return, especially at night, without anyone knowing."

"How did she do that?" And had she told anyone her secret route? A route that didn't depend on Lord Theo's possibly missing key.

"How would I know? She didn't tell me."

"How long had she known about it? And how often did she use it?"

Lady Kaldaire looked at me with admiration.

"She found it a few months ago, and no, she didn't use it often. It's damp. She was always afraid she'd ruin her gown."

"And that's all you know about it?"

"Yes. She said even their very loyal butler didn't know about the escape route."

"Did her husband know about it?" This route raised more questions in my mind. Damp. A tunnel, perhaps?

"Possibly. I don't think so. He wouldn't have needed it, as assured of himself as he was."

"How did she find it?" I couldn't picture the notorious

Lady Roxanne with her perfect uncalloused hands searching for a way out.

"One of the maids told her. Once Roxanne used it, the maid started blackmailing her. Called it a usage fee." Lady Ravenbrook smiled at her own words.

"Was there a reason she had to sneak out without the family or staff knowing?"

"Not really. She wasn't a prisoner."

"Did she owe someone something she couldn't pay back?"

"No." She turned away from us. "That's all I know. Leave me alone."

"Who poisoned the punch, my lady?"

She looked at me, her eyes wide with feigned innocence.

"Someone wants you dead. Or perhaps they don't care who they kill and you were in their way." A frightening thought I didn't want to follow.

"The punch." She fell silent for a minute. "I don't know anything. Go away."

When it became obvious we'd get nothing else, we left. Once outside, I said, "She's lying. She knows who poisoned the punch, and I think she may know a debt Lady Theodore couldn't repay." My mind grabbed on to a second thought. "Or a debt Lord Theo owed when he died that someone wanted his wife to pay."

"What do we do now?" Lady Kaldaire said. She sounded entranced by our newest discoveries.

"We'll visit Lady Westkirk, and then you are going to tell your friend the Duchess of Wallingford about the escape route while I go back to work."

Amazingly, she didn't argue.

We arrived at Westkirk House a quarter of an hour earlier than the three o'clock Lady Westkirk had commanded. When we rang the bell, the butler informed us we would have to wait for a short time and put us in the gloomiest of old-fashioned drawing rooms. It hadn't been redecorated since the old queen became a widow.

The wallpaper was a smoke-stained yellow now faded to muddy beige. Upholstery was stained with wine and fire soot. A vase had been inexpertly mended and displayed a spiderweb of cracks.

Lady Kaldaire and I looked at each other and sat. We'd only been there a few minutes when the door opened. An elderly man wearing a single-breasted morning coat and straight-cut waistcoat, both so out of date only my grandfather could appreciate them, peeked around the door and then came in. "Bianca should be back soon. It's nice to have her friends visit, especially the pretty young ones," he said, looking me over. "I'm the sixth Lord Westkirk."

We both rose and curtsied. "How do you do. I'm Lady Kaldaire, and this is Miss Gates. I thought Lady Westkirk said last night that she'd be here now." Lady Kaldaire gave him a beatific smile.

"You were at the Blackford ball, were you? Beastly things, balls. You're expected to dance, you know."

I was startled by his words, not seeing any reason to attend but to dance. However, Lady Kaldaire was ready for his pronouncement. "No one dare expect me to dance."

The ancient man came over and took Lady Kaldaire's hand, leading her to a sofa. "A woman who knows her own mind. Good for you."

"Did Lady Westkirk go for a ride?" I asked, not wanting to waste time. "It's such a lovely day out."

"No, she had business to take care of. Always taking care of business, my Bianca."

"Surely, you have a man of affairs to handle that," Lady Kaldaire said.

"I do, but Bianca doesn't trust him. Says being the fourth wife of an old man means she has to watch out for herself. She and Willard don't see eye to eye."

"Who's Willard?" I asked. I couldn't believe this elderly aristocrat was telling complete strangers all this. He must be in his dotage.

"My heir. Son from my first wife. I have three children. Two from my first wife and one from my second. There would have been more, but she died in childbirth. These last two women have been disappointments. Good to see a woman become a mother."

I wondered if his last two wives would have agreed. Then I looked at the shaky, wrinkled old man, considered the marriage bed, and shuddered.

Fortunately, his attention was back on Lady Kaldaire. "I'm sure Lady Westkirk and your son have much in common," she said.

"Oh, no. He calls her a money-grubbing adulteress. I'll have to leave her something in my will, because Willard will chuck her out into the street before I'm in the ground." He cackled, and the sound made me shudder.

"Surely you've made provision for her already," I said.

"Oh, no. Plenty of time. That way she won't poison me. I understand if she stabbed me, it would leave a mark. That's why poison is a woman's weapon. All clean and neat and tidy."

"It has that going for it," Lady Kaldaire agreed.

At this point, I wondered about the sanity of both of these older aristocrats.

On the other hand, could Lady Ravenbrook have poisoned the punchbowl at the ball? And then fallen victim to it herself? She could have made certain to only imbibe enough to make herself sick, while others might have died. But why would she plan to kill random people at a ball in honor of her sister? That didn't seem to be at all sane, although it might be an efficient plan to a crazed mind.

The old man continued without prodding. "Willard's daughter is older than my wife. She didn't—"

"My goodness, Hamish, what are you telling our guests? Good afternoon, Lady Kaldaire." Lady Westkirk breezed into the room, pulled the bell rope, and sat across from her husband and Lady Kaldaire. I sat at an angle to all three, so I saw the look of loathing Lady Westkirk gave her husband while he looked at Lady Kaldaire.

"I'm afraid we arrived early, so your husband has kindly entertained us until you returned." Lady Kaldaire glanced at her hostess with her eyebrows raised.

"Thank you, Hamish, but this will all be women's talk. I'll have tea taken to your study."

"With those little cakes I love?" he asked his wife, his voice as eager as a little boy's.

"Of course."

A maid answered the bell. Lady Westkirk gave the orders for tea and had the maid help Lord Westkirk out of the room.

Once they were gone and the door shut, Lady Westkirk said, "I'm afraid he's totally confused, but he's harmless. Now, what is so important, Lady Kaldaire and friend?"

I gave her a frozen smile while Lady Kaldaire introduced us. Then she added, "We need to know what you know about Lady Theodore's murder."

She gave us both a steely look. "Nothing."

"You were a good friend of hers. You spent time in the Marlowe Club with her. Surely, you know who she'd quarreled with. Who she owed money to," Lady Kaldaire insisted.

Lady Westkirk rose. "You misjudge our acquaintance and my tolerance for gossip. I think you should go."

"Then I shall have to tell the police what I know," I blurted out.

The young lady gracefully sank into her chair, her black hair a lovely contrast to her pink and white afternoon gown. Her dark gray eyes narrowed as she said, "And what is it exactly that you think you know?"

"We know what's been going on at the Marlowe Club and at the balls. I think you should tell us everything," I told her. As a bluff, I thought it was quite good. I had no idea who had poisoned the punch and I'd been told I was much too innocent to understand what happened at the Marlowe Club.

"Fine. Wait until the tea arrives and then I'll share all the gossip that I've heard," Lady Westkirk said.

Chapter Sixteen

We sat in silence, punctuated by the ticking of the clock and Lady Kaldaire tapping one shoe while we waited for the tea to arrive. Every time Lady Kaldaire began to speak, Lady Westkirk silenced her with a look. All I could think of was the amount of work awaiting me at the shop.

Finally, the tea service was brought in by a maid, and Lady Westkirk began the laborious task of pouring and adding bits of sugar and splashes of milk. She took her time about it, making me think she was waiting for someone or something to save her from answering.

Once that was finished, I said, "Now, my lady. You have something to tell us."

"Have you heard the name Victoria, Lady Abbott?"

"She was the youngest child of the Earl of Winterset. She died almost two months ago. In a late-night carriage accident, I believe," Lady Kaldaire said.

"Don't believe everything you hear. She married Lord Abbott last autumn after a single season, and before that, she had spent all her time in the country. She was an innocent suddenly set free on all the sport London provides."

Lady Westkirk took a sip of her tea while I said, "How did Lord Abbott take to his wife's taste of freedom?"

"He'd recently resigned his commission when he

inherited the peerage so he was new to London, too. They went to the Marlowe Club and were quickly seduced by the gaming and the drugs. Some people don't know when enough is enough."

She shook her head and continued. "Within a month, they had become good friends with Theo and Roxanne. Then one night, Roxanne gave Victoria a mixture of brandy and laudanum and, when she could barely stand, took her to one of the rooms on the second floor where Theo was waiting."

"Oh, dear," Lady Kaldaire whispered.

"Somehow, Lord Abbott found them and beat Victoria to death and injured Theo and two of Lucky Marlowe's stronger manservants."

"Then why does Lady Kaldaire think Lady Abbott was killed in a carriage accident?" I asked.

"Victoria's body was found in an overturned carriage early the next morning, which explained her injuries and removed any need for Scotland Yard to investigate her death or the Marlowe Club." She gave me a satisfied smile.

"Did Lord Abbott then enter Wallingford House and finish Theo off?" I asked.

"Doubtful," she said in a dry tone. "He shot himself before Theo died."

"Other than revealing how repulsive Lord and Lady Theo could be, why are you telling us this?" This painful story didn't seem to move us toward the name of the murderer.

"At Blackfords's last night, I thought I saw Hugo Watson, one of Victoria's brothers. He has sworn to get to the bottom of what happened to his beloved little sister and to make people pay."

I could understand the desire to see justice done. I hoped he hadn't obtained justice on his own. "Are you sure it was him?"

"No. I only caught a glimpse of him. I'm not even sure he's in London. He wasn't when his sister died and only returned the day of the funeral."

"Were you a good friend of Lady Abbott?" Lady Kaldaire asked.

"I tried to be, but Victoria didn't heed my advice."

"Do you know which dancer stepped on one of the gowns and ripped the hem out at the Blackford's ball?" I asked.

"No. I missed the event of the night. Playing cards," she told us in a dry tone.

She fell silent for a minute, and when we didn't ask any other questions, said, "I'm supposed to go out to an at-home soon, and I must get ready. If there's nothing else?"

We rose and said our good-byes. Before we left the room, I had a question. "We've heard there's a secret entrance to Wallingford House through the back garden. Do you know anything about it? Did Roxanne mention it?"

She gave me a smile and seemed to relax now that we were leaving. "No, Roxanne never mentioned it to me."

We were out on the pavement, the door shut behind us, before I said, "I should have asked if Lord Theo had mentioned the secret entrance."

"Never mind, Emily. We know about it, and I can have the staff at Wallingford House find it and brick it up." Lady

Kaldaire started in the direction of her friend's home. "Coming, Emily?"

"No. I've done my bit. It's time for me to get back to work making hats."

Jane was glad to see me return, as we had three customers in the shop, and two of them were aristocrats. I began to serve one and we soon had all ruffled feathers smoothed. After Jane left for the night, I spent time in the shop with my sketch pad, working on new ideas for spring and summer hats. By the time dinner was over and I had spent more time putting pencil to paper, I had solved the millinery problems of several of my customers.

When I heard a knock on the door, I hurried to open it, expecting James. Instead it was my cousin Garrett. "You need to come with me now."

"What's going on?"

"Grandfather said to tell you to come now. Come on."

His words convinced me I was in trouble. "Noah," I called out, "my grandfather wants to see me. I'll be back in a little while. Don't worry. Garrett is escorting me."

"Mind you both take care," he said as I hurried to put on my hat and grab my bag and gloves.

We hurried off in the dark to catch an omnibus. As much as I asked Garrett, he wouldn't tell me anything. Only that "Grandfather said to bring you to the stable," and "You'll find out soon enough."

The stable was actually my grandmother's, while my grandfather conducted business at the house. We wandered down the narrow alleys of the East End until we reached the stable from the rear. Cousin Tommy sat beside the side door with a lantern. Garrett opened the narrow door and all three of us piled in.

The horses all appeared to be dozing in their stalls, ignoring the humans gathered in one area around the hay bales. There were several men standing in the barn, half of whom I'd never met. In the middle, lying on fresh hay spread on the ground, was Lucky Marlowe.

Marlowe was a mess. His evening suit was dirty and torn, his face was bloody and already sprouting bruises, and dried blood stuck to his hair. Uncle Thomas had a bucket and rags and was using them to wash off the worst of the damage.

He no longer appeared to be Satan, all powerful and untouchably evil. He looked like a man who'd received a beating.

Grandfather said, "Emily is here now. I'd like you to tell her what you've told us."

"Your granddaughter?" came out slightly muffled through swollen lips.

"Yes." Grandfather waved to me to join him on a hay bale.

I sat down, trying to find a comfortable spot, and looked at the man lying before me. "Mr. Marlowe, what happened?"

"Your family found me and brought me here so neither my attacker nor the police would find me." He lifted one bloody hand and grabbed mine. His grip was strong. "Stay away from this business with Lord Theo and the murder of the notorious Lady Roxanne."

Everybody seemed to be advising me to do that. "Who

attacked you?"

"I don't know him."

"Everyone involved in the murders is a regular at the Marlowe Club," I told Marlowe.

"Not him. Ow!" Marlowe gave Uncle Thomas a dirty look.

"Are you certain this was because of the murder of Lady Theodore Hughes?"

"He said it was because of my role in the murder. She's the only murder I know of."

"What about Victoria, Lady Abbott? She was killed in the Marlowe Club," I told him.

"What?" He looked at me in confusion. "No, she wasn't. She died, yeah, but not murdered."

I stared at Marlowe, as confused as he looked. "What did you hear about the cause of her death?"

"Carriage accident. It turned over and crushed her. Late at night, after she left the Marlowe Club."

"Did you see her leave?"

"Well, no, but—" He frowned as he fell silent.

"Is it possible Lady Abbott was killed in the club?" I gave him a hard stare.

"I pride myself on knowing everything that goes on in the Marlowe Club. That is my business. Mine." He jerked twice on the hand he was holding, nearly pulling my arm from the socket and pulling me off the hay bale.

"Are you sure all of your employees are loyal?" I asked. I was rewarded by seeing Mr. Marlowe squirm around on the floor to look at the men I didn't recognize. His efforts left visible expressions of pain on his face.

"We're all loyal," one of them finally said, "but there's no telling about the maids. Wave enough money in their faces and they'll look the other way. It's usually sex, though." The speaker glanced at me and reddened before hurrying on. "I don't know of anyone who'd look the other way if it's murder."

"Ask around the club. I want to know what happened to Lady Abbott," he growled. "Someone must know something."

The men nodded and three of them left the stable.

"Do you know about a secret way into Wallingford House from the back garden?" I asked.

Again, he looked puzzled. "No. Why would I?"

"I don't know. I just hoped it might answer something I wondered about." I looked at my grandfather. "You wouldn't know about a secret entrance into Wallingford House, would you?"

"Really, Pet." He smiled. "Of course, that would be a useful piece of information, but it could only be used once."

Oh, dear. Now the entire Gates clan would be listening for any hint of a secret passage into Wallingford House, or any other of the grand houses in the area.

Uncle Thomas, on Marlowe's other side from my grandfather and me, tossed the rags into the bucket and said, "You won't look pretty for a few days, but then, you didn't before."

Mr. Marlowe and Uncle Thomas grimaced at each other.

"Not much real damage, Marlowe," Uncle Thomas said

to his patient. "You want to try to sit up?"

"Give me a hand, Gates."

My uncle helped the man sit against a hay bale and then checked his head. "You've got quite a knot there."

"Hit it on a wall. The wall did me more damage than that toff." Marlowe gingerly touched the back of his skull.

"Good thing there's nothing there to damage," my uncle said.

"If the wall hadn't been in my way, I would have gotten the best of that man. And I may still."

"I'm sure," my uncle told him, "but for the next few days, take it easy." Uncle Thomas stood and walked off with the bucket.

"Anything else you need to know, Pet?" my grandfather asked.

"Who the man was who attacked Mr. Marlowe, and what really happened to Lady Abbott. Somehow, I think it will lead us to who killed Roxanne. Or I should say Lady Theo."

"How will it do that?" Marlowe asked. His eyes narrowed and he sounded as if he were weighing my words.

"I don't know yet. But in my search for who killed Lady Theo, I found Lady Ravenbrook and Lady Westkirk. Then Lady Westkirk mentioned Lady Abbott's death and how she thought she saw Lady Abbott's brother at the ball where Lady Ravenbrook was poisoned. The next thing I know, you're beaten up by a strange man."

"Pet, you're going to find yourself in serious trouble if you keep investigating this murder." My grandfather looked more than a little worried.

I looked away. I didn't want to mention the reason Lady Kaldaire could force me to help her find the killer. Instead, I asked, "Did you know Lord and Lady Theo well?"

"What's your interest?"

"The lady who came with me to the Marlowe Club is very close to the mother of Lord Theo Hughes and has involved herself, and me, in making certain no harm comes to her friend."

He shook his head very slowly, as if trying not to cause himself any more pain. "Not good enough."

"I found Roxanne's body. She was killed rather brutally, and I want to see someone pay for the crime." I held his gaze until he finally looked away.

"What happened to her?" He kept his face turned toward the horse stalls.

I told him. When I finished, Mr. Marlowe looked shattered, and even my grandfather looked sickened. "Pet, you should never have seen that."

"Well, I did, and I can't unsee it." I watched Mr. Marlowe until he stopped wiping at his eyes and put away his handkerchief. "What was the notorious Lady Roxanne to you?"

"A customer."

"So was Victoria, Lady Abbott, and you weren't affected by her death. There's a Jeb Marlowe inside Lucky Marlowe, and I want to know who Lady Theo was to him. To the man inside the club owner."

In a voice I could hardly hear, he murmured, "I loved her."

Chapter Seventeen

Lucky Marlowe had the attention of everyone in the barn. When the silence lingered, I asked, "Did she know?"

"Yes."

"What about...?" my grandfather asked.

"I was over her a long time ago," Marlowe said in a rush. Then he grinned. "Really, she was over me."

"Was the notorious Lady Roxanne willing to leave her husband, her wealth, and her title for you?" I asked. Lucky Marlowe was devilishly handsome, emphasis on devil, and I could see how he could appeal to some women. Including a woman who seemed to thrive on notoriety.

"Yes."

A couple of the men, including Petey, made scoffing noises.

"It's true. She couldn't stand her husband, and the title was just a courtesy one," he said defiantly and then expanded his story. "He was always gambling, always drinking, always taking cocaine. And his family didn't see what a danger he was to everyone. I had already begun to wind up my business affairs when her husband died." He stared straight into my eyes. "She was free, and we were going away together."

"Is that why he had to die?" I asked.

"No. She'd have left if he were dead or alive."

"You're certain of that?"

"Yeah, I am." He gazed into my eyes, and I found I believed him.

"Where were you planning to go?" Where could the widow of a duke's son and a man from the East End escape to be together?

"Australia. We had booked passage on the *Queen of the Orient* sailing in a few days."

"Did Lord Theo's family know? She was still living in their house."

"She said she hadn't told them yet, and I don't know if she would have even on the day we sailed."

He might still be able to tell me details that would help find Roxanne's—find Lady Theo's—killer. And I was curious. "What was Roxanne like?"

"She was bold. Outspoken. Honest. Funny. That was what originally drew me to her. She had only been married a month or two when they came into the club the first time and was still trying to learn how to be part of the Wallingford family. The duchess and the family were pulling her one way, constantly finding fault with her words, her behavior, her walk. Theo and his friends pulled her the other way, into debauchery."

He shook his head. "She didn't like either way, and she was unhappy. She tried to please her husband, but there was no pleasing him. She tried to please his family, but that got her nowhere. Even when she took the blame for a couple of his idiotic stunts."

"Such as?"

"The infamous carriage race down Pall Mall. Lord Theo made the bet, and Lord Theo drove their carriage. After the crash, Roxanne put Theo inside the carriage and took the reins herself. The police never knew Theo was hiding inside on the floor of the carriage. The duke got the police charges dropped because he knew it was his son who'd caused all the damage, but he never told his family who'd been driving and he never thanked Roxanne for her quick thinking."

"The poor woman." To be blamed unfairly must have stung, especially since she saved the family's reputation.

"After a while, she began to stay away from her husband. Then she began to refuse his demands. She wouldn't place bets for him after I refused him any more credit. She showed me the bruises he'd given her for not convincing some woman to climb into bed with him."

"When did she stop bringing him women?" I asked.

"Several months ago, when she found Lord Theo was promising her to his friends in exchange for placing bets for him and buying him cocaine. She refused to have anything to do with their—games."

That didn't tally with what Lady Westkirk told me. Lady Abbott only died recently. "What can you tell me about her friends?"

"The people who come to my club don't have friends. More like accomplices." He sounded disgusted.

"The women she was closest to."

He settled back against the hay bales and said, "Lady Ravenbrook was all right, but lately she's become too fond of cocaine. I think Lord Ravenbrook has been frightened by the deaths of both Lord and Lady Theo and is trying to get his wife to go away to their country house for a while."

He thought for a moment and added, "Lady Westkirk is a tough bird. I think she's lining her pockets for the time when she's a widow."

"Why do you say that?" I broke in. I was thinking the same thing, but I suspected Mr. Marlowe knew her better.

"She always seems to have money."

"And money is important to her?"

"It's important to all these fancy people who come to gamble at the club. They want flashier jewels. An automobile. Travels to the Continent or to Africa," he told me.

"Do they all end up owing money to you for their sins?" I asked.

"No." Marlowe sounded as if he was scoffing my words. "Some of them are short on funds from time to time, but few of them run up much of a tab. Well, Lord Theo was an exception. I was having to rein in his credit." He waved a hand. "No, I didn't kill him because he owed me money. I wouldn't."

"And Lord Armstrong? I've heard he doesn't have a penny to his name."

"His wife must give him a huge allowance, because he's never short of funds. He's one of the richest men in the club."

"All of whom end up chasing strong spirits or cocaine or someone else's wife." That's what I'd heard about the Marlowe Club.

He shook his head. "That's not true about most of

them. They come in occasionally to taste what they believe is the wild life, and then go back to their respectable lives. They want the fantasy for an evening."

"But Lord Theo Hughes, Lady Ravenbrook, and Lady Westkirk want it for longer than an evening?" I wondered if I understood them.

Marlowe huffed out one laugh. "Lord Theo was insane. He liked the Marlowe Club because it was less sane than his home or his club. He fit in better. Lady Ravenbrook wanted the club for an occasional indulgence, but it's beginning to take over her life. She'd better watch out. Lady Westkirk only wants the Marlowe Club for what it can do for her."

"Such as what?"

Mr. Marlowe looked me in the eye. "I don't know. I don't think I want to know."

"Are you going to Australia?" Uncle Thomas asked. I hadn't heard him return.

"I finalize the sale of my share of the club in a couple of days, and then I'll be off shortly thereafter."

"Who did you sell your share to?" I asked.

"That, Miss Gates, is none of your business." He grimaced. "I hadn't planned on going alone, but I think it's time for me to leave London."

"Why is it called the Marlowe Club if you're only a part owner?" I didn't know how, but I thought the information might help me find Roxanne's killer.

"I'm the face of the club. Everyone assumes I own the place, which makes my partner happy."

"Your partner?"

"No, Miss Gates. No more questions."

Uncle Thomas held out his hand. "I've known you as long as I've known anyone. I wish you well. I'll miss you, my friend."

"We all will," my grandfather added.

As they said their good-byes, I thought about what he'd said concerning Roxanne. He saw her much differently than the woman the Duchess of Wallingford saw her late daughter-in-law. Their descriptions might have been of two different women entirely. The question was, who was right?

My grandfather shifted on the hay bale and my bag fell open on the dirt. As he picked it up, the little gold case I'd taken from Lady Ravenbrook came out.

He looked at me through frozen features. "What is this?"

"I got that last night from Lady Ravenbrook. I was going to give it to James, to Inspector Russell, but I forgot. What is it?" I had my suspicions.

Grandfather looked at the powder, put a tiny bit on his finger, tasted it, and then wiped his tongue on the back of his hand. His expression was a mix of horror and disgust. "Cocaine."

Immediately, my family all spoke at once. "Are you crazy, Em?" "What are you thinking?" "What a fool."

And Petey's comment, "Gran's gonna whup you."

"No, she's not," I told him. "I have to give that to Inspector Russell. Or return it to Lady Ravenbrook, though I think that's not a good idea. I don't want it."

"That stuff's poison, Pet," my grandfather said.

"I know. That's why I'm turning it in."

He dropped it back in my bag. "You'd better. Taking cocaine is a terrible habit. And one that's hard to break. Don't try it, Pet."

I looked at Lucky Marlowe. "Who's selling cocaine in your club?"

"No one." He looked around him at all the angry stares. "No one. They bring it in to the club, sure, but it's not illegal."

I shook my head. "Someone is selling it in your club, but no one has told me who. Yet."

"Murder. Selling cocaine. Do you have any idea what's going on in your club, Jeb?" Uncle Thomas asked.

* * *

We were busy all the next morning in my shop. When things finally settled down, I sent Jane off for her lunch and waited on our only customer present, Marjorie Whitaker, the Dowager Marchioness of Linchester.

"Since I'm in town at the moment," she said, settling in to one of the chairs, "I've decided to visit you for a new hat or two."

Lady Kaldaire and I had been guests at her country estate for a few days while hiding out from Lord Kaldaire's murderer. The current marchioness had been very kind to me, and the dowager's younger son—well, that was another story. I hoped Lord George Whitaker had found another young lady to be enamored with.

"Are you remaining in mourning for this season?" I asked, bringing up the first non-Lord George subject that popped into my head.

The dowager was dressed in black from head to toe, and while I knew Lady Kaldaire was counting the days until she could shed her mourning wear, Lady Linchester was a more conservative soul.

"Of course."

"Let me show you something I've designed for Lady Kaldaire and you let me know if you might be interested in something similar."

I went into the storeroom and came back with it a moment later. I felt confident Lady Kaldaire would come by the shop that day and I looked forward to showing her the new hat.

"It's lovely, but how far down does the veil go?" Lady Linchester asked.

I set the hat down on the center table. "It doesn't. The netting is only there to give the impression of a veil. However, for you I would attach a light veil that would reach to your shoulders. Also, I would use a wide-brimmed, rounded, shallow-crowned hat for you since that seems to be the style you favor. With perhaps a few black roses at the side of the crown, like this?"

"I think I would prefer a blackbird."

I winced. I hated the habit of killing birds to put on ladies' hats. This was going to take some fancy talking, to convince a marchioness she didn't want something she wanted.

"That's so unlucky," I said, trying to think of something to divert her with. "Flowers are much luckier. And ribbons are so much more stylish. With just perhaps a few feathers for an extra bit of style."

We both turned when we heard the bell over the shop door ring. Lady Kaldaire strolled in and brightened as soon as she spotted her old friend. "Marjorie, when did you come back into town? It's so wonderful to see you again."

"Roberta, I'm thrilled to see you. And your new hat is wonderful. I'm so glad you recommended Emily's shop to me." Lady Linchester took both of Lady Kaldaire's hands in her own.

Lady Kaldaire shot me a look. "Where is my new hat?"

"Sit down in the other chair and I'll fit it on you in just a moment," I told her.

"Go ahead," Lady Linchester told me. "I'd like to see it on Roberta."

I gave her a nod and began to work on setting Lady Kaldaire's hat. Of course, she had to be wearing a different hair-style that day, so I had my work cut out for me, adjusting the hat to her reshaped head. "Have you heard who the dancer was who stepped on the hem of a ballgown at the Blackfords' ball?" I asked.

"No. Why do you keep asking about this ripped hem?" Lady Kaldaire asked.

"It's possible the ripped hem was used as a signal for the jewel theft," I told her.

"Emily is so clever. I never would have thought of that," Lady Linchester said.

"People get hems ripped all the time at balls. There's never enough room for all the dancers," Lady Kaldaire grumbled.

I was nearly done and had so far avoided sighing over

what should have been a simple task when Lady Kaldaire said, "We found the secret entrance."

"What? Where?" asked the marchioness in an eager tone.

"Wallingford House," Lady Kaldaire said.

"Of course. Didn't you know? The old duke, the one before the current one, had a tunnel put in to visit his paramour without the duchess knowing. She had all the doors watched, but she never learned about the secret exit," the marchioness told her.

"It had to have taken a great deal of effort to put in the tunnel and the hidden staircases," Lady Kaldaire said in a dry tone. "I don't see how she never found out."

"Pay servants well enough, and they can keep any secret," the marchioness said.

I was working on a particularly difficult angle in the brim and asked, "Even murder?" without thinking.

I could have heard a feather fall in the silence. Then Lady Linchester said, "Roberta? What is going on?"

"You must have heard Lady Theodore Hughes was murdered most scandalously, and Lord Theo may have been murdered as well," Lady Kaldaire said.

"I heard she would have faced the hangman if she hadn't been murdered," the marchioness whispered.

"I've heard she was innocent and another was guilty of the crimes she's been blamed for," I told the old woman in a sharp tone.

"Emily, what have you heard?" Lady Kaldaire demanded.

If I told her, I'd have to tell her who told me, and she

would never believe anything good from Lucky Marlowe. "I can't tell you yet because it hasn't been verified, but I heard something that makes me think we're looking at this all wrong."

"Then who is the killer?"

"I don't know. Yet." I felt sorry for Roxanne and Lucky Marlowe, if his story was true. And if true, I was more determined than ever to find Roxanne's killer. She deserved a better life than she'd had.

"But where did the secret tunnel lead?" I was still wondering about this hidden exit.

"To the carriage house. There was a matching staircase at that end. The tunnel was bricked so Roxanne could have passed through there in a ballgown to leave Wallingford House," Lady Kaldaire said. "Of course, she'd have to be careful since dampness leaked in throughout the length."

"And this long-ago duchess didn't notice all this activity?" That I could not believe.

"Not so long ago. Just one generation back. Supposedly it was done while she was in the country giving birth to a sibling of the current duke," the marchioness said. "And no one told her about it when she returned."

"What a scoundrel," Lady Kaldaire said.

Neither of us disagreed with her.

"Why did Lord Theo marry Roxanne Starley?" I asked. "It couldn't have been an arranged marriage, because Roxanne wasn't from an aristocratic family."

"The family was desperate for Lord Theo to marry.

They thought it would settle him down," the marchioness told me. "The duchess had a very pliable young lady from a baronet's family lined up. When she told Theo, he raced out of the house, found Roxanne, whom he knew quite well," at that she raised her eyebrows, "and proposed. Roxanne, not knowing any of this, thought he was sincere."

"What did the duchess do when she learned of this engagement?" I asked.

"She took to her bed for a week," Lady Kaldaire said.

"She does that quite a lot." I remembered the first time I'd met her. "And I imagine she took out her displeasure on Roxanne even before the wedding."

Lady Kaldaire nodded, her head lowered.

I was developing a great deal of sympathy for Roxanne. "Can we find anyone who will tell us the entire truth about this wretched business?"

Chapter Eighteen

"The Duchess of Blackford became good friends with Lady Theo. She might know more than she's told us," Lady Kaldaire said.

"Can you arrange an opportunity for us to speak with her again?" I asked. I couldn't believe how eager I was to abandon my shop in the hunt for the truth. Someone had slashed Roxanne's neck and stolen her clothes and her dignity. Someone needed to pay.

And I wanted help to rescue James's position and reputation. The Blackfords could aid me with that.

"Yes. Now, would you please finish fiddling with my hat?" Lady Kaldaire sounded as eager as I was to find out what was going on.

It took me only moments to finish her hat. Both ladies were pleased with the result. Lady Kaldaire paid me, and with a promise to contact me later and to see Lady Linchester for tea, she was off carrying a new Duquesne's Millinery eight-sided hatbox.

Jane returned before I finished designing the dowager marchioness's hat with an exclamation of "There's a horseless carriage out front." Our customers were traditional. They arrived in carriages, or were dropped off at our door and picked up later.

"That's my son's," the marchioness said. "He's very proud of it."

"Lord George Whitaker is here?" My voice went up in a screech.

"He's visiting a tailor down the way, but then he said he'll come by and collect me. He's looking forward to seeing you again."

I had met Lord George, as I thought of him, when Lady Kaldaire and I hid away from London at the Linchester country home, and later when Lord George had driven his mother up to London. George had a charming crush on me, which I was glad wouldn't go anywhere since I was in trade. He was a dim overgrown puppy. I took a deep breath and let it out before I lied. "It will be nice to see him, too."

Jane looked from one of us to the other, shook her head, and checked on supplies in the storeroom. She was back out in the shop when Lord George entered.

Her eyebrows went up a notch as she looked at me. George was looking a little plumper than before and just as vague. He walked straight toward me with a big, goofy grin on his face. "Miss Gates. I am so pleased to see you again. Is this your shop?"

Jane rolled her eyes and walked over to adjust a display.

"Yes, it is. Your mother seems pleased with the hat I'm designing for her. Did you have good luck with your tailor?"

"Yes. Would you like to see my motor? It's new since you visited us."

"I'd like very much to see it. Let me finish with your mother's order and I'll walk out with her." I was glad to hear George was spending his money on motor carriages and not in places like the Marlowe Club. He'd definitely get fleeced in a gaming club.

As I finished the drawing and received Lady Linchester's approval, she said, "George, you knew Theo Hughes. What can you tell Miss Gates about him?"

"I hadn't seen him since his wedding, and I'm glad." He sounded petulant.

"You didn't like him?" I asked in a gentle voice. I suspected George responded better to calm when he was forced to think.

"No. We were at Eton together. He was always taking my things and making fun of me." His lower lip went out and I thought I heard a sniff. Poor Lord George. He must have had painful memories of Eton.

"What a terrible beast." That would be like bullying a child.

"He wasn't much fun to be around." He seemed to be warming up to a litany of complaints, which wouldn't help. I was about to redirect our conversation when he said, "And he liked doing cruel things to animals. And small children, although he complained they were harder to get."

Lady Linchester gasped. "Oh, George, I can't believe that."

The two of them began to discuss George's truthfulness, but I was thinking about what Dorothy had said concerning Theo keeping her from her crying child.

On the night Theo died.

Could Dorothy, in a panic, have accidentally killed Theo who was preventing her from reaching her injured child? This was something else I needed to talk to the Duchess of Blackford about.

It was then I remembered I hadn't yet spoken to the Wallingford nursery maid. I needed to get her details from Lady Kaldaire as soon as possible and visit the nurse.

"Miss Gates? Did I offend you?" George called me back from my thoughts.

"Not at all. I was just thinking how shocking Lord Theo Hughes was. How long have you had your new motor?"

It was the right thing to say. I didn't need to speak as I ushered the Whitakers out of my shop and into the motor carriage. Lord George promised he'd give me a ride in his motor whenever I liked. I thanked mother and son and sent them on their way.

Then I gave a big sigh.

When I reentered the shop, Jane gave me a big smile. "That's the lord who was courting you not so long ago?"

"He wasn't exactly courting me." I made a face while I tried to think of a way to describe what Lord George had been doing. "Bumbling" would have been a good adjective.

Now that I saw another way to investigate Lady Theo's murder, I wanted to get moving. However, that was not to be. The rest of the day sped by as we served a steady stream of customers. Wives of peers and wealthy commoners needed hats to go with their new spring wardrobes. Once I closed the shop with a sigh of relief and Jane left, I told Noah I'd have to go out for a short time and would be back to dish up dinner.

He gave me a skeptical look and went back to reading his newspaper. Annie looked up from her doll long enough to give me a smile.

I put on a wide-brim, summer straw hat done in white with blue ribbon trim, pulled on my gloves, and headed outside. I hadn't taken two steps when I ran headlong into James Russell.

"Where are you going?" he asked, falling into step with me.

"Lady Kaldaire's." I began a quick pace, wanting to reach her before she set up a meeting with the Duchess of Blackford.

"If it's important enough for you to be running down the street, I'm going along," James said, matching me stride for stride.

When I didn't say anything for the next block, James said, "What's going on?"

It couldn't hurt to have James use the capabilities of Scotland Yard to find the children's nurse if the address Lady Kaldaire had been given wasn't useful. "I heard a comment by Lord George Whitaker, you remember him from Rolling Badger—"

"Oh. Yes. Still courting you, is he?"

I glared at him. "Inspector Russell."

"Sorry. Go on." He gave me a grin.

"Lord George said that Lord Theo Hughes liked to tease and mistreat animals and small children. The night he died, his nephew ended up on the floor of the nursery and the nurse was beaten. The nurse was let go immediately and no one has ever asked for her version of events. I'd like to talk to her."

James studied the pavement, scowling as he walked. Finally, he said, "What does her ladyship have to do with this?"

"The day she and I went over to Wallingford House, she got the nurse's details. We've never followed up."

He smiled. "I'm glad I bumped into you. Once we have the woman's name, I'll see what we can find out about her location."

"I want to talk to her first."

"She might have information concerning a crime."

"Which she hasn't reported yet. I believe I'll have more luck than you will. I'm a woman. I have no official standing. I hope to be able to get her to talk." I smiled at him then. "And I have a weapon you don't have."

He looked at me, puzzled for an instant, before he shut his eyes. He opened them and said, "Lady Kaldaire."

Still, he continued with me to her house. Lyle opened the door to our ring and looked at James in surprise. "Her ladyship hoped you'd stop by. She has news for you, miss."

"And I have news for her. Is she here?"

"If you'll wait in the morning room." He gestured us in, still looking at James in confusion.

As soon as he saw us in, Lyle disappeared. Whatever he said sent Lady Kaldaire to us much faster than usual. "Emily. Oh. Inspector Russell. What brings you here?"

"I learned something from Lord George Whitaker after you left," I told her. "Now I think it's imperative I speak to the children's nurse that the duke fired the night

Lord Theo died."

"But we know how the killer entered the house now, and the duke is having the passageway closed." Lady Kaldaire gracefully sat and indicated with a wave that we should sit, too.

"I want to know who killed Lady Theodore Hughes. The more I hear, the more I think she was the victim of a great deal of misunderstanding."

"You're wearing your stubborn expression, Emily."

"You don't need to come with me, or write her, or anything. I'll take care of it. All I want is the name and address you obtained from the Wallingford butler." I gave Lady Kaldaire a smile.

"No. There's no need to stir that up again."

"It wasn't stirred up the first time. When the child and the nurse were both injured," I said.

"I want to speak to her. Officially." James had put on his formal police inspector tone and expression. "Either you give me the information or I'll have to bother the duchess for the nurse's name and address. Since you don't want your friend disturbed, you may decide this would be a better way for me to learn her contact information."

Lady Kaldaire matched him in attitude. "You don't need to talk to her. She was long gone before Lady Theo died."

"I get to decide who I interview. Now, you can make this easy for your friend, or I will make it difficult." He stared at her until she threw up her hands and marched to the secretary in the corner. She reached into one of the pigeonholes and came back with a piece of paper that she handed to James.

He glanced at it before he put it in his pocket. "Thank you."

"Lyle said you wanted to speak to me, my lady," I said.

"The Duchess of Blackford said she will see us at two o'clock tomorrow afternoon."

"I look forward to it." And if I were lucky enough to speak to the nurse first, we might finally get to the bottom of this problem.

And I could go on working on hats, unencumbered with the feeling I had failed to obtain justice for a young woman who'd been both murdered and misjudged.

Lady Kaldaire rose. I noticed she hadn't offered us any tea. "If there's nothing else?"

"No, my lady." James was on his feet in an instant and I wasn't far behind him.

As soon as we left, James took the paper from his pocket. "This village is just a few miles west of London. We can catch a train and be there in half an hour."

Noah was surprisingly self-reliant for a man if he had to be. When Annie got hungry, he'd dish up her dinner and have her wash her plate. If he was also hungry, he'd dish up his dinner, too, and leave me all the plates. As well as complain loudly that I'd abandoned them. "All right," I told James. "Let's find this nurse."

We went to Paddington Station and caught the next train carrying London's workers home to their families in the countryside. Half a dozen men dressed like James in suits, vests, ties, and bowler hats left the train at the station for the nurse, Elizabeth North's, village.

The address Lady Kaldaire gave us was one in a row of narrow stone two-story houses. As we approached the door, walking past a tiny strip of dirt with the green heads of plants poking out, I could hear raised voices inside. However, I couldn't make out any of the words.

Either James was used to the sound of arguments or he couldn't hear the voices, because he walked up to the door and loudly rapped on it three times with a studiously neutral expression.

The voices inside suddenly stopped. A moment later, a woman opened the door a few inches. "Yes?"

"Miss Elizabeth North?"

"I'm Mrs. North."

"I'm Detective Inspector Russell, and this is Miss Gates. We've come to ask Miss North a few questions about her employment in the Duke of Wallingford's nursery."

"Oh. You want Betsy. I knew she'd bring trouble to our door." The woman turned her head and bellowed, "Betsy."

Another woman, a little younger, and both taller and thinner, appeared in the first woman's place. "Yes?"

Behind her, we could hear the first woman shout, "Come on, you lot. Tea's on."

James went through his introduction again as if the inside of the house wasn't full of running feet, crying, and loud voices.

Miss North paled and looked down. "I knew he wouldn't let it go."

"Who wouldn't?"

"Lord Theo."

Chapter Nineteen

I glanced at James, who seemed not to want to give anything away. "Why did you think Lord Theo wouldn't let it go?" I asked the former nursery maid.

"Because he told me, before he smashed my head against the wall, that no one would believe me. That he'd see to it that I didn't get a good reference from the family if I didn't—submit." She made a face as she glanced over her shoulder into the narrow house. I could see a cloth doll on the floor and the back of a wooden chair nearby. "Not that they believed me. And now he's come to you to get me into more trouble."

Betsy North twisted her hands in front of her, but she looked us in the eye when she spoke. She stepped out on the stoop and shut the door behind her. "Let's walk down to the green."

We fell into step next to her as I asked, "Did you get a good reference?"

"The duke came to my room and said I was to be gone by breakfast time. And there would be no reference. He shoved a quarter's worth of wages into my hands and told me to get out."

"Was this before or after the doctor checked your head wound?" I hoped they had at least done that much.

"The doctor was concerned about my head injury and told the duke I should rest for at least two days. As soon as the doctor was gone, the duke told me to leave."

She shook her head. "It's the little boy I worry about. Lord Alfred. I doubt they're protecting him from that madman."

"What madman?" I asked.

"Lord Theo."

I stared hard at James until he relented. "Lord Theo Hughes died the night of the attack on Lord Alfred and you."

"Oh, thank goodness." Her posture relaxed.

"What do you mean, thank goodness?" James asked, giving her a hard stare.

"The child is safe. But why won't they give me a reference? I'd never say anything bad about the family. I'd like to go back to work, and the only thing I've been trained to do is be a nursery maid."

I gave her a smile. "It sounded like your sister-in-law can use your help."

"And I give it to her, but she begrudges me every morsel that goes in my mouth. I sleep with my two older nieces, but she wants me gone so she can put the youngest girl in there too and get her out of my brother and sister-in-law's bedroom."

I winced. Betsy's life sounded miserable. But I hoped she had more to say. "Tell me about Lady Theo."

"You mean Lady Roxanne? I know we're not supposed to call her that, but that's what the servants called her. Just among ourselves, and to Lady Roxanne when the family wasn't around."

"She approved of you calling her something other than her courtesy title?"

"Yes. I don't know how she put up with that family." She took a few steps, looking at the street, before she spoke again. "They didn't give me a reference, so I suppose I can speak out. They were rude to Lady Roxanne if it was just the family and servants around. And Lord Theo was brutal to her. Beating her and cursing her. And his mother saying it was all Roxanne's fault. That she deserved the beatings."

"Did the servants like Lady Roxanne?" I wondered how she treated people who weren't in her class.

"Yes. She didn't put on airs or make silly demands on us. Not like the rest of the family."

I decided to find out what else Betsy North knew about Roxanne's life. "Did she use the secret passage much to escape the house?"

"Lady Roxanne wasn't a prisoner. She or Lord Theo used the tunnel once or twice a week. Of course, that cow Sally charged anyone who used that exit. It didn't matter if you were servant or master. Sally considered that passageway her own little toll road."

"Who is Sally, and how would she know who used the tunnel?" Could she know what happened the night Roxanne died?

"Sally is the head housemaid. She's in charge of the linen cupboard where the tunnel comes out into the house, and I've heard she's always in sight of the entrance."

I needed to talk to Sally, but later. Right then, I needed to find out everything Betsy North knew. "Where was Roxanne the night Lord Theo attacked you and Lord Alfred?"

"Did he attack Lord Alfred that night?" Betsy asked me.

"You didn't see Lord Theo hurt the baby?" I asked with as much surprise in my voice as Betsy had in hers.

"No. Lord Alfred was in his cot when Lord Theo struck me down."

Had I been assuming too much, that since Lord Theo had attacked Betsy and was accused by both Betsy and Lord George Whitaker of being a danger to Lord Alfred, he also attacked the baby immediately after? "Where was Lady Roxanne that night?"

"Her mother was taken ill. Her family came from the north around York. Lady Roxanne left to see her mother the day before Lord Theo attacked me. I have no idea when she returned, because it was after I left."

"The family hasn't been forthcoming about that," I muttered.

"Has something happened to Roxanne?" She looked from me to James.

"Her throat was slit and she was found in the park across the street wearing only her corset," he told her.

Betsy's hand went over her mouth. I couldn't blame her, not the way James had worded it.

She took a couple of deep breaths. "When?"

"A month after your attack." James wasn't making this easy for her.

"And she could have been so happy if she could have just gotten away from that family." Her hand went over her mouth again once the words came out.

"How do you know she could have been happy?" I asked.

At first, I didn't think she'd answer, but finally she said, "It's nothing I could point to, but there were moments when she thought she was quite alone that I would see her smile to herself. As if she were in love. As if she had a secret no one else knew."

"How did you, a nursery maid, see Lady Theo when she thought she was alone?" James asked.

"She'd come up to the nursery to play with Lord Alfred if none of the other family was about. I think she wanted one of her own."

"Did you mention this to any of the other servants?"

"Only to the head nurse, Mrs. Coffey. We guarded her secret visits to the nursery. That's how I learned…" Her hand went to her mouth again.

"That your work would double?" I said.

She shook her head. "We all knew Lord Alfred would get a sibling almost from the moment it happened. Lady Frethorton was sick from the start and it made her hysterical."

We were circling the green. The tiny leaves on the trees were a light green fuzz when I looked at them across the expanse of grass and the garden beds were nothing but well-raked soil. With the sun going low in the sky, I knew if we didn't soon find out everything Betsy knew, she'd go in for her tea and we'd never discover this secret. "Then what was it you learned from Mrs. Coffey?"

"I shouldn't say."

"Why not? You don't owe them anything. They didn't give you a reference after their son injured you." James pushed her to speak again.

I didn't think it was the right way to proceed. "Mrs. Coffey overheard something about Lord and Lady Theo, didn't she? I know the duchess defended Lord Theo even when he didn't deserve it and blamed Roxanne for everything, but surely the duke wasn't so blind."

"He wasn't. There were rows in that house. I will tell you that."

"You liked Roxanne, didn't you? I never met her, but I'm determined to find out who killed her. Surely you can help me." I wasn't above begging for any information she had.

After a moment's reflection, she nodded. "Mrs. Coffey heard a man, she didn't know who, in the duke's study threatening legal action against Lord Theo if the duke didn't pay for the damage. He mentioned a huge sum, so it wasn't just some broken china. And he mentioned a scandal."

"Was the duke angry?" I asked, hoping to keep Betsy talking.

She nodded. "I heard him the whole way up in the nursery when the man left. Later, one of the other servants told Mrs. Coffey the duke had begun looking for a private asylum to put Lord Theo in. We were all warned not to tell the duchess."

"An asylum for the insane?" Would the duke have

gone so far as to put his son there?

"That's what one of the footmen heard. I think it was all the drugs he was taking."

"What was he taking?" James asked.

"Cocaine. All the servants knew it."

If the duke was willing to have his son locked up, why did he throw the night nurse out of the house without a reference? Did he know he wouldn't have to lock Theo away? But what story did he fear Miss North spreading? Cocaine was legal. Theo wasn't the only young man from an aristocratic family who was wild and irresponsible. "What time did the duke tell you to leave? That your employment was terminated?"

"It was nearly daylight. I must have been carried to my room, unconscious, from the nursery. After I awoke in my bed, the doctor came in and looked at my head. He called for more lanterns, since there is no electric light in the servants' area. When he left, he said there wasn't any more need for the lanterns. I looked out the window and saw pink in the sky."

"Up to that point, you hadn't seen the duke or the duchess?"

She shook her head. "That was when the duke came in. The two men conferred for a moment in the doorway before the doctor left. The duke said since it was almost light, that he'd have a tray sent up, but as soon as I ate, I was to leave and never return. That was when he paid me, for all the good it did."

I looked at the young woman, who glanced down the street at the narrow stone house where she lived. "Your sister-in-law, Mrs. North, took your money?"

"No. She made my brother take it. Said they needed the money to keep me." Bitterness flowed out of her tone.

I turned to James. "What time did the doctor put on Lord Theo's death certificate?"

"A quarter past two in the morning." He glanced at Betsy. "The death certificate says he died from an accidental fall."

Betsy looked puzzled. "If Lord Theo was already dead, why was the duke in such a hurry to throw me out without so much as a reference? Nothing I said could affect Lord Theo."

"I don't know. Maybe the duke was afraid if you were nearby at another house, you might let something slip and the duke's plans for Lord Theo would get back to the duchess." I stopped and studied the dirt path along the edge of the green. "It doesn't make sense since Lord Theo was dead, and it doesn't seem fair."

I stared at James until he gazed back at me and said, "I don't see what the police can do except continue to investigate Lady Theo's murder."

"So, nothing I said makes any difference." Betsy started to hurry away.

"Betsy," I called. "Wait."

She turned and waited until I caught up. "If you tell the duchess what I said, you'll ruin my chances of ever getting a reference. I need a reference. I need to get out of here." Then she strode the rest of the way back to her brother's house.

I was about to chase after her when James put out a

hand to stop me. "We'll get nothing else from her. I doubt she knows anything else."

"And nothing that will help solve Roxanne's murder." We walked slowly back to the railway station while I thought about all the night nurse had said. James was silent, too. I'm sure he was thinking as hard as I was.

During our train ride back to London, I told James, "Lord Theo isn't the only one. At Blackfords' ball, Lady Ravenbrook's purse fell open and a small case landed on the floor. My grandfather says it contains cocaine."

"Do you have it now?"

I shook my head. "Not with me."

"Give it to me the next time you see me and I'll get rid of it for you," he replied. "Cocaine is dangerous. I don't want you anywhere near it."

* * *

At two the next afternoon, Lady Kaldaire in her mourning black from head to toe and I in a green suit with a matching green toque decorated with a few feathers, presented ourselves at Blackford House. Once again, the butler showed us to the small drawing room just off the main hall as he took our damp umbrellas.

Lady Kaldaire sat in what I was beginning to think of as her chair in this room near the cheery fire and peeled off her short gloves. I took a seat a little distance away, expecting to wait for a while to see the duchess.

Not more than two minutes later, the Duchess of Blackford walked in and said, "I've asked for tea, if that is all right with you ladies."

"That's very kind, Your Grace," I said, not expecting

quite so warm a welcome. She must have learned from Lady Kaldaire that I had some hard questions to pose about the highest levels of the aristocracy.

The duchess sat down so that she faced me, forcing Lady Kaldaire to swivel around in her chair to see us. "What do you want to know?"

"First, to get it out of the way, has any complaint been lodged with Scotland Yard over Inspector Russell's failure to protect your jewelry on the night of the ball?" I was ready to plead for James's career if necessary.

The duchess smiled at me. "You needn't worry about your friend, the inspector. The duke put in some very complimentary words about his professionalism and quick thinking."

I sagged in my chair in relief. "Thank you."

"There is something you need to know," the duchess told me. "It has nothing to do with your investigation. I first met my former assistant, Emma, when she was about thirteen and a second-story burglar for an East End gang. She helped burglarize a house where a murder had just taken place."

I looked at Lady Kaldaire and probably turned bright red. I met her when I broke into her house and found Lord Kaldaire attacked and dying.

"The police caught the burglary ring and assumed they were the killers. Our detection group, the Archivist Society, was hired to find the real killer. That's when I met Emma. Friends convinced the judge to release her into my custody, and we've been close ever since. The duke and I, and Emma, understand why you took Annie in. If you ever have need of legal assistance to keep nosy officials away, let me know. I can help."

I gave her a big smile. "Thank you. I'll definitely remember that," I told the duchess.

"What did you want to know about the murder that brought you here?"

"The truth, Your Grace," I replied, gazing into her eyes.

"How much do you know?"

"I've heard two different stories. One from the Hughes family and their aristocratic friends, and one from Lady Theo's commoner lover. Since she was going to run away with him, I tend to believe him. Am I right? Was Roxanne, was Lady Theo, a decent person?" I asked.

Lady Kaldaire rose and turned her chair to face us, pulling it a little closer. I knew her well enough to know she didn't want to miss a single word.

The duchess turned toward Lady Kaldaire. "I know you and Louisa have been friends for decades, but Louisa had a blind spot when it came to Theo and Roxanne. Theo was a beast. He didn't deserve Louisa's protection."

"She knew he wasn't perfect—"

The duchess eyed Lady Kaldaire coolly. "He was sadistic."

"Oh, now..." The door opened and Lady Kaldaire fell silent.

The tea tray came in and we remained quiet as the duchess poured. Once we each had our cups and saucers in hand and the door was shut, Lady Kaldaire immediately began to argue. "Sadistic? I think not. Lulu always described him as high spirited."

"I once arrived at Wallingford House with Roxanne to find Dorothy in tears on the stairs and the sounds of the duke and Theo shouting at each other coming from the study. Dorothy told us Theo had taken Alfred from his nurse and locked the two of them in his room. Alfred had been heard screaming all over the house."

"What happened to the baby?" I asked, cringing inside.

"When Mathers unlocked the door, they found Theo had been brushing Alfred's bare feet with a stiff scrubbing brush. Babies have tender feet with soft skin on the bottom."

I gasped. "That poor baby." Theo was a monster. Betsy, the nursery maid, was right. Lord Alfred was safer with Theo dead.

"I'm sure Lulu put a stop to that," Lady Kaldaire said.

"Louisa joined us after we'd calmed Dorothy. When Dorothy told us what happened, Louisa said Dorothy was hysterical and to pay no notice of what she said. A moment later, Theo walked out of the house, ignoring his mother as she called to him. Then the duke walked out and apologized to me for having to witness this family squabble. I thought it sounded more like a disaster."

"And Roxanne? What did she say?" I asked.

"She was wonderful with Dorothy, calming her down and holding her while she cried. Louisa told the duke this was all Roxanne's fault. If she were a better wife, these things wouldn't happen. Roxanne said if Louisa were a better mother, Theo would have been locked up years ago."

I sat there with my mouth hanging open. Even Lady

Kaldaire was speechless. When the duchess stayed silent, I had to ask, "What happened next?"

"Louisa slapped Roxanne."

Chapter Twenty

"She what?" I exclaimed. My family seemed respectable by comparison, and they were a bunch of crooks. Even Lady Kaldaire looked shocked at her friend's behavior.

"Louisa slapped Roxanne, who stalked out of the house without a word," the Duchess of Blackford told us.

"She sounds like more of a lady than the Duchess of Wallingford," I said, glaring at Lady Kaldaire as if this were somehow her fault.

"That doesn't sound like Lulu," Lady Kaldaire murmured. "What happened then?"

"Dorothy burst into tears again and raced up the stairs. There I stood with the duke and duchess, wondering what to say or do. The duke stalked away, and then Louisa asked me if I'd like a cup of tea." The Duchess of Blackford raised her eyebrows and then took a sip from her cup.

"Good grief." Aristocrats certainly put up a calmer, quieter front to the world than my crazy and outspoken family.

"What else would you expect Lulu to say?" Lady Kaldaire asked.

"I didn't expect her to strike her daughter-in-law." Our

hostess sounded scandalized.

Lady Kaldaire shook her head. "I don't understand it."

"But it does explain why Roxanne was leaving Wallingford House especially now that Theo was dead," I told them.

"Nonsense. Where would she have gone?" Lady Kaldaire asked.

"Australia."

"Why would you say that?" the older lady asked me.

I didn't want to tell her how big a role Jeb Marlowe said he played in Roxanne's life. "Her lover claimed they had already made plans."

"She'd never get a penny out of the duke."

"I don't think she wanted his money." I sighed and continued. "She just wanted to escape these crazy people who treated her so badly."

"But Roxanne would have wanted to get money from somewhere before she left," the duchess told us. "Roxanne was middle class, just like me. She understood how necessary money is."

"A subject Emily has been teaching me," Lady Kaldaire said. She turned to me then and smiled. "I am trying to learn."

"Would the Duke of Wallingford have cut her off without a shilling if she asked him for some money to emigrate?" I asked both ladies.

"I'm not sure," the duchess said.

"No. The duke wouldn't have given her money to travel to Australia," Lady Kaldaire said. "I can see him setting her up in her own household near her family in the north, but Australia? Never. He doesn't believe in women traveling to the colonies. He sees it as men's work to tame the natives. Make their fortunes. Women are to wait at home for the men to return."

The duchess, who'd once run a bookshop, and I, who ran a millinery shop, looked at each other as if to say *Men can be so foolish.*

"Then, knowing Roxanne as you did, do you believe she would have gone elsewhere for money to take with her to Australia?" I asked.

"Yes, and I'm sure her family would have helped her, but with her mother's lingering illness and the sad state of the family brewery, I doubt they could give her much. And I don't know anywhere else she could get money," the duchess said.

"How about her friends at the Marlowe Club? Lord and Lady Ravenbrook? Lady Westkirk? Lord Armstrong?" I asked.

"What about Lucky Marlowe?" Lady Kaldaire said.

As the duchess gave us both puzzled looks, I replied, "I've heard he might have lent her money for her passage. I think the ship will sail soon." I really didn't want to give away my contact with the club owner.

"And you think she would have gone elsewhere for more money?" Lady Kaldaire asked.

"I would have," I said. "Setting up life in a new place halfway around the world can be expensive."

"I would have also," the duchess said. "I wonder if she pawned her jewelry."

"According to Lulu, some of her jewelry was missing."

When we both looked at her, Lady Kaldaire said, "They thought her death was some sort of robbery, so that was the first thing they checked. Especially since the jewelry wasn't really Roxanne's."

"Whose was it?"

"The Hughes family's. Theo didn't have any money to buy jewelry for his wife," Lady Kaldaire said.

I looked at the duchess. "Would Roxanne have pawned jewelry belonging to her mother-in-law?"

"I'd have been very surprised if she had," the Duchess of Blackford told me. "She was very honest."

Lady Kaldaire made a harrumphing sound.

"Most of the tales told about Roxanne weren't true," the duchess said. "The drunken carriage race? That was Theo. After the crash, Roxanne shoved Theo inside the carriage and dealt with the police and the damage to the carter's wagon. The constables never knew Theo was there."

"I bet Her Grace didn't thank her, either," I said.

"Is this true?" Lady Kaldaire demanded.

"Yes. And the debutante who was the worse for wear at one of the balls? Roxanne didn't get her into that state, she was trying to get the girl home without incident and without her becoming a plaything for Theo." The duchess snapped at Lady Kaldaire, "Shall I go on?"

"There's no point. But how could all of these stories be told about Roxanne if they weren't true?" Lady Kaldaire asked.

"Would the Duchess of Wallingford know?" the Duchess of Blackford asked, skepticism in her tone.

"I don't think so. She believed them, but she didn't spread them. Those stories reflected badly on the family, and the reputation of the family means everything to her," Lady Kaldaire told her.

"Someone must have started them," I said, angry at this unknown person.

"But how would we figure out who this someone is?" Lady Kaldaire asked.

"Let's talk to Lady Margaret Ellingham, the duchess's daughter. She's almost as proud of her heritage as her mother. If we give her what we know, I suspect she'll help us by narrowing our search for the culprit," the duchess said.

"Because she'd be most likely to know who Roxanne's enemies were outside of the Hughes family?" I asked.

"Because she's very observant where the interests of her family are concerned," the duchess told me. "Shall we find out what she's observed?"

I nodded. "And between the two of you, I'm hoping you can help with something else. Do you know which dancer stepped on and ripped the hem of a gown at your ball?"

"Emily, will you stop with the ripped hem?" Lady Kaldaire said.

The duchess spread her hands in a vague manner. "I heard Lord Armstrong, or Lord Stapleton, or Lord Walters, who is the clumsiest man I know. I'm afraid I didn't see the accident."

Lord Armstrong might have stepped on the gown as a signal. I'd never heard of the other two in relation to the

Marlowe Club, and suspected if they had trampled on the woman's gown, it was by mistake.

A few minutes later, after the duchess gave instructions to the staff and put on her hat and gloves, we walked out of Blackford House, holding our umbrellas against the drizzle, and climbed into the ducal carriage.

"The duke isn't back with the fancy carriage, so I'm afraid all I can offer is the family coach," the duchess said. The carriage was plain black with a thin gold line painted along the edges of the sides and the door. The seats were a close woven beige and brown plaid and a little hard. The carriage didn't give a comfortable ride, but it was dry, and I considered that to be the important thing.

The home of Lord and Lady Ellingham was only three streets away. I'd have thought nothing of walking that distance in worse weather than this light rain, but apparently ladies didn't risk their fine clothes and expensive hats on the tiniest bit of water.

The Duchess of Blackford led the way up to the door and rang the bell. When the butler opened the door, the duchess gave our names, starting with hers, as she handed him her calling card. He must have been sufficiently impressed, because he bowed us in and escorted us up the stairs to the main drawing room.

As he went off to inform his mistress of her callers, I looked around. The decor was a mixture of Victorian and Edwardian. The furniture was large and heavy, but I guessed this room had been twice as crowded in the late queen's reign. The curtains had recently been replaced by a lighter fabric in a pale blue that wasn't yet dulled by smoke.

Lady Margaret Ellingham walked in a few minutes later in a gown of gray and violet for second mourning that made her look more than ever like her mother, the Duchess of Wallingford.

The duchess walked up to her and said, "Margaret, I'm so glad to see you relieving your mourning a little. I hope your heart is a little lighter, too."

"Thank you, Georgia. I think I would be reconciled to all that has happened if Mama could let go of her grief and anger."

"That is to be prayed for. And along those lines," the duchess said, "I'm convinced that Roxanne didn't kill your brother and didn't do half the things she was accused of."

Lady Ellingham turned away and walked toward the door. "I wish that were true, but she was undoubtedly guilty."

"Margaret, did you personally see Roxanne do any of the things she was accused of?" Lady Kaldaire asked.

"Do you remember when the Smith girl had to be removed from the Castlewells' ball? I overheard Lady Westkirk berating Roxanne afterward for her part in it."

"Do you remember exactly what she said?" I asked. It could be useful, although I had no idea why at that moment.

"Bianca Westkirk said…" Lady Margaret scrunched up her face in thought. "She said Roxanne shouldn't interfere in other people's lives. Roxanne replied that Bianca was an expensive whore, but a whore nonetheless."

"How do you know they were talking about that

incident? They could have been talking about something entirely different. The two women didn't get along, did they?" I asked.

"They didn't," Lady Margaret Ellingham agreed. "They never mentioned the subject of their disagreement, but it seemed reasonable to assume they were talking about the girl who'd been helped out not five minutes before."

"I'd heard from someone who saw the incident that Roxanne acted quickly to keep embarrassment to a minimum. If that's so, then it was good she did interfere," the duchess said.

After a moment of silence, Lady Kaldaire said, "I didn't want to believe it either, out of loyalty to your mother. But I've been persuaded that most of the crimes and bad behavior Roxanne was accused of in gossip was only that. Gossip."

"But who would start such malicious tales? And who really carried out these dangerous pranks?" Lady Ellingham said, turning to face the room again.

"We were hoping you could help us. Who wants to harm your family? Or perhaps harm Roxanne?" the duchess asked.

"Everyone knows my mother detested the notorious Lady Roxanne. There was no way to harm our family by making her look bad."

"What started the feud between your mother and Roxanne?" I asked.

"My mother had arranged a marriage for Theo with the daughter of one of her friends. Then Theo insisted on marrying Roxanne. My mother thought it made her look foolish, but of course it couldn't be Theo's fault." Lady Ellingham sounded bitter as she said the last words.

"Who did she want him to marry?" Could this be the answer?

"The prospective bride? Priscilla Lawson, daughter of Sir Leonard and Lady Lawson."

"Who is Miss Lawson friends with? Has she married?" I asked.

"She was very good friends with Lady Victoria Abbott, who died two months ago or a little more. Priscilla is now engaged to Hugo Watson, Victoria's brother."

I felt certain this was important, but I couldn't figure out how. Unless someone told Priscilla the secret of the hidden passageway and she or Hugo Watson used it to kill Roxanne or Theo. I could understand why either of them might have wanted to kill Theo for Victoria's death, and if they believed the story about Roxanne's involvement, they would have wanted to kill her, too.

"Was there anyone else who was close to Priscilla Lawson or Victoria Abbott?" the Duchess of Blackford asked.

"Certainly no one close enough to want revenge by killing Theo and Roxanne," Lady Ellingham said.

"It makes no sense," Lady Kaldaire said. Then she stared at Lady Ellingham. "Have your parents closed up the passageway to the carriage house?"

"Yes. At least, Father ordered it sealed up after he learned of the tunnel. I don't think the work has begun yet."

That meant one good outcome of our sleuthing. "Your

Grace, could you arrange for Lady Kaldaire and me to interview Miss Lawson and Mr. Watson?" I asked.

"Of course," the Duchess of Blackford replied.

"Why?" Lady Ellingham asked, glaring. I couldn't tell if she was always skeptical or this was just her reaction to me.

"If your brother and his wife died because of Victoria Abbott's death, or rumors about her death, Miss Lawson and Mr. Watson may know something that will help us get to the truth," I told her.

"And why do you want the truth?" Lady Ellingham asked, leaning forward slightly with her hands planted on her waist and staring hard into my eyes.

I stared back, certain I was coming close to hearing the truth. "Because I believe Theo died when someone tried to protect baby Alfred from harm, and because Roxanne may well have died because of a rumor started about her."

Lady Margaret Ellingham paced for a moment, her skirt swirling around her ankles. "No one killed Theo. His death was an accident. My parents assured me no one was to blame in his death. He fell and hit his head."

"Your parents saw this, my lady?" If she said yes, I would consider that to be the end of any concern I had that someone had killed their son.

"No. My father arrived to find Theo on the floor, lying on his stomach, with the back of his head broken and bloody. The night nurse was also sprawled on the floor with a head injury, but still alive. Dorothy was kneeling next to Alfred, picking him up, rocking him, and screaming hysterically. The baby was whimpering. The nursery was in shambles, with the fireplace tools spread out on the floor and a chair laying on its side."

"I've spoken to the night nurse, who claims to have been attacked by Lord Theodore. He apparently gave her the head injury and she was unconscious for whatever transpired later." Not hiding my disgust, I added, "The injured nurse was thrown out of the house at daybreak without a reference by the duke, making her unemployable."

Lady Ellingham shook her head, as if she couldn't take in any more.

I continued, "That leaves Lord Theo alone with Lady Frethorton, who would do anything to protect her baby." I looked at the three ladies standing around me. "I believe we can assume, having heard of Lord Theo's rough treatment of small children and pets, that Lady Frethorton may have pushed Theo to get him away from Lord Alfred."

Lady Margaret sucked in her breath.

"He may have stumbled or tripped and hit the back of his head on the way down, and landed on his stomach."

Seeing the expression of relief on Lady Margaret Ellingham's face, I knew I was right. Dorothy struck Theo over the head to save her child. I couldn't condemn a mother to the gallows for protecting her infant. "When I was in the nursery, I saw that the fireplace shovel and the poker were dented. You said that the fireplace tools were spread out across the floor. Which did Lady Frethorton use on Lord Theo to stop him from hurting her baby?"

Lady Ellingham shuddered. "The poker. When we calmed her down, Dorothy told us what happened. It's not fair for Dorothy to be punished for protecting an innocent child."

I wasn't certain if this qualified as self-defense under British law, but it was close enough for me. "Obviously just a terrible accident."

Lady Ellingham let all her air out and dropped into a chair. Lady Kaldaire patted her shoulder. The duchess held Lady Ellingham's hand. All three women watched me in silence.

"There's no reason to believe anyone broke into Wallingford House and murdered Lord Theo, since it was an accident, but then who," I looked at each lady in turn, "killed Roxanne? And where? And why?"

Chapter Twenty-One

"What is this rumor you've heard about Roxanne?" Lady Margaret Ellingham asked, gesturing us to sit.

When I told her, she made a face. "She was wild, but I never thought Roxanne would do anything that disgusting, even for the benefit of my brother. Where did you hear this story?"

"Lady Westkirk," I said.

Lady Ellingham made a scoffing noise. "I wouldn't put too much faith in what little Miss Bianca says."

"Why do you say that?" I was truly interested in how Lady Margaret Ellingham saw other members of the aristocracy.

"Bianca Casale wasn't above telling lies to better her position. Her father wasn't an Italian aristocrat, he was a peddler who worked near the docks. She learned Lord Westkirk had a dead granddaughter who had traveled to Italy, and she told him lies about being friends with this granddaughter. Bianca's never been near Florence."

"Surely, she was just stretching the truth to better her own position," the duchess said.

"Georgia, I know you have great sympathy for the lower classes," Margaret said, "but you've never lied about your antecedents. That's why we like you. You don't pretend to be anyone other than yourself."

"Does Lady Westkirk?" I asked her.

"Yes," Lady Kaldaire quickly responded before Lady Ellingham could. "She acts as if she can trace her lineage back to the Conquest. While it doesn't bother Lord Westkirk—he finds it amusing—his son Willard grinds his teeth every time she puts on airs. And quite frankly, so do I."

"So do a lot of us," Lady Ellingham said.

"She's trying to fit in by being more royal than the king, when, if she just trusted us a little, we might find we like her," Georgia, Duchess of Blackford and former bookshop owner, explained.

"Was she a friend of Lady Victoria Abbott?" I asked.

Lady Margaret Ellingham laughed aloud. "Bianca put Victoria down at every opportunity, especially to Bartholomew Abbott before the two married. Lord Abbott wasn't a lord yet, but he certainly was handsome in his naval uniform. Bianca chased him quite blatantly, but he only had eyes for Victoria."

"That wasn't what Lady Westkirk told Lady Kaldaire and me," I said.

"Of course not. She probably acted like she loves her husband and is everybody's friend, but don't get taken in by her," Lady Ellingham told me. "She chases everything in trousers."

"That can't be too pleasant for Lord Westkirk," Lady Kaldaire said.

"We never see Lord Westkirk out in society, so

perhaps he doesn't know," the duchess said.

"And if I talk to Priscilla Lawson and Hugo Watson, what do you think they will tell me?" I asked.

"Talk to them and see if they agree with me. They— Victoria Abbott, Priscilla Lawson, Lady Westkirk, and Roxanne—were all about the same age and came out in society at about the same time. Or married into it without benefit of being presented to the king and queen." When Lady Margaret Ellingham smiled at me, I was reminded of her mother. Her mother who hated Roxanne. "Would you care to stay for tea?"

"I would, if after tea, you might prevail on your father to allow us to see the tunnel before it's closed up," I said.

"Why do you want to see that cursed tunnel?" Lady Margaret asked.

"We've been thinking Roxanne left by way of the tunnel to meet the person who killed her. But what if she met the person in the tunnel? Has anyone searched it for clues to Roxanne's death?" I asked the ladies.

"No one has, and it certainly can't hurt," Lady Kaldaire said. "We wouldn't have to bother your parents if the tunnel is still open."

Lady Ellingham smiled, this time not looking at all like her mother. "It's still open. There's been some debate about how to close it up so that it never caves in. After tea, we'll inspect the tunnel and you'll see there's nothing there."

"And would it be possible for me to talk to the housemaid Sally while we are there?" I asked.

"Why?" Lady Ellingham was immediately on her

guard again.

"Supposedly Sally knows more about who came and went by that tunnel than anyone else in the household," I replied.

Lady Ellingham made a sweeping gesture with one hand that I took to be assent.

"Do any of you know of any other deaths of young people in aristocratic families in the past six months?" I asked.

All the ladies shook their heads. "That's why the deaths of the two couples were much talked about. First the Abbotts, and then Theo and Roxanne's deaths," the Duchess of Blackford said. "No one in their age group had died in the past two years. And then four deaths in the space of less than two months, all under questionable circumstances."

"Bartholomew Abbott would have died by hanging if he hadn't shot himself, so I'm not sure he should count," Lady Kaldaire said.

"Oh, he should, since there should be another hanging." I looked at the ladies. "Roxanne's killer."

"You think it was an aristocrat?"

"I don't think it was a common thief. Especially since we still don't know where she was killed. Have the police checked all over Wallingford House?"

Lady Ellingham groaned. "As much as my father would allow. Hearing him tell the police inspector that he would give his word that Roxanne was not butchered in his bedchamber, or that of his wife, is not something I'll soon forget."

"I suspect the inspector won't, either," Lady Kaldaire said with a smile.

After much social chatter, Lady Kaldaire, Lady Ellingham, and I joined the duchess in her carriage and rode the short distance to Wallingford House. The duchess sent the carriage home while Lady Margaret led the way into her childhood home and surprised the butler when she said, "We want to see the tunnel, Mathers."

"But my lady, your father doesn't want anyone going down there."

"If he asks, you can tell him you knew nothing about this."

Mathers's stiff demeanor cracked for an instant as he smiled. "Yes, my lady. Oh, you'll be glad to hear Lord Alfred is crawling and standing again." Then he put on his unflappable expression and stood back while we entered.

"That is good news, Mathers. Dorothy must be over the moon," Lady Margaret responded.

"Indeed, my lady."

I was a stranger to the house but I murmured my thankfulness, after the duchess and Lady Kaldaire, at the happy news that the baby had recovered from his injuries.

Lady Margaret Ellingham and the butler exchanged broad smiles before she led the way and we followed her down one hall after another and then down stairs.

Finally, she opened a door that appeared to allow entrance into a linen cabinet and pushed out the back. She picked up a lantern and lit it. Then we followed her down a steep flight of wooden steps between two narrow stone walls that continued down a corridor.

I took the lamp from Lady Ellingham and slowly walked the passageway, looking down at the dirt floor while she quickly walked the distance to the other set of stairs going up.

Suddenly, the Duchess of Blackford cried out from behind me. Even Lady Kaldaire, chatting about how cleverly the passage was hidden, fell silent. I looked up to find the duchess pointing about waist high on one wall just ahead of where I stood. Searching carefully, I found what appeared to be blood-stains splattered on the rocks. In front of me, the dirt was packed down, but it was a different color. As if something had poured into the dirt. Blood, perhaps?

"I think we found the spot where Roxanne was murdered," I said in a quiet voice.

"I think we need to show this to Scotland Yard," the duchess said.

"Send a message to Inspector Russell. He'll take care of it without upsetting the household," Lady Kaldaire said.

We carefully stepped over the spot and walked the rest of the way single file to climb the stairs and open the door in the carriage house. To one side were the duke's carriages, while on the other were his horses. A man looked up, surprised at being joined while he was mucking out the stalls.

Lady Ellingham sent him to find a bobby and send the bobby off to take word to Scotland Yard that Inspector Russell was needed at Wallingford House. Then we left the carriage house to walk along the alleyway and return to the front door of the house.

Mathers, to his great credit, managed to not appear surprised at our second appearance on the doorstep.

"You're going to have to tell your father what has transpired, and I doubt he'd want a duchess to see his reaction. I'll go now, but please call for me if I'm needed." The Duchess of Blackford squeezed Lady Margaret Ellingham's hands and walked home across the side street.

"My lady?" Mathers said to the daughter of the house.

"Is my father in his study?"

"Yes."

"Please show these ladies into the small parlor and have someone bring them tea." Margaret walked off, pulling off her gloves as she did so.

The small parlor was near the front door and overloaded with Victorian furniture. Heavy curtains in a green brocade darkened by coal fires hung by the windows, giving the room a gloomy look and a stuffy smell. This didn't appear to be a room where guests were served tea.

Nevertheless, Lady Kaldaire and I were enjoying a cup of good Darjeeling when the Duke of Wallingford burst into the room, followed by his daughter. "What is the meaning of this, calling the police back to my home?" He roared rather than spoke.

We both sprang to our feet. "Your Grace," I began, "we seem to have stumbled across the site of Lady Theo's murder in the tunnel. And like all good English people, we informed the police so they can make progress in finding the murderer. A murderer who broke into your home to kill."

Mercifully, the duke fell silent.

At least until the first constables showed up to view the tunnel. Then the duke returned to his apoplectic roar. I suggested they go to the carriage house and have someone show them the entrance to the tunnel. Blood on the stone walls and mixed into the dirt on the floor marked the spot they should show to Inspector Russell.

The two uniformed constables looked grateful to escape. Lady Margaret gave me a smile before she suggested to her father that he return to his study.

He nodded to us and stalked away.

We had only a few minutes' wait before James Russell knocked on the door, a group of policemen behind him. Before the butler could send him away, I hurried into the hallway and said, "I'll show you where the tunnel comes out in the carriage house. This way you won't disturb the household."

James didn't look pleased to see me, but he gestured for me to precede him. Surprise flashed in his eyes when not only Lady Kaldaire followed me out, but also Lady Margaret Ellingham. We made a strange parade on the Mayfair pavement, with two ladies, a milliner, and a line of police officers, but people in Mayfair never stop and stare, no matter how much they may want to.

The ladies waited at the top of the steps, but I followed the police down into the tunnel.

"Miss, you should go back up," the first bobby I reached at the bottom of the stairs said.

"Have you found the location?" I asked.

"Let her through," James said. When I reached him, he

said, "What made you think to come down here?"

"You've searched the house and the outside for the place where Roxanne was murdered. Not too many people knew about this tunnel. If her killer did…?" I shrugged.

"Awkward place to kill someone and undress them." He studied the tunnel with its lack of width and height, lantern light flickering patterns on the rocks. "It would have taken two to move her to the park."

"Couldn't one strong man do it?" I asked.

"We know from the body she wasn't dragged. She was carried. And there's no room for a man, no matter how strong, to lift her and carry her in this tunnel and up those steep stairs. It would have taken two, one at her shoulders and one at her knees."

"So, we're looking for a pair who wanted Roxanne dead and wanted her moved out of the tunnel." I was going to have to think about pairs among the people who wanted Roxanne dead.

"Why didn't they just leave her here? Did the family use this tunnel often?" James studied the tunnel again, being careful not to hit his bowler on the timber ceiling.

"No. Do you think they wanted the body found?"

James held my gaze. "She was found quickly enough in the park, even with the rain. Here, she might have remained undiscovered for days, perhaps."

"At least that long," I agreed.

James nodded as if mulling over his thoughts. "Then it must have been important that the body be found quickly."

"Why?"

"If I knew that, I'd be in clover."

I gave James a smile and left the police to do their work. When I reached the top of the steps, I found the two ladies waiting for me.

"What did you learn?" Lady Kaldaire demanded.

"It took two people to carry her out of that tunnel and they must have wanted Roxanne found quickly. How often did anyone use that tunnel?"

"Back in the day, perhaps once a week," Lady Ellingham told me. "Perhaps less often."

"Why would it have been important for Roxanne's body to be found the day it was?" I asked, but neither lady could give me an answer.

"Could I speak to Sally now, Lady Ellingham?"

"I'll get Mathers to fetch her. Lady Kaldaire, would you like to wait with me in the drawing room? I think Sally can be more easily persuaded to tell what she knows if she's only faced with one person."

Once more, we walked around to the front door and entered Wallingford House. At Margaret Ellingham's direction, Mathers sent for Sally and the two of us were soon seated in the housekeeper's office.

Sally appeared older than me, with large, roughened hands and a face full of freckles. She stared at me, waiting for me to let her know why she'd been called away from her work.

"I understand that you are in charge of the linen closet down the hallway."

"Yes."

"And you keep a close eye on it."

"I don't want nobody to steal the duke's sheets."

"And you don't want anyone to use the tunnel behind it without paying you a toll."

"Can't have anybody wrinkling the sheets. I have to iron them."

"The night Lady Theo died, she left by the tunnel."

She gave me a calculating look. "Did she?"

"We know she did. She was murdered down there. Her blood's on the stones."

"Coulda been anybody."

"Do people routinely get butchered down there?"

Her skin paled as she swallowed.

"All I want to know is what time did Lady Theo go down there that night?"

"I don't know."

"Really? How do you collect your toll if you don't know who's using the tunnel?"

"How much trouble am I in?"

"I'm not going to squeal on your little money maker. Not if you honestly tell me what time Roxanne went into the tunnel, or why you don't know."

Her defiance seemed to leak out of her. "I can keep an eye on the cupboard during the day and evening, but not at night. Then I have to rely on the valets and lady's maids telling me. Roxanne's lady's maid told me she went out, all dressed up, through the tunnel about eleven."

"Did you collect your toll for that trip?"

"Couldn't, could I? She was dead by then."

Sally didn't have anything else useful to tell me. I went back upstairs to meet with the two ladies. "We can't do any more until we can talk to Miss Lawson and Mr. Watson. And I need to get back to work."

I stared at Lady Kaldaire. "Please send word when we can interview those two." Then I turned to the other lady. "Lady Ellingham, thank you for making it possible for the police to learn where Roxanne was murdered. And now I have a pretty good idea of the time of her death."

I knew I was being abrupt, but I needed to get back to my millinery. Finding Roxanne's killer, as much as I wanted to, wouldn't pay the bills.

As I turned to leave, Lady Margaret said, "I'll speak to my father about giving Miss North a reference. None of this was her fault."

I smiled at her. "Thank you. Miss North will be very glad."

* * *

Things went along peacefully until eleven the next morning, when a liveried servant of the Duke of Blackford brought me a note. *Miss Lawson will see us at three today,* it read. *Mr. Watson won't meet us and finds our curiosity about his sister's death morbid. He has forbidden Miss Lawson to speak of his sister.*

It's been years since I was involved in an investigation. I look forward to assisting you with this one. Roxanne, also known as Lady Theo, deserves justice.

We'll take my carriage.

Georgia Ranleigh, Duchess of Blackford

I read it through twice. A duchess was involving herself in an investigation insisted upon by Lady Kaldaire. I doubted there was any reason for me to tag along. Still, if

Roxanne really was going to get justice, I'd better be a part of this.

Just as important, someone had to ask what really happened to Victoria Abbott.

Chapter Twenty-Two

At twenty minutes before three that afternoon, a shiny black carriage with a gilded crest painted on the door pulled up in front of my shop. Jane peeked out the window and whistled. "You'll be traveling in style today."

"Wish me luck. I don't want to have to do this again." Through the window I could see people across the street openly staring. I didn't want to step out onto the pavement and have my neighbors crowd me in their desire to gaze inside the carriage. "How do I look?"

"Like an aristocrat."

I deliberately wore violet and gray, the colors of second mourning. My clothes were slightly out of date, but mourning clothes were less likely to be stylish even though frequently worn, and wouldn't be so out of place in a room full of the titled and wealthy. Plus, with my reddish hair, the combination looked good on me.

I pinned on my wide-brimmed gray hat with the violet ribbon roses and feathers, pulled on my gloves, crossed my fingers, and with a cheery good-bye, walked out to the carriage.

Thank goodness we didn't have any customers in the shop at that moment.

When I was handed up by the footman, I discovered

the seat cushions as well as the curtains in this carriage were a plush dark blue velvet. The decorative edgings were gold. The Duchess of Blackford and Lady Kaldaire had the forward-facing seat, so I sat with my back to the horses. Fortunately, the rocking of the carriage didn't give me queasiness as it did to so many.

This must have been the carriage the duke had used the day before.

The Lawson residence was not far from Regent's Park. The footman was sent up to ring the bell and present the duchess' and Lady Kaldaire's cards before helping us down from the carriage. As usual, I went last, giving me a chance to notice the relative newness of the buildings and the cheerfulness of the early spring flowers set out in pots and along the edges of the buildings.

The manservant, still a boy really despite his livery, escorted us up to the main drawing room. Two women were already waiting in the blue and cream-colored room.

The younger of the two rose when we entered and said, "I'm Priscilla Lawson. I will warn you again that Hugo, Mr. Watson, does not want me to make any statements about Victoria's death." She was small and delicate and had the slumped shoulders of someone who carried a great weight with her all the time.

I wanted to meet Mr. Watson. Was he the great weight she carried?

The older of the two rose and said, "I'm Lady Marian Lawson. Welcome to my home."

We greeted Lady Lawson while she curtsied to the duchess in the small space between a heavy table and a massive sofa. Lady Lawson still preferred decorating in the style of our late queen.

After we were seated and the tea was poured, no one knew quite how to begin a conversation concerning Miss Lawson's guilt or innocence.

As usual, I leaped in. Unlike these other ladies, I didn't have all day. "I understand you were a good friend of Victoria Abbott."

Priscilla gave me a shy smile. "Yes, we were close since the days when she was Victoria Watson."

"Did you see much of her after her marriage? After all, you were both in London all the time, weren't you?"

She shook her head. "We were both in the country for the autumn. Then we met again at the Watson estate for the Christmas season. Bartholomew, Hugo, and one of Hugo's brothers were about the same age and served in the navy together."

"Was it after Christmas that Victoria and Bartholomew began to frequent the Marlowe Club?"

Her glare was full of fury. "They never frequented the Marlowe Club. They were only there a few times."

"And that quickly, Victoria was dead."

The fury in her eyes melted in unshed tears. "It wasn't right."

I softened my tone. "What wasn't?"

"Vic—"

"That's enough, Priscilla," her mother said sternly.

"Priscilla, tell us," I said.

"I forbid it," Lady Lawson said.

"Do you want Victoria's killer to go free?" I glared at

the thin older woman.

"It's not seemly." She folded her hands in her lap.

"Murder isn't seemly," the duchess said, "which is why it must be punished."

All heads turned to look at her, sitting demurely while holding a teacup. She gave Lady Lawson a regal nod.

"If you know anything, you must tell us," I told Priscilla.

"Why? What can you do?" she demanded.

"See that justice is done," I replied. It sounded grandiose, but I hoped it would work.

"Hah." Obviously, Priscilla didn't fall for my sweeping claims.

"What makes you think I can't?"

"Because he's dead."

She stopped me, but she didn't stop the duchess. "Who is? Bartholomew or Theo?"

"Both," Priscilla replied.

"They were in it together?" I sounded amazed to my own ears.

"No. Victoria was already dead when Bartholomew found out what had happened after gambling all night. He went after Theo. Theo taunted him with not being there to protect his wife. Theo laughed at him and said Bartholomew failed her." Priscilla let loose one loud sob.

I felt ill at all the ruined lives Theo was responsible for. "How did Victoria die?"

"She just stopped breathing." Priscilla's voice faded as she looked down.

"Was she strangled?" I asked.

She nodded, still looking down. "She resisted Theo and he choked her as he..." Priscilla burst into sobs.

"I hope you're happy," her mother snapped at me.

"How could anyone be happy over Victoria's death?" I asked.

"Digging up gossip." Lady Lawson glared as she leaned toward me in her chair.

"How did she end up in the carriage?" the duchess asked.

"You'll have to ask Hugo," Priscilla said between sobs.

"I'll have the duke ask him." The Duchess of Blackford spoke serenely.

"You wouldn't dare," Lady Lawson said.

"Of course I would."

I looked at the duchess in admiration. I wondered if James could be as accepting a husband as the duke.

Priscilla looked from one to another of us and then said, "Hugo bribed one of the men who works at the club, who said he helped put her in a carriage. Then two carriages raced off, Lord Theo driving one of them, until he got into an accident with a delivery wagon."

"Miss Lawson, was Victoria in the carriage that was in the accident?"

"No," she told me, shaking her head as she wiped away a tear, "she was in the other carriage that overturned later. It was in a park and no one saw who was driving or who freed the horses. The carriage was stolen."

"Who did the man from the Marlowe Club say was driving the second carriage?"

Priscilla looked down. "Lady Westkirk."

"Why would Lady Westkirk steal a carriage and drive off with Lady Abbott's body?" Lady Kaldaire's tone made clear she didn't understand any of what happened.

The young lady burst into tears. "I don't know. All I know is Victoria was my friend and now she's dead because of Lord Theo Hughes."

"Did Hugo or any of the Watson family attempt to get revenge on Lord Theo?" I asked.

"It certainly would have been understandable," Lady Kaldaire muttered.

I shot her a dark look as Priscilla said, "No. I asked Hugo and he promised me he wouldn't. He said he'd like to shake the hand of the man who killed him."

"Hugo doesn't know who killed Theo?" the duchess asked.

"No." Priscilla shook her fair head. "And neither do I. But I know who killed Victoria, and he deserved to die."

"And his wife? Did Roxanne deserve to be murdered?" I asked.

"Theo killed her, not Lady Theo." Priscilla turned her head at the sound of voices in the front hallway. "Hugo's here. Now you can ask him yourself."

Hugo Watson blew into the room, a big man looking to be in high temper from his reddened complexion. He glared at the three of us before standing next to Priscilla and laying a hand on her slumped shoulders. "Have you been badgering Miss Lawson?"

"Hello, Mr. Watson," the duchess said with a smile. "Miss Lawson has just been telling us how distressed you both are at your sister's death."

"What else has she been telling you?" he asked.

His fiancée flinched.

"That someone did you both a favor and killed Lord Theo before you had a chance to," I said. "What she didn't have a chance to tell us is whether you two killed his wife, Lady Theo."

"The notorious Lady Roxanne? Why would we do that? She had nothing to do with Victoria's death." His tone didn't waver from belligerent. They obviously hadn't heard the story we had.

"I have no idea," I told him. "But I do know it would have taken two people to move her body from where she was killed to where she was found."

"Well, it wasn't us." His lower jaw stuck out. I wondered if that was his normal pose or if he was trying to frighten us off. The three aristocratic ladies sat in their customary straight-backed position, looking as though we were discussing the weather.

"And it wasn't your brothers?"

"Why would they?"

"Why would they, indeed?" I smiled at the couple, aware of Lady Lawson glaring at me. "And I suppose you'll tell me you weren't the one to give a beating to Lucky Marlowe, the owner of the club where Victoria died?"

Hugo looked around the room to find all of us staring at him. "Yes, I did, but that's all I did. He deserved worse, running a club like that. Once he knocked himself out on a wall, I kicked him a couple of times." He glared at me. "He was alive when I left."

"If you're quite finished here, I'm sure Priscilla and

Hugo and I have preparations to make for the wedding," the older woman said as she rose.

We also rose and said our farewells. I was impressed at how gracefully Lady Kaldaire and the duchess could leave a place they were not welcome. I made a pale imitation of their exit.

"Well," the duchess said as we climbed back into the carriage, "that was a good guess, Emily. But what will be our next step?"

"We've ruled out one pair who could have carried Roxanne out of the tunnel and across the street. We need to think of some others," I said.

"As much as the Duchess of Wallingford would approve, I doubt she and the duke are the pair you seek," Lady Kaldaire said in a dry tone.

The duchess chuckled. Then with a sigh, she said, "Bartholomew Abbott was dead before Theo, so he couldn't be involved. Perhaps Lucky Marlowe and one of his henchmen?"

"He seemed surprised to learn that Victoria died in his club rather than in the carriage accident," I told them.

"And you believe him?" Lady Kaldaire asked. "He's nothing but a ruffian."

"Ruffian or not, he sounded sincere," I replied. "What about Lord and Lady Ellingham? Or the duke's heir and his wife? Oh, wait, no," I said as I pictured hysterical Dorothy. "She couldn't manage to move a body without going insane. But I bet Lady Margaret Ellingham could."

"She wouldn't," Lady Kaldaire said.

"How can you be certain?" I asked.

"That's not the sort of thing she'd do. Order Roxanne's clothes to be packed in a trunk and deposited on the pavement. Snub her. She would do something direct. Margaret didn't need to kill her. She would just see that Roxanne was banned from polite society," Lady Kaldaire told me.

I was glad to see even Lady Kaldaire could give Roxanne her own name and not call her Lady Theo, a name the poor dead woman must have found hateful.

But here we'd found another pair that failed to meet the requirements of Roxanne's killers. As we rode along, I had one more thought. "How about Lord and Lady Ravenbrook? Or Lord Armstrong and Lady Westkirk?"

"Why would they kill Roxanne?" the Duchess of Blackford asked.

"I've been told she was going to emigrate and that takes money. Perhaps she was blackmailing them and they either couldn't or wouldn't pay."

"That sounds like Lady Westkirk, but not Lord Armstrong. He has to be circumspect or his wife, the royally born Lady Armstrong, could have him cut off without a penny and banned from the royal court. The kiss of death for a man in Armstrong's position," the duchess said. "He has a title, but absolutely no money of his own. And Lady Armstrong made certain before they wed that he could never get his hands on hers."

"Does he get an allowance from her?" It made sense to me that Lady Armstrong would give him a large one in the hopes of keeping her husband out of trouble and the penny press.

"A very small one. Lady Armstrong works on the principle that her husband can't get into trouble if he doesn't have the money to afford it." The duchess shook her head. "From the amount of gambling he does, Lady Armstrong thinks he's either very lucky or owes a great number of people who will soon show up on her doorstep."

I knew Lucky Marlowe wouldn't be one. He said Lord Armstrong always had a full purse. "Then I suppose we need to talk to Lady Ravenbrook again." I looked from one lady to the other.

The duchess knocked on the ceiling and when the footman responded, she gave him directions to the Ravenbrook address. As she settled back in her seat, the duchess said, "Let's hope she's not out calling on friends. That would make it difficult to find her, and she seems to be part of our likeliest pair for Roxanne's murder."

If it wasn't the Archers, as they called themselves at the Marlowe Club, I was out of suspects. It seemed so unlikely that a random housebreaker would find out about the tunnel, find Roxanne there, kill her, and then undress the body and put it in the park across the street. Too unlikely to be believed.

The killer had to be someone who knew her well. If it wasn't, we'd never figure out this murder, and Roxanne's killer would go free.

Chapter Twenty-Three

We arrived at the Ravenbrook residence a few minutes later. This time, before the duchess could send up her card with the footman, Lady Kaldaire said, "I think we should just ring the bell, don't you? She's not expecting us. Less chance of her not being at home."

I knew if members of the aristocracy didn't want to invite you into their drawing room, they had their servants say they weren't at home. I suspected Lady Kaldaire would march past the footman into the house, making it harder for Lady Ravenbrook to deny being home.

As it turned out, I needn't have worried.

We rang the bell, the ladies handed the footman their cards, and he escorted us to the drawing room. Lady Ravenbrook bustled in a few minutes later, dressed elegantly and appearing energetic and in command.

"Lady Ravenbrook, I'm so glad to see you've overcome the effects of the poison," Lady Kaldaire said.

"Thank you. Won't you sit?" our hostess said. "You're lucky to have caught me in."

"Are you traveling?" I asked.

"Yes. Lord Ravenbrook and I are going to our country estate to avoid the hot weather in London."

We were still months away from any hot weather. I didn't believe her, but there was no point in saying that and having us thrown out of Lady Ravenbrook's drawing room. "Has Scotland Yard had any luck in finding out who poisoned the punch?"

"Not that I'm aware of," I said. "And you don't believe the attack was aimed at you personally?"

"No." The idea seemed to startle her as her eyes widened and she smoothed her green skirt. "I have no enemies who would want to kill me."

"But you do have enemies." I made it a statement and watched her reaction.

She lifted her head. "Everyone has enemies."

"Roxanne had enemies. I suppose that's why she planned to emigrate."

"Roxanne? Emigrate?" Frown lines appeared on Lady Ravenbrook's forehead. "She never told me that, and I think she would have told me."

"Why do you think she would have told you?" I was curious about their relationship.

"We got along well. Two bored married women disliked by our husbands' mothers and looking for a little excitement to break up the monotony of our lives. We tried to help each other survive." She relaxed a little and unhunched her shoulders. The tension in her face disappeared.

"Would Roxanne have left her husband? He was, by all accounts, brutal."

"She knew she could never escape him. She was in it for life. She half expected him to lash out and kill her at any moment. Which was why she was so relieved when he died."

"Relieved?" I sounded surprised, but if Lady Ravenbrook's words were true, I could understand Roxanne's gratefulness.

"Yes. She spoke once after Theo died about going back to northern England, where her family lives, and putting Wallingford House behind her. She said she was sick of London. Theo had been brutal to her, to the servants, to his nephew. And he was getting worse."

"Then why would she have taken an...overindulged young lady to him in the upstairs of the Marlowe Club?"

She laughed. "Not Roxanne. She wouldn't have done it anyway, but the woman who takes care of all those arrangements at the Marlowe Club is Lady Westkirk."

"Lady Westkirk took Victoria Abbott to Lord Theo? Not Roxanne?" If so, it changed everything I'd thought about these deaths.

"Of course it was Bianca Westkirk. Lady Beatrix indeed. She was born to be a madam." There was scorn in her tone and something else. Anger? Fear?

Then her words hit me. "Lady Westkirk took care of all of the arrangements between willing participants at the Marlowe Club?"

"Of course. Sometimes she arranged unwilling participants, too. That was what Roxanne told me. She was as disgusted by Bianca as she was by Theo."

Lady Kaldaire gasped. The duchess looked ill.

I was having trouble picturing this. "And it was Lady Westkirk who drove Victoria's body away from the club in a stolen carriage? She couldn't have done all that by herself."

"I imagine Lord Armstrong or a couple employees of the club did the heavy lifting, but Lady Westkirk was the brains behind the carriage ride," Lady Ravenbrook said. "She bragged to me about it later."

"It sounds like Lady Westkirk was in a powerful position at the Marlowe Club. Almost an owner. Why did Lucky Marlowe let her do these things?" I asked.

Lady Ravenbrook spread her hands apart and shrugged her thin shoulders. "Because there was a need for someone to carry out these tasks, and Bianca was born to please men. For the right incentive, of course. With Bianca, that incentive was money."

Why Marlowe let her do this was a question I also needed to pose to Uncle Thomas. "What did Lord Abbott do about Lord Theo and Lady Westkirk treating his wife that way?"

"He had been losing heavily at the gaming tables for weeks and when encouraged that night to help himself to the brandy bottle, he was in no condition to know where Victoria was until it was over and she was dead." Lady Ravenbrook shook her head. "Victoria was a sweet child and should never have been treated that way."

"Child? She was old enough to be married," Lady Kaldaire said.

"But she was so innocent. She'd been well chaperoned until the day of her wedding, and Abbott gained the title only the week before. They both had a lot to learn." Lady Ravenbrook stopped and looked at each of us in turn.

"What does this have to do with who poisoned me?"

"Maybe nothing," I admitted. "Tell me about Lord Armstrong."

"He was there when I went into the dining room during the ball." She shook her head. "I don't remember much after that."

"What's he like?"

"As dissolute as Lord Theo Hughes, but not as cruel. Armstrong is more of a prankster, but his jokes quickly become annoying. His wife is ready to have him jailed in the colonies so not to embarrass her cousin the king."

"Drastic, but effective," Lady Kaldaire said in an approving tone.

"How would that...? Oh, the London papers would be less likely to hear about his incarceration," I said as I figured out where this would lead.

"Who are Lord Armstrong's friends?" the duchess asked.

"I don't think he has any real friends. Lord Theo Hughes and Lady Beatrix are the closest thing he'd have to a friend."

"Lord Theo is dead and Lady Westkirk has her hands full with Lord Westkirk," I replied, and Lady Ravenbrook nodded. "So who are his friends now?"

"Certainly no one at court. I suspect he no longer has friends," Lady Ravenbrook said.

Which ruled him out as part of the pair to move Roxanne's body. I was running out of possibilities.

"Lady Ravenbrook," the duchess asked in a quiet voice directly to our hostess, "are you and Lord Ravenbrook going to the country to separate yourselves from the dangers of cocaine?"

"Planning to gossip about me?" our hostess asked, her arms wrapped around her waist as if protecting herself from an assault.

"I was the victim of too much gossip as a newlywed to ever gossip about another. I was merely going to say if you are, that's very wise." The duchess gave her a smile and Lady Ravenbrook lowered her head for a moment.

When she raised it, she said, "That is good advice. Helpful to a large number of people. I'll keep it in mind." And then she returned the duchess's smile.

"You and your husband had no reason to kill Lady Theo Hughes, did you?" I asked. The expressions on the ladies' faces told me I'd been too bold.

"What a monstrous thing to say," Lady Ravenbrook snapped at me.

"You and your husband were the last pair I could think of who had any contact with Lady Theo," I tried to explain.

"Why a pair?" she sounded surprised.

"We know to move her body from where she was killed to where she was found would have required two people. I've been searching among everyone who knew her for those two people." My shoulders sank from a great weight. "I'm out of ideas."

"It wasn't us," she told me. "I liked Roxanne. She deserved better. I wish you luck in finding her killer."

* * *

Once we were in the carriage, I asked, "Can you ladies talk to the Hughes family and the servants, away from the

Duchess of Wallingford, and find out if anyone knew that Roxanne was planning to leave the house or leave England? Did she confide in any of the servants?"

"Of course. What are you going to do, Emily?" Lady Kaldaire asked.

"I'm going to talk to someone about Lucky Marlowe and his employees."

I reached the shop in time to find out from Jane about the orders that had come in while I was gone. Then I closed up, took my sketch pad up to the flat, and started getting the dinner ready that Mrs. McCauley had left for us.

Noah and Annie came in a few minutes later from the workshop. "Does this mean we'll have dinner on time tonight?" he asked.

"Of course." I made it sound as if I'd dished up dinner on time every night recently.

"So, you've stopped chasing after a killer?"

"Not at all." I gave him a smile. "I need to talk to my grandfather after dinner."

"Is he as unhappy as I am about your investigation?" He glowered at me.

"If anything, he's even more unhappy. If you'll watch dinner for a minute, I'll change into a dark muslin frock."

"So you're harder to see, I imagine," Noah said as he tasted the chicken.

Dinner was a quiet affair. I did the dishes with Annie's help and then put on my hat and gloves.

"Emily, I don't like this. Be careful," Noah called out to me as I was closing the door.

"I will."

The omnibus ride was uneventful. I left the bus not far from my grandfather's house so I could use the alley shortcuts. It was still light out enough to see activity on the streets, but the alleys were already filled with shadows. Ominous shadows. I quickened my steps, keeping a sharp lookout around me.

An ashcan half a block in front of me rattled and I froze. A moment later, a cat, or a big rat, ran across the alley. I took a deep breath and hurried on.

I reached the cross street and felt tension leave my shoulders as I looked around. Just normal traffic. No cats, rats, or men carrying lethal-looking knives. I sped up my pace.

In the next block, I thought I saw a shadow move. I stopped and waited, but there was nothing else. I continued on my way, glancing all around me.

I was nearly to the next street, thinking I would be safe when I reached the busier thoroughfare, when I was grabbed around the waist from behind.

Someone forced me toward a carriage that was just pulling up on the street. I screamed at the top of my lungs.

Whoever he was stuck a dirty hand over my mouth. I bit down, and as he loosened his hold on me, elbowed him in the stomach. Then I swung around to smash him in the mouth.

He let go of me completely, but then someone else put a knife to my throat. That seemed to be a good time to stop resisting.

"Watch her," the first man said. "She's got a nasty right hook."

"That's what you get for grabbing a lady," I said in a soft voice, afraid to aggravate the person with the knife.

More shadows jumped out from behind the carriage and the man who'd first grabbed me fell to the brick paving. The second person pushed me away. I hit the bricks and rolled away, glad I'd changed from the nice afternoon frock I'd worn earlier.

I looked up to discover a man swinging his blade at anything that moved. The shadows stayed out of range. Then the man jumped onto the carriage. A whip cracked and the carriage sped away. My first attacker limped away into the shadows.

"What are you doing here, Emily?" my cousin Tommy asked, holding out a hand to help me rise.

"I've come to see Grandpapa and your father, since they seem to know Jeb Marlowe better than anyone."

"Let's get you to the house and then I'll get my dad." Two other cousins followed Tommy and me down another alley and then to my grandparents' home, where the glow of the gas lights welcomed me.

Gran welcomed us at the door with "What happened to you?"

"She was attacked by two men with a carriage."

"There had to be more than two. Who was managing the horses?"

"Oh, you think you're so smart."

"Wow, can she fight." My cousins all talked at once, over and on top of each other until I couldn't tell who said what.

"My cousins rescued me," I said and turned to face

them. "Thank you."

"They're good lads, all of them," my grandmother said. "Let's get you straightened up and set down with a cuppa," she added as she escorted me into the kitchen. The kitchen was her territory. I'd never been allowed in that room since I was little.

I washed my hands at the sink, brushed off my dress, and repinned my hair while she fixed us each a cup of tea.

"I got a letter from your brother in the mail yesterday."

"Oh, good, Gran. What did he have to say?" I could tell by her smile she was thrilled to receive a letter from Matthew.

"He misses my cooking and looks forward to his next break so he can eat dinner here."

"I'll be sure to bring him over. And stay for dinner, too," I said and gave her a warm smile. I was glad to see the thaw in our frigid relationship grow.

My grandfather hurried into the kitchen, a stricken look on his face.

Gran and I both leaped to our feet. "What's wrong?" I asked as Gran tried to help him into a chair.

He resisted her efforts. "Tom's been kidnapped."

Chapter Twenty-Four

It took me a moment to find my voice. "Are you sure Uncle Thomas has been grabbed?"

"I don't know if they're our enemies or involved with this investigation of yours, but I'm sure he's been kidnapped. When Tommy and Garrett went to get Tom, since you wanted to see us both, they got there just in time to see him being forced into a carriage at knifepoint."

Gran sank into a wooden chair with a thud.

"Was it the same men and carriage they just rescued me from?"

"They think so." Grandfather sat next to Gran and took her hands in his. "We'll get him back."

"Who would do this?" she murmured.

"We have enemies."

"But they've never done anything like this before, have they?" I asked.

He shook his white head, looking ten years older than when I last saw him. "Zach raced back here and brought the whole family the message while Tommy and Garrett followed the carriage. They'll send us word when they can."

Zach was Uncle Thomas's youngest. At ten, he was

skinny, fast, and an expert at sneaking through anywhere to bring messages. He'd be the one to pass word once my older cousins learned where the men with the carriage had taken my uncle Thomas. With my thoughts tumbling, I asked, "Jeb Marlowe. Could he do something like this?"

"He's crazy enough," Gran said, frowning.

"Why would he?" Grandpapa asked.

"Uncle Thomas knows him the best of everyone in the family. And if Marlowe knows what we discovered, he may not want me talking to Uncle Thomas."

"This is about those toffs getting murdered?" Grandfather sounded enraged. Probably at me, since I was the one who brought this problem to their door.

"Maybe," I said, not wanting to admit this trouble was all my doing. "How long have you known Marlowe?"

"Since he was a tot. Why?"

"He came from this neighborhood. How did he manage to acquire a gaming club?"

"He saved his money, obtained some investors—"

I interrupted him. "Anyone you know?"

"Well, no." He gave me a level stare. "What are you thinking?"

"What if his partner was a toff?" Lord Theo and Lord Armstrong came to mind. And if it was Armstrong, the two men could have moved Roxanne's body easily. But that raised the question in my mind of where Lord Armstrong, having only a small allowance, would get the money to start up a gaming club.

"It's possible." My grandfather rubbed his wife's hands.

"Is there anyone around here that Marlowe is still close to?"

"Tom, I suppose. They've been friends forever. I don't know of anyone who'd be closer to him than Tom. He doesn't have family anymore." Grandfather studied the well-scrubbed kitchen table for a while. Finally, he said, "I don't know what happened to that girl."

I half jumped from my chair. Could he have known Roxanne for a long time? "What girl?"

"The tart," Gran said.

"Now, Aggie."

"Well, she was." Gran scowled at him. "Going after any man she could to get anything she wanted at that moment. And then dropping that man to chase after another who had even more money in his pockets."

"Do you remember her name?" I asked Gran.

"No. She was always the tart to me."

I looked at my grandfather. "Do you know her name?"

"No. She was from the area close to the docks. Italian, I think. A lot younger than Marlowe. He was wild about her."

"She was almost young enough to be his daughter," Gran said with a sniff worthy of an aristocrat.

I remembered where I'd heard that description before. Was it possible? Could the Italian girl be Lady Westkirk, and could she and Marlowe have killed Roxanne? They were in the perfect position to hide the details of Victoria Abbott's murder. One had taken the girl to be slaughtered, and the other provided the location.

But Marlowe said Roxanne was going to go to

Australia with him. Was she really going to leave? "I need to talk to some people in Mayfair."

"Pet, I can't let you run all over England. We've had one kidnapping tonight—"

I interrupted him. "If I get the answers I expect, I'll know who kidnapped Uncle Thomas and why. Did Uncle Thomas keep his automobile?"

"Yes."

"Can you drive it?" I asked my Grandfather. This would only work if he could.

"No, but your father can."

For a moment, I almost said no. I was still furious with him for not bothering to send word to my mother when she was dying. Even if he was in jail and couldn't come to see her, he could have sent words of encouragement.

But Uncle Thomas, and my grandparents, deserved better than for me to refuse to work with my horrible father. "Get him."

My grandfather rose and pushed one of the buzzers on the board on the kitchen wall that connected to my father's and various uncles' nearby homes.

My father appeared in a minute and a half, buttoning up his waistcoat. "What's wrong? I..." His voice trailed off when he saw me. "Emily?"

"Can you drive Uncle Thomas's motor-car?"

"Better than he can."

"Good. You're driving me to Mayfair. I'll explain on the way." I rose and headed toward the barn where the motor-car was kept.

"Wait. I'm coming with you." My grandfather hurried

out after me, my father following with a puzzled expression.

He cranked over the motor and the vehicle started. We all climbed in, me in the back seat, and started off at a good clip.

"What's going on?" my father asked, raising his voice to be heard.

Grandpapa filled him in on the kidnapping, and then I told them both about how it would have taken two people to move Roxanne's body up the stairs without dragging her, and what I'd learned about the disposal of Victoria Abbott's body away from the Marlowe Club.

"How did you get mixed up in murder, Emily?" my father asked.

"Lady Kaldaire found out about you. She threatened to tell all my customers about my criminal relatives if I didn't help her find Roxanne's killer." Well, not exactly, but my explanation was close enough.

"That's blackmail." He growled and shifted gears to go around a goods wagon.

"I thought you called it 'persuasion,' Father."

"Both of you stop right now," my grandfather said. "After we get Tom back safely, you two can fight all you want." His tone was feeble, as if his heart wasn't in it.

Traffic was light until we reached the West End, and then my father drove through the crowded streets with an expertise that surprised me. "I'm getting to be an excellent getaway driver," he told me, pride in his voice.

Then he spooked two carriage horses, who tried to bolt. "If you can't manage your horses better than that," he muttered.

I resisted saying what I thought of his criminal activities or his driving and instead gave him directions to Blackford House. When he pulled up, I climbed out and said, "Wait here." I dashed up the steps and rang the bell.

The butler opened the door and I jumped inside before he could shut me out. "Is Her Grace home?"

"Not to callers."

"I only need to see her for a moment. It's a matter of life and death."

The duke and Mr. Sumner came down the hallway toward us, both looking solemn in their evening jackets. "Life and death?" the duke asked with raised brows.

"My uncle was kidnapped tonight, by men who tried to abduct me first. I'm sure Lucky Marlowe is behind it. I asked the duchess to find out something about Lady Theo for me today. I wondered if she learned anything." My words tumbled out as if I'd been running.

"Take a deep breath," Mr. Sumner said, looking as frightening as he did before. "I'll take care of this, Your Grace, if we could have a moment of Her Grace's time."

The duke shook his head slightly as he walked off. Less than a minute later, the Duchess of Blackford appeared, looking more beautiful than our Queen Alexandra and wearing enough jewelry to dazzle my relatives.

"I've talked to Lady Margaret Ellingham and Lady Dorothy Frethorton, and they both said Roxanne wasn't making any plans to leave for Australia. Margaret then talked to her father, and Wallingford admitted they were making arrangements with Roxanne for her to establish a household in the north near her family. She sounded to him to be quite relieved for things to end this way."

"They're both certain," I asked, "that she wasn't running away with Lucky Marlowe?"

"Yes. She'd mentioned him to Margaret in a derogatory manner."

"Thank you, Your Grace." The pieces of this sad tale were coming together.

"What are your plans?" Sumner asked me.

"I'm going to get my best ballgown and go back to my grandparents' house to wait for my cousins to report where they've taken my uncle. I suspect it will be the Marlowe Club."

"You think Lucky Marlowe killed Lady Theo?" the duchess asked.

"With the help of Lady Westkirk."

Both the duchess and Sumner looked stunned.

"Marlowe has known her since long before she married Westkirk. Remember the story about her father, an Italian immigrant, being a peddler on the London docks? And I think we'll discover it's Marlowe and Bianca Westkirk who plan to run off to Australia. Thank you for your information. Now, I have to hurry."

I ran out of the house and down the steps to the automobile. My father drove us over to my shop at breakneck speed, frightening horses pulling carriages as we passed them with a roar.

I gathered up what I needed from our flat for my role in freeing Uncle Thomas. Then I added the little gold box that I needed to give to James to my bag. Noah wasn't happy about my planned return to the Marlowe Club, but he wished me and the Gates family well. I told him not to wait up.

Then we drove back to my grandparents' home. Gran was waiting with Garrett, Tommy, and the rest of the family.

"We followed them to the West End. To a club in Mayfair. They took him through a back door into the basement," Garrett told us.

"We'll need to break in the back way and get him out," Uncle Wilbur said.

"I've been in there once. An assault won't get you in or free Uncle Thomas. We'll need a diversion. Maybe two." I'd been quiet on the ride back, thinking. Now I laid out my plan.

Grandfather, who knew more about timing than I did, made some corrections and one very big addition. Then we all scattered to dress for our assault on the Marlowe Club.

Gran helped me dress for the part of a wealthy heiress and did my hair. As a final touch, she pulled out a diamond and blue sapphire necklace and earrings.

"No, it's too dangerous," I told her. "I might lose them. They must have cost the earth."

"Don't worry about that, Emily. The important thing is to get Tom freed without any of you getting hurt. And as your grandfather says, carrying out a con requires looking and acting the part. Now, do us all proud." She gave me a wide smile.

"Yes, ma'am." I couldn't fail her. Not when she was

counting on me.

I walked out to the drawing room to whistles and applause. My father looked particularly proud, which annoyed me. Why couldn't he have been there when I was alone after my mother died, trying to nurse Matthew through his illness and running the millinery shop at the same time?

Some of my cousins were dressed in black from their hoods to their shoes. My grandfather and my cousin Joe, who had Grandfather's elegant looks, were dressed in evening jackets and white tie. Gran straightened ties and tucked in hoods.

"Zach," Grandfather asked the youngest of my "working" cousins, "are you ready to deliver this message to Scotland Yard? Into the hands of Detective Inspector Russell and him alone?"

The boy stood up straight and puffed out his scrawny chest. "Yes, sir."

"Good lad. You may have the most important role of the night."

Grandfather might think getting James and the police involved with rescuing Uncle Thomas was a good idea, but I was afraid it would end any friendship between the detective and me.

It had been decided Grandfather, Cousin Joe, and I would go in the front door as newly arrived visitors from Canada, where we made our fortune in timber. Our other cousins, led by Uncle Wilbur, would go in the back when we created the diversion. My father would drive us in style up to the front of the club.

The first step went according to plan, except for a horse pulling a hansom cab rearing and nearly turning over the cab as we approached in our noisy motor-car on a particularly dark street. Then, as soon as my father dropped us off, the automobile engine died. My father then began the laborious task of tinkering with what was reputedly a temperamental contraption, drawing the eyes of the doorman to him and the car, and away from the inside of the club.

My grandfather glanced around as he began his old man act, introducing his grandchildren to the city of his youth. Joe and I did our best to look awed at our surroundings while locating the exits, searching for the best place to cause a loud distraction, and any possible way down to the basement.

Having been inside once, I signaled the location of Lucky Marlowe's office with a nod. It was important he not see us. Marlowe would recognize Grandfather and me, which would destroy any possibility of surprise.

The entire ground floor was decorated in red brocade, and there were tables for all sorts of gaming in every room. A huge bar was set up in the second room with an average-sized bartender. The waiters, however, all appeared to be weight lifters, despite their evening attire.

We each took a flute of champagne and began to mingle with the other "guests."

A couple of young women in gowns that showed their assets circulated the rooms. One of them latched on to Joe, making him appear to be flustered. I knew it was because he was supposed to be part of a caper. At least, I hoped he wasn't having his attention drawn elsewhere.

I was across the room from Joe and had lost sight of Grandfather when Lady Westkirk came out of Marlowe's office carrying a satchel. I had to make sure she didn't see me, since I was the only one of the family she would recognize.

Appearing to wander around a craps table, I stood behind the largest man there and peeked out from around his shoulder.

At that moment, Grandfather walked into the room and glanced around. When his gaze fell on Lady Westkirk, he froze.

She looked at him, took a step back, and then hurried to a doorway near the bar. I guessed it led downstairs.

Grandfather mouthed "Marlowe's Italian girl."

My cousins might not yet be ready to act, but we had to put our plan into action. My uncle's life depended on it.

Chapter Twenty-Five

I threw my champagne flute into the air in the direction of the gaming table and I screamed. The bubbly liquid spilled on a lady in a green silk gown who cried out nearly as loudly in shock and dismay before the glass landed on the felt covering on the table as I bellowed "Rat" at the top of my lungs.

Women, holding up their hems, screamed and hopped around, getting in the way of the waiters who were trying to find and eliminate the beast. Men began to hustle their wives or girlfriends out of the room, getting in the way of each other.

Somewhere I heard a car horn blast. *A-oo-gah. A-oo-gah.*

I dashed to the door Lady Westkirk had entered, my grandfather behind me. It led down a dark wooden stairway, but I could see faint light at the bottom.

As I reached the bottom, I heard shouting from my left. I ran forward and shoved open the wooden door at the end of the hall. It stopped after only moving a foot.

Then it swung the rest of the way open and I found myself looking down the barrel of a gun. As I started to raise my hands, the man holding the gun sank to the floor. I found myself facing one of my masked cousins, holding a coal shovel.

He swung back into the fight as I grabbed the gun off the floor and stepped into the melee. My cousins were dressed alike in black with hoods that covered their noses and mouths. They were used to working together in crowded quarters and poor lighting. I didn't ask, but I suspected it came from doing burglaries.

They battled Jeb Marlowe and several of his employees. My grandfather pushed past me into the room, saying, "Hold on to the gun," as he passed. One of my cousins freed Uncle Thomas, who had a bloody nose and cuts but otherwise looked all right, while all around them men fought.

Uncle Thomas jumped into the fray as I heard a noise behind me. I turned to find Lady Westkirk carrying a satchel and tiptoeing toward the stairs. "Stop right there."

She smirked at me. "You wouldn't use that. The Gates clan doesn't believe in hurting people."

"While you've killed how many?"

She gave me a saucy smile. "It doesn't matter. They shouldn't have stood in my way."

She turned and ran up the stairs. I followed as quickly as I could, holding the gun in one hand and my skirts in the other. I reached the top in time to see her wallop Joe with the satchel and then run past him. The hold-all gave a rattle as she swung it through the air and a clank when it connected with my cousin's face. Barely glancing at Joe as he struggled to regain his wits and his feet, I went after her.

The ground floor of the gaming club was empty as she

ran up to the first floor with me on her heels. As she hurried up, I reached for her and she kicked me. I lost my balance and tumbled down the steps.

Fortunately, I landed in a heap on a thick Persian carpet. Joe had disappeared and there were sounds coming from Lucky Marlowe's office. Leaving that to Joe, I rushed up the stairs again to check every room on the first floor, clutching the gun.

I found no one as I gasped to catch my breath. My gown was designed for a fashionably thin waist and Gran had pulled my corset as tight as she could, making it hard to breathe. Neither of us had expected me to be as active as I'd been tonight.

I passed bedroom after bedroom of red flocked wallpaper, red velvet curtains, and unmade beds with sheets in a tangle as if they had been abandoned in a hurry. Here and there was a forgotten item of clothing.

I heard a squeak over my head and I took off running up another flight of stairs. These rooms weren't as luxurious. Red was still the dominant color, but the mattresses and the carpets weren't as thick. Curtains and bed covers were smoke stained and threadbare and the tangled sheets looked gray.

I walked into one of the rooms. Running footsteps below in the alley attracted my attention and I walked over to look out the window. The people below were only shadows. As my cousins would appear in their black outfits.

The door shut behind me.

I turned, pointing the gun with my finger on the

trigger.

"Oh, Miss Gates," Lady Westkirk said, holding a revolver of her own with more assurance than I could muster, "do put that gun down before you hurt yourself."

"After you."

"I think not."

"Where did you learn to handle a revolver?" I asked. Anything for a distraction.

"On the London docks. It's a handy skill. One you should learn."

"You came up here for your luggage?" A trunk sat near her along the wall.

"It was a good place to store it until we were ready to leave."

"You and Jeb." We were still aiming our guns at each other. I hoped if she kept talking, she wouldn't shoot. I hoped someone would come upstairs and grab her from behind. I hoped tomorrow would find me alive.

"Yes. We were planning to quietly leave after the club shut down tonight. Instead, the help has run off in all the excitement. Now I don't know how I'll get my trunk to the ship."

I felt no sympathy for her and her problem of moving her wardrobe to Australia. "Why did Jeb Marlowe tell me he was leaving with Roxanne? He sounded very convincing."

Lady Westkirk smiled. It was frigid. Cruel. "Jeb's always been a good actor. We didn't want anyone to link us together. It would make leaving that much easier if my husband and his cursed son didn't know. And Australia is far enough away for us to disappear."

"Why do you want to disappear?"

"It beats hanging. Now, get on your knees before I have to shoot them out from under you."

The click of the hammer cocking made me decide she meant it. As I was lowering myself, she grabbed the gun I held. Then she tore down the drapery ties and began to tie me up in them.

This was one of the many games my cousins and I played as children at my grandparents' house. If you hold your hands and wrists just right, you can slip the bonds right off.

She pulled the drapery ties tight, not realizing it made no difference. As soon as I moved, I'd be free.

"What really happened to Lady Abbott?"

"Poor little innocent Victoria. And she was an innocent, even though she was looking for excitement. She and that lump of a husband of hers. He might have been big and handsome, but he was totally useless when she needed him. That night, Theo and I both got into bed with her. She got frightened and started to scream. Theo shut her up immediately, but then we had to get rid of the body."

I felt ill. How could she be so indifferent to the murder of a girl right in front of her?

"Jeb and Theo moved her down the back stairs to where the carriages were parked. And so began the famous carriage race."

"Jeb and Theo drove?"

"No, Theo and I did. Later, Jeb came to the park and

helped me unhitch the horses and flip over the carriage."

I had thought Lord Theo Hughes was terrible, but this woman in front of me made me think she was just as bad, if not worse. The world would have been a better place if Lord Theo and Lady Westkirk had never met. "Anyone accustomed to carriage races could have tried to run me down near the Marlowe Club on my first visit."

"You need to learn to move faster."

I looked over my shoulder to see her gloat. I needed to keep her talking. "What role did Lord Armstrong play? Is he part owner of the Marlowe Club?"

"Haven't you figured it out? Armstrong's the one with the contacts to get all the magic dust we want. That's how he's now full owner of the Marlowe Club and we have the money to get out of town." I heard her move to the window to check the alley below. Before I could act, she was back, pulling on my bonds.

Magic dust? "You mean cocaine?"

"Of course. Lady A keeps him on a tight leash, so he takes care of others' needs in order to build his own fortune."

"And the monarchy says they're above trade. *Hmmpf.* They're just like us." Could I get her on my side?

"There is no 'us.' You're a plodding, boring, middle-class shop owner. I'm a free spirit. I take what I want." She gave a final tug on my bonds and stepped around me, still pointing the gun at me.

"What good did it do you to kill Lady Theo?"

"Lady Theo? Hah. Roxanne suited her much better. Jeb, fool that he is, told her all our plans. They were friends. He liked her. Fool. Stupid, stupid fool. If we didn't want to be followed to Australia and brought back in chains, she had to be silenced."

"Why did you take off her clothes and leave her outside in her bare feet?" It made no sense to me.

"To shame her. She was so proud of her clothes and her looks. It was so important to her. She'd have been embarrassed. Served her right." She pointed the gun in my face. "She was a bothersome little wench. Like you."

I had to move fast. I slipped out of my ties, grabbed the gun and her hand, and swung it around away from me.

The gun went off with a thunderous sound. The room smelled of burned fabric. In shock, I loosened my grip and she swung the gun back toward me as she stepped back.

"Now you're gonna pay."

The door began to open behind her. I hoped it was the police, Lady Kaldaire, my cousins. Anybody. I started to shake as my breath caught in my throat.

It was Jeb Marlowe.

"We need to get out of here. Now," he told her in a tone both demanding and panicked.

She never took her eyes off me. "Clean out the safe and meet me in the alley. The carriage is waiting." When he didn't move, she added, "Hurry."

"Lock her in and let's go."

"That's not smart." Her voice was cold.

"Do you want to hang? We don't want to leave any bodies here or the police will follow us the whole way to Australia."

"What about your friend Tom?"

"His family freed him."

Thank goodness Uncle Thomas was safe.

"You incompetent fool." Her scorn showed in her voice.

When she didn't move, he said, "Get going. That shot you fired woke up the neighborhood. The police are bound to find our carriage at any moment."

"What about my trunk?"

"Forget it. You can buy anything you want in Australia. We need to leave now."

He grabbed her arm without the gun. She tried to pull away, but he dragged her out the door. A second later, I heard a key in the lock.

Another game my cousins and I played with our grandfather. I had the door unlocked in about three seconds, thanks to a hairpin. When I heard footsteps on the stairs, I went out in the hall to follow them.

Staying to the side of the hall and then the stairs to avoid squeaking boards, I listened as Jeb said, "I'll clean out the office and meet you in the alley in a couple of minutes."

Two sets of footsteps went off in different directions. I followed the lighter tread of Lady Westkirk. I had almost caught up to her when she peered out a window overlooking the alley. "Wonderful," she murmured. "Bobbies."

Her footsteps came toward me. I slipped behind a large leafy potted fern and hoped she didn't notice me in the shadows.

She went right past me and I waited, holding my

breath until I could tell which way she went. Through the empty rooms and toward the front door.

When I was sure she was near the front door, I ran after her. I reached the open front door to find her on the outside steps. She started to turn, the gun swinging toward me, as I leaped out and landed on top of her.

She partially broke my fall, but all the air had been knocked from my lungs. She lost her grip on the gun, which landed next to the satchel.

Lady Westkirk recovered faster than I did. Just as my fingers touched the metal barrel, she grabbed the gun, snatched up the satchel, and stood up, pointing the gun at me.

Before I realized what was happening, my father grabbed her from behind. She whirled around and fired. My father went down in a spurt of blood.

Chapter Twenty-Six

How dare she kill my father? I may have hated him for years for abandoning my mother on her deathbed, but he was my father. I wasn't about to let her escape now. I was barely aware of shouts from the street. All I saw was her and that gun. I went after her.

Before she could aim to get off a second shot, I punched her in the jaw. "How dare you, you…"

She dropped the gun but stomped on my foot. I was hopping when she punched me just above the waist.

Didn't she know you never punch anyone in the corset? Gran had pulled my corset tight. It was like wearing a brick wall. I could barely feel her blow, while she certainly felt it in her hand. Bianca clutched her fingers while I, undamaged, slugged her in the face again.

She staggered back, cursing. Blood flowed down from her nose. I went after her and punched her again. This time she went down and stayed there.

Only then did I realize police whistles were shattering the calm of the West End neighborhood. I looked up to see several uniformed constables and Inspector James Russell surround us.

"She shot my father," I told anyone who would listen.

"It's all right," my father said, endeavoring to sit up as

he gripped his arm. "It just hurts." His expression was pitiful. "And there's a lot of blood."

"Someone get a physician. And arrest her. She killed Roxanne Hughes," I told James, pointing at Lady Westkirk as he reached me. "She and Jeb Marlowe."

"Who is she?" James asked as he handed the pistol to a sergeant.

"I'm Lady Bianca Westkirk." She sat up then, her face bloody, her hair falling about her shoulders, and her dress torn and dirty. But as she spoke, she lifted her chin and looked down her nose at James.

"We were sent over here to find you, Lady Westkirk. Your husband, Lord Westkirk, has been found dead. Murdered. You're to come with us," James told her.

That feeble old man? He could barely remember what day it was. I hardly knew him, but I was sorry to hear of his passing. That he was murdered sounded incredibly unfair.

At James's signal, one of the constables went to handcuff Lady Westkirk and she slapped him. A second bobby tried to help and was struck for his efforts. Finally, four burly constables were needed to restrain her.

Meanwhile, another constable brought the satchel over to James. "There's a lot of money in there, sir. Maybe one or two thousand pounds."

"Where did the money come from? Was it Lord Westkirk's?" James asked the handcuffed woman.

The fight out of her now as she sat on the pavement, her arms clamped behind her, Lady Westkirk pouted and looked away.

"It probably came from the Marlowe Club. You might want to go inside and find out how they raise money," I told him. "I went upstairs, and it is even more interesting than the gaming on the ground floor."

Lady Westkirk faced me then, giving me a look that should have struck me dead. Since she was handcuffed and the police had the gun, I made a face back at her.

James ignored us as he sent two constables and another detective into the club.

Then as James was arranging transport to Scotland Yard for Lady Westkirk, the gun, and the money while a physician from the crowd surrounding us saw to my father, more noises came from the front of the house.

A battered Jeb Marlowe, no longer looking lucky, came out of the club closely followed by Mr. Sumner. I realized Marlowe's arm was twisted up behind his back in his captor's grip. "Someone want to arrest this kidnapper?" Mr. Sumner asked.

"Who are you and who did he kidnap?" James said, walking over to them with two constables.

I hurried after them. "Inspector Russell, this is Mr. Sumner, assistant to the Duke of Blackford. I told the duke and duchess that my uncle had been kidnapped, and the duke sent Mr. Sumner to assist us in freeing him."

James looked over the larger man with the massive scar along one side of his face and then looked at me. "How did you know your uncle was here? And where is he?"

At that moment, Uncle Thomas wobbled out the front door of the club, looking worse than when I'd seen him in the basement. "Could someone help me?" he asked in a piteous tone.

A constable rushed over and helped him down the stairs.

"Why don't you assist your uncle while I deal with this," James said, looking askance at the confusion around him.

I hurried over to Uncle Thomas. "Why don't you sit on the steps while the inspector organizes things?"

The constable walked away to help his colleagues.

My uncle sat on the second step and then looked up at me with a grin. "Why don't I?"

I looked over my shoulder and found James couldn't see my uncle's face. "Are you all right?"

He gingerly felt his nose and then rubbed his right knee and ankle. "Nothing that time won't heal. How's Henry?"

At least he didn't call him my father. "He was shot in the arm."

He looked horrified. "Merciful heavens. Criminals are getting more violent all the time."

"How are Grandpapa and my cousins?" None of them had appeared with Uncle Thomas.

"Well away from here by now. We're letting Mr. Sumner take the credit," Uncle Thomas assured me.

I was immediately suspicious. "Why? Is there a reason why you don't want anyone to know they were here? A tangible reason?"

In the light of the streetlamp, I could see my uncle grin. "Ah, Emily, don't ask questions you don't want the answer to."

That told me all I needed to know. They'd stolen something while they were in there. Maybe a lot of somethings. Jewelry. Cash. Artworks. I decided to change the subject before James joined us. "Had you met Mr. Sumner before tonight?"

"No, but he's a handy man to have in a fight. Military trained and served in the colonies, I'd guess, but I think he's been in London for years doing something else. At any rate, we were glad to make his acquaintance."

James came over, bringing Mr. Sumner with him. "Mr. Sumner tells me he heard a cry for help in the back and went to investigate, but you, your father, and the rest of the people in the club were all out front. I wonder who he heard."

"My grandfather and my cousin Joe came with me and they went to the basement looking for my uncle while I looked for him upstairs. Mr. Marlowe has several thugs in his employ and there was quite a to-do trying to free my uncle. I believe it was Joe who called for help." I tried to look innocent, which was difficult in a ruined ballgown.

I gave Lady Westkirk a look that said I would destroy her for the damage to my gown. In return, she gave me a wicked smile.

"Where are they now?" James asked, sounding as if he didn't believe me.

"Joe took Grandpapa home. He was injured trying to free Uncle Thomas." Injured could mean anything. I wasn't lying. Not really.

"Inspector," I added, "I have something for you." I reached into my bag and pulled out the little gold container.

"Thank you." James signaled for one of the constables, murmured something to him as he handed off the gold box full of cocaine, and turned back to us as the constable hurried away. "I'm going to need statements from all of you, but it's late. I'd like for all of you to come to Scotland Yard tomorrow morning to give your account of this evening."

Sumner turned away.

"Mr. Sumner, if you would give your details to this constable here, you are free to leave for this evening," James told him.

Sumner nodded to James and spoke to the constable who hurried to us with his notepad and pencil. Then the former soldier strode away.

James turned his attention back to us. "I already have your details. I want you two, your father, your grandfather, and everyone else from your family who was here tonight to be at Scotland Yard in the morning. Am I clear?"

"Completely, Inspector. Now, if you will excuse me, I'll see about getting my father and uncle home to their families. They're both in need of medical care." I helped my uncle to stand.

"And be sure to take care of that jewelry you're wearing. There are plenty of thieves about," James said.

I nodded, my cheeks on fire. James suspected my jewelry had been stolen sometime in the past. I couldn't deny I had the same thought.

As my uncle got his feet firmly under him, the other

inspector came out of the house and murmured to James. They conferred a little while, glancing from time to time at Lady Westkirk and Jeb Marlowe, who were now both handcuffed. After watching them, I whispered to my uncle, "What did they find in the club?"

"From the looks on their faces, I suspect a whole list of charges for both Jeb and his lady friend." Uncle Thomas put a hand on my shoulder to help him walk as he limped forward.

"How did you get injured after you were freed?"

"The fight continued another minute or two, and I was struck on the leg with a coal shovel. Unfortunately, it was wielded by Petey."

I swallowed my laughter. "He is clumsy."

Uncle Thomas grumbled as he winced in pain.

"Is Bianca Westkirk the woman Mr. Marlowe was in love with a few years ago? The one Gran called 'the tart?'" I asked.

Uncle Thomas chuckled before groaning. "The very same. And it does appear Mum was right."

We joined my father, whose arm was bandaged. His jacket lay on the ground next to him, and I could see his shirt was bloody.

"You're a mess, Henry," my uncle said.

"I'm still prettier than you," my father said with a grin that ended in a grimace as he moved his arm. "Help the old man up, will you?" he said to me.

It took both Uncle Thomas and me to get my father standing, and then we moved the few feet to the automobile. "So," my father said, tossing his jacket on the back seat, "who's going to drive?"

The two men looked at each other and their bloodied limbs and burst out laughing. I knew it would be a long night.

I looked around for James to say good night to him, but he was disappearing through the front doorway of the club with the other inspector. I wondered what they had found.

Then I watched my father and his brother try to figure out how to get into the automobile and, more important, drive. And then there was the matter of cranking the engine to start it.

I knew I'd be better off walking home.

Chapter Twenty-Seven

When my father and uncle were ready to leave, I climbed into the back seat. It required lifting my skirt obscenely high in front of the bystanders who lingered, but it was late and I was too tired to care. I suspected I'd have to climb out and walk. I muttered my opinion, but my father insisted that I have faith.

Fortunately, a constable was still available out front of the Marlowe Club who knew something about motor-cars and enjoyed working with them. My uncle convinced him to crank the motor while my uncle reached over from the passenger seat and fiddled with the choke as well as other buttons and levers I didn't know the name of. My father sat in the driver's seat and worked the pedals.

When the auto roared to life, my uncle gave the bobby a jaunty wave and we drove off, nearly sideswiping a carriage as we left. The constable shook his head, the carriage driver shook his fist, and the horses pranced skittishly down the street. I tried to ignore how close we had come to disaster.

Our drive across London was salvaged only by the lateness of the hour. My father and uncle tried to synchronize their movements in driving the automobile, but this only resulted in the vehicle hopping as the engine made grinding noises.

Steering was problematic. With both men trying to maneuver the vehicle, and with different ideas about where the vehicle should be, we came dangerously close to other objects. We nearly collided with a goods wagon, causing shouts and threats. At one corner, we bounced off the curb and nearly took out a streetlamp. The few pedestrians out stared at our weaving path and ran into alleys if we came too close. By the time we reached the East End, the two brothers were cursing at each other.

If they weren't so busy trying to keep the automobile from stalling, they would have come to blows.

Steering became particularly difficult in the narrow alleyways near my grandparents' house, but by then both men had figured out how to cooperate on their steering while shifting gears and working the pedals.

When we pulled into the barn and were greeted by the whole family, half of them holding lanterns, the brothers collapsed into each other's arms and slapped each other on the back. All their anger was forgotten once they accomplished their task and made it home.

Garrett and Tommy helped me down from the back seat. "Wow, what happened to you?" my cousin Petey asked. "You look like something the cat dragged in."

"I ruined my best ballgown in the service of catching a killer and rescuing Uncle Thomas," I told him, my nose in the air.

"Well, come in the house and let's get a look at all of you," Gran said. "And we'll see if we can't repair the gown."

"I need to get home. I've got to open the shop in the

morning," I told her.

"Nonsense," my grandmother decreed. "Sleep here. I'll find something for you to wear to bed. I've already sent a message to Noah to tell him you'd spend the night here so he wouldn't worry."

I looked at her, surprised she'd been concerned that Noah might be anxious. "Thank you."

She smiled and put her arms around my waist. "Thank you for helping to bring the whole family back safely tonight."

I hugged her. "That's what families do."

* * *

At sunup, I declined an offer of a wonderful-smelling breakfast and hurried home in the plain dark muslin gown I'd worn to my grandparents' house before I had put on my evening gown. Once back at the flat, I changed into a green dress with white lace trim that went well with my reddish hair and fair complexion and joined Noah for some tea and toast.

"I got the message from your grandmother. You must have had quite an evening," Noah said. "Pass me the jam, please."

Images from the previous evening—Uncle Thomas tied up and bloody, fighting with Lady Westkirk, my father bleeding from a gunshot wound—flashed through my mind. "Nothing I want to repeat. And I have to go to Scotland Yard this morning to give my statement."

"Which of your father's clan has been arrested?"

I smiled. "None, actually. They've arrested the two people who killed Lady Theo Hughes and kidnapped my uncle."

"Why did they kidnap him?"

I felt suspicion grow in the back of my mind. "I suppose I'll find out this morning. Will you and Jane be able to manage without me for a few hours?"

"We'll have to. You can't ignore a summons from Scotland Yard. We'll say you're out on an appointment." He took a sip of his tea. "Will you see Inspector Russell this morning?"

"I hope so." After seeing me aid my father's family last night, I wasn't sure he wanted to see me.

After I opened the shop and gave Jane a brief account of where I'd be and what to expect in the shop that morning—gossip being a staple of aristocratic life—I put on my green spring hat with plenty of white roses on the flat brim and traveled by omnibus to Scotland Yard.

From the gate, I was escorted to one of the entrances and led upstairs to a hallway where I was told to sit and wait. I wasn't sitting in one of their wooden, straight-backed chairs for long before my grandfather, Cousin Joe, Uncle Thomas, and my father joined me.

We greeted each other and then Uncle Thomas sat next to me and asked, "Have you seen Jeb Marlowe?"

"Don't you mean Lucky Marlowe?" I asked.

"Bet he doesn't feel too lucky today," Joe said.

My grandfather silenced him with a stern look.

"I've always known him as Jeb," my uncle said. "And I'd really like to talk to him now, away from her ladyship."

"Why did they kidnap you?" I couldn't figure out the reason.

"They were afraid if the two of us talked, you'd realize they were the ones who'd killed Lady Theo, or Lady Roxanne, or whatever her proper name was, and have the police stop them from sailing for Australia."

"They said that?" I was amazed. If they said that in front of my uncle, that must mean they didn't expect him to live long enough to tell what he'd heard.

"Yeah." He exchanged a look with my father, who grimaced.

"When is the ship supposed to sail?"

"Noon today."

We'd stopped them just in time. I didn't want to think how close the killers had come to escaping.

At that moment, I heard men's voices coming toward us. As they came around the corner, I saw a middle-aged man in a well-made black suit and vest with a high white shirt collar haranguing a uniformed constable. "—should be hanged," he was saying.

"If you'd please wait there, sir—"

"My lord. I'm Lord Westkirk now."

"My lord," and with that the constable gave him a slight bow, "the inspector will see you soon."

The new Lord Westkirk looked us over. Uncle Thomas had obviously been in a fight, my father's arm was in a sling, and Joe was sporting a black eye. Even my grandfather looked bruised. He nodded to me and sat in a chair a little distance from us.

"My condolences on the death of your father," I told him. "I'd met your father recently and he was a lovely man."

"He was completely barmy, marrying that woman." He stopped to stare at me. "You're not a friend of that woman, are you?"

"If you mean Lady Westkirk, no. We were involved in stopping her from escaping until the police arrived," I said, gesturing to my father and his family.

"Good. She should hang for what she did."

"What did she do to your father?"

"She killed him." He folded his arms over his chest and scowled.

I decided to try again. "How did she kill him?"

The man's face twisted in grief for a moment. "Early last evening, she sent the nurse after a glass of milk for my father, and when the nurse returned, my father was dead and that woman had fled the house."

"Are you sure he didn't die naturally?"

"There were marks from a small pair of hands around his throat."

"Oh, dear. I'm sorry," I told him. And if she'd murder her elderly husband, was there anyone she would hesitate to kill? Her actions were as reprehensible as anything I'd read about in the penny press. She and Lord Theo were a pair, and Lucky Marlowe was no better. I was glad none were free any longer to hurt their fellow man.

"Yes, well, thank you." He cleared his throat. "So why are you here?"

"To give our statements to the police about my uncle's kidnapping and my father being shot by Lady Westkirk."

The new Lord Westkirk looked from one of us to another. "Heavens. Is he going to live?"

"She just winged me," my father said and grinned.

Uncle Thomas murmured "Oh, well," earning a dark look from my grandfather.

"Then you had a very lucky escape from her," the new lord huffed out.

At that moment, James came down the hall with a constable and stopped in front of my uncle. "Mr. Marlowe wants to speak to you and your niece. You may have a few minutes while I speak to Lord Westkirk."

A bobby led us down a corridor and then opened the door to a stuffy, windowless room that smelled of fear and sweat. Marlowe sat on one side of a heavy, scarred table, and there were two straight-backed chairs on the other side for us. Another constable stood by the door and shut it once we were inside.

Marlowe glared at the bobby. "Can't you give us a minute alone?"

The uniformed policeman shook his head. Otherwise, he remained motionless.

"Why'd you do it?" Uncle Thomas asked.

"I kept getting dragged into things after the events had already started. God help me, I love her, but I didn't kill anyone and had no intention of ending anyone's life. And I didn't want to kidnap you. None of this was my idea."

"Did you know she murdered her husband?" I asked.

"What? No." Marlowe looked stunned. "Why would she kill that harmless old fool?"

"Were you going to run away together?"

"Yes." He slumped dejectedly in his chair. "We should have boarded the ship this morning."

"Australia? *Queen of the Orient*?" Uncle Thomas asked.

Marlowe nodded.

"How much did you really know about Victoria Abbott's death?" I asked.

Marlowe nodded his head toward the constable.

I started to choke. Rather convincingly, I thought. After I was pounded on the back, my uncle got the constable to get me a glass of water.

The second he was gone, Marlowe said, "The first thing I knew, she was dead. Bianca said Hughes killed her, but she had taken Lady Abbott up to the room he had hired for the night."

"Was that her role in your club? Taking innocent young women to men like Lord Theo?" I kept my voice down, but my distaste carried.

"She did—assist people. I didn't keep track of what she did. Guess I didn't want to know. That particular night when I found the three of them, they were in bed in various stages of undress."

Good grief. No wonder my grandfather didn't want me to find out what was going on in that club. And they were all married. To other people. Aristocrats had a lot to answer for.

I was sitting there shaking my head, angered at what Jeb Marlowe had said when the constable came in and handed me a cup of water. I took a sip and thanked him.

"Were you friends with Lord Abbott?" I asked.

"No. I barely knew either of them."

I raised my eyebrows at him.

He leaned forward. "Really. They didn't come in

often."

"When did you complete the sale of the club?" Uncle Thomas asked.

"Last night," Marlowe replied.

"Was that the satchel of money Lady Westkirk was carrying?" I asked.

He scrunched up his face this time when he nodded.

"She wasn't supposed to run off by herself with the money, was she?" I asked.

He shook his head with just the tiniest of movement.

"Who did you sell the club to?" I asked.

"My former partner. Armstrong," he murmured so the policeman couldn't hear.

"Why did you tell us you were leaving the country with Roxanne? You were very convincing," I told him.

"Bianca had told me to say that if anyone asked. She didn't want Willard to hear of her plans to leave. I felt badly when I learned Roxanne died. I liked her. I really did."

"You didn't feel so badly that you were unwilling to help move her body after Lady Westkirk slit her throat," I said, glaring at him.

Uncle Thomas flinched before he leaned forward to stare directly into Marlowe's face. "You fool. Why did you help her? You used to be so much better than this."

Marlowe lowered his head, unable to meet his old friend's gaze. "I know I'm a fool. The worst of it is, I still love her."

James came in then with another detective and we were escorted out. A sergeant took my statement with little interest and few questions before I was shown back into the hallway to await the other members of my family.

According to Jeb Marlowe, Theo Hughes had killed Victoria Abbott. Unknown to the police, Theo had in turn been killed accidentally by his sister-in-law, Lady Dorothy Frethorton. The current Lord Westkirk was certain Lady Westkirk had murdered the late lord. But what about Roxanne? Poor Roxanne had been killed to ensure her silence, left dead in the park with neither clothes nor jewelry.

Jewelry that the Duchess of Blackford said Roxanne wouldn't have pawned since it didn't belong to her. Jewelry that was missing.

I looked around me as I remembered the rattle when Lady Westkirk hit Joe with the satchel. "Excuse me, constable. Has anyone examined the satchel Lady Westkirk was carrying?"

"Don't worry, miss. We'll look into it." He started to walk away from me.

"I need to see Inspector Russell now. It's important."

"He's busy now, miss."

"This will only take a second," I told him in my most reasonable tone.

"I'm sorry." He walked off.

As soon as he was far enough away, I jumped up and ran down the scuffed black and white flooring to the room where I knew James was. I threw open the door and said, "Inspector Rus—" before I was grabbed by the constable, quickly aided by the sergeant.

James rose from his chair, as did the other two men in

the room. The policemen started to drag me away.

"Wait," James said in a commanding voice. "What is so important?"

"Have you examined the satchel the money was in yet?"

"We counted the money."

"No." I wiggled away from the policemen and tried to catch my breath. "The satchel. The lining. I think there may be stolen jewelry in there."

James Russell glanced at the sergeant. "Bring the satchel to my office."

Chapter Twenty-Eight

I was ordered back to my chair in the hallway while James, the sergeant, and the other detective strode away. My grandfather, who'd been sitting in the hall watching all this, murmured, "What's going on, Pet?"

"I was at the Duchess of Blackford's ball when some of her jewelry was stolen. When we tried to talk to Lady Westkirk a short time later, she shoved us out of her way as she rushed from the house. I think she might have jewelry she's taken from various people, including the duchess and Lady Theo, hidden in the satchel she carried away from the club last night."

I hoped she did. She was taking that hold-all away to Australia with her. I'd be very embarrassed if she wasn't taking the jewels, too.

If she'd already sold them, I would look foolish.

Joe and then my father rejoined us after they were questioned, as we all waited in the hall on hard chairs to find out if my guess was correct. Then the three policemen returned and walked into an office with the satchel.

Unable to contain my curiosity, I walked into the office, followed by my relatives. The money had been moved elsewhere, making it easier for James to feel around in the bottom of the empty bag and then cut the fabric with his pocket knife.

With a look at me, he began to lay out fabulous necklaces, bracelets, and rings on his desk.

My grandfather peered over my shoulder and said, "I think you'll find the ruby necklace belongs to the Duchess of Wallingford, and the emeralds belong to the Duchess of Blackford."

"You're familiar with them?" James asked, his tone dry.

"I have a fondness for beautiful jewelry," my grandfather replied without an ounce of irony.

"I'll bet." James turned to the sergeant. "Notify both Wallingford and Blackford we may have recovered their missing jewelry and to identify it here at Scotland Yard. However, we'll need it for court proceedings before we can return their property."

He turned to the other inspector. "We'll need to tag each item of jewelry found in here and put it back in the strong room. And Sergeant," he added, "please escort the Gates family out of the compound."

We went quietly. As we exited Scotland Yard, I heard my father and uncle both give a sigh of relief. Cousin Joe looked back and said, "I wonder where the strong room is."

"No," my grandfather said, "some things are not meant to be thought about."

Joe walked on, his head down.

Uncle Thomas put his arm around Joe's shoulders. "We've all had those thoughts when we were your age. But believe me, private houses and clubs like the one last night are much safer. And just as lucrative."

"My cousins did all right, then, last night?" I asked and immediately regretted my curiosity. I could feel my cheeks growing hot.

My uncle winked at me. "They did, all thanks to you."

I wasn't sure I wanted to hear this, but I asked anyway. "What happened after I chased Lady Westkirk out of the club?"

"Jeb Marlowe ran upstairs, leaving his goons to fight us. Garrett and Tommy slipped upstairs and saw Lady Westkirk and you leave by the front door. They waited for Marlowe to come out of the office with another satchel. We were right. Apparently, he didn't trust the fair Bianca with all of the funds for their new life." Uncle Thomas had a smile on his face.

"And?" I asked through tight lips. I felt certain I would not approve.

"Joe took care of Jeb Marlowe, while Garrett and Tommy took care of the satchel. Hearing steps coming toward them, Garrett and Tommy went out the office window, leaving Joe with an unconscious club owner to face the footsteps alone. It was Mr. Sumner."

"Jeb woke up, saw Mr. Sumner's scarred face, and meekly followed his directions. I told Mr. Sumner I was going to care for my grandfather, and that is exactly what I did." Joe gave me a cheery grin.

"Then there is no reason, you little scamp, for trying to take on Scotland Yard and their strong room," my grandfather said in a stern voice. Then he ruffled Joe's hair.

We walked a short distance before my father said,

"Inspector Russell was quite willing to listen to you and let you enter rooms he wouldn't let us get within a mile of." His gaze was penetrating. "Emily, what's going on?"

I felt my cheeks heat. "I'm sure James—"

"James?" My father's eyes widened as his brows went to his hairline.

Now my cheeks were on fire. "I've worked with Inspector Russell before."

Joe and Uncle Thomas burst out laughing. My grandfather wore his cherubic expression.

"You've been working with a Peeler?" The smoke I saw coming out of my father's ears was not all due to my imagination.

"Not—just—working," Joe gasped out as he guffawed and clung to his uncle so he'd not fall onto the cobblestones.

"Harry," my grandfather said, "Detective Inspector James Russell has been courting your daughter. Get over it."

"Get over it?" My father could probably be heard across London.

"It's her business and none of ours." Then in as stern a voice as I'd ever heard, Grandfather said, "Leave her be. And you two," he pointed at Uncle Thomas and Joe, "stop it now."

Then Grandpapa winked at me.

* * *

Amazingly, I managed to work uninterrupted by murder the rest of that morning and half the afternoon. It felt wonderful to talk to customers and create hats without the threat of having to chase down clues.

Then Lady Kaldaire paid a visit to my shop, accompanied by the Duchess of Blackford.

After a round of curtsies, followed by Lady Kaldaire greeting my other customers with her usual grace and charm as she made comments on their choice of hats, she said, "I've just heard from the Duchess of Wallingford. It seems Scotland Yard has recovered the jewelry stolen from Lady Theo the night she was murdered."

One of my customers, I don't know who, gasped. They all leaned forward without looking directly at anyone else.

"I know," I said in a neutral tone. I wasn't about to entertain my customers with tales of gunshots in the night, kidnappings, and stolen gems.

"I thought you might." Lady Kaldaire's gaze burned a hole in my brain.

I kept working, concentrating on the slant of a businessman's wife's hat and not looking directly at Lady Kaldaire. "Do you still want me to come over for tea after I close the shop?" I asked. That was a hint for her to be quiet about the murders here and now. I'd tell her all later, over tea and scones and jam.

There was dead silence for ten seconds before Lady Kaldaire brightened and said, "Yes. You're busy. We'll talk at tea time." She then gave us all a farewell that made me think of royalty leaving.

"I'll see you later," the duchess said to Lady Kaldaire with a smile. "I'd like to order a hat. May I sit over here?" she asked me.

"Yes, Your Grace. I'd be honored." Not certain what the

situation called for, I curtsied again.

Jane and all three of our other customers stared at me and then at the duchess.

"Oh, I'll wait with you. Who knows what ideas I may get for my own hats," Lady Kaldaire said and sat next to the Duchess of Blackford as if they were the closest of friends. The duchess kept a neutral expression but her eyes gleamed with amusement.

I knew I needed to get my business back on track, especially with statements from Lady Kaldaire that left people wondering. "Mrs. Kerrick," I asked Jane's customer, "how do you like the fit of your hat?"

* * *

The shop was closed for the evening and Jane had gone home when there came a knock on the door. I opened it to find James on the doorstep, his bowler hat in his hands. "May I come in?" he asked as if we were strangers.

I stepped back and held the door open for him. He entered and shut the door behind his back.

"Am I forgiven?" he asked.

"Forgiven for what? You haven't done anything wrong." Unless he'd arrested someone in my family and I didn't know about it yet.

"Claiming your successes as my own. Or at least not setting the record straight. The thought in Scotland Yard is that I was called to a ruckus at a private club and recovered stolen jewels and a killer who was about to escape justice. No one is giving you or Mr. Sumner any credit. 'Just a little assistance from private citizens,' they're saying."

"That's wonderful. You can use the good opinion of your colleagues. I don't care, and my father's family doesn't want any notoriety." I ducked my head to hide my blush. Notoriety was the kiss of death for a conman.

I hurriedly continued. "Mr. Sumner is an employee of the Duke of Blackford, and when the duke heard I was going over to the Marlowe Club because I suspected there might be stolen jewels there as well as my kidnapped uncle, the duke sent Mr. Sumner over to look out for the duke's interests." Well, that wasn't too far from the truth.

"A handy man to have on your side," James said in a neutral tone. I knew he didn't believe me, but he didn't press for the truth.

I nodded. "How are you going to prove Lady Westkirk killed Roxanne, I mean Lady Theo?"

"I'm not. The only death we can pin on her is that of her husband." When I let loose a sigh, James put his hands on my shoulders. "She can only hang once."

"But she told me—"

"The barristers would call it hearsay. They could say she was joking."

I decided I didn't like barristers. "Are you certain you can get a conviction of Lady Westkirk? She's very elegant and personable. She's young and exotic. She'll charm the judge and the jury." I stared into his eyes and he gave me a confident smile.

"Emily, we have a lot of evidence, as well as witnesses to her dislike of her husband, her craving wealth, and her actions last night. Juries don't like women who are too greedy and disdainful of their husbands. It makes them nervous. Makes them worry about their own wives."

"Then Lady Theo's killer will be punished, even if it's not for her murder." I slipped my arms around his neck. "Thank you."

"What about Lord Theo's killer?" James asked me. "You kept telling me that he was murdered, too, and not dead from natural causes as the death certificate says."

Chapter Twenty-Nine

"I was wrong." Wrong about Lord Theo Hughes, timid Lady Dorothy, and all of the Wallingfords. I couldn't let him suspect what I had guessed, that a woman had accidentally killed Lord Theo while protecting her baby. "His death was due to injuries, but they were all caused by a simple accident. The doctor was right."

"Good. I don't want to dig around a duke's home again, looking for evidence. Especially for evidence you now tell me isn't there." He pulled me in tightly and whispered into my ear. "I'm glad this case is over and we can get back to courting without Lady Kaldaire interrupting."

I hoped she wouldn't interrupt again. Somehow, I knew I couldn't be so lucky.

He kissed me then. We didn't talk for a long while, but when he finally pulled away, curiosity made me ask, "Can you tell me what Jeb Marlowe and Lady Westkirk said when you questioned them?"

"Marlowe wouldn't be quiet. He told us about Lady Victoria Abbott dying in bed with..." he stopped and reddened.

I decided not to tell him what I knew about that episode.

"Never mind," he hurried on. "She was dead when he

was called by one of the maids, with only Lord Hughes and Lady Westkirk in the room. Marlowe didn't want to call us, it'd be bad for business, so Lady Westkirk said she'd take care of everything and to send Lord Armstrong upstairs.

"Marlowe thought that sounded like a bad idea, letting someone else in on the secret, but Lady Westkirk said he was reliable. Marlowe lent them the use of the back stairs and went down to his office. He said it made him nervous, but they assured him Lady Abbott became overexcited and just swooned and died."

I had never heard of a woman dying that way. I suspected men were gullible, or overconfident, at heart. Dying from overexcitement, indeed.

"He swears he knows nothing of the carriage race or the stolen carriage that Lady Abbott's body was discovered in. He says he didn't know she was strangled, which we had already learned from our pathologist." James squeezed my hand when I shuddered.

"Lady Westkirk told me a different story this morning when she was questioned. She said Jeb Marlowe helped get rid of the body and tip the carriage over in the park with Victoria's body inside." He shook his head.

"Once again, we can't charge anyone on such little evidence and so many charges and countercharges."

"It sounds like the only people who could have strangled her were Lord Theo or Lady Westkirk," I said.

"I'll get to the rest of Lady Westkirk's statement in a minute. Marlowe had a lot to say about Lady Theo's death, too."

"Did he admit he and Lady Westkirk carried her out of

the tunnel and over to the park?"

"Yes, but he says Lady Theo was already dead when he reached the tunnel."

I felt my eyes widen. "Neither one admits to killing Roxanne?"

"Yes. Marlowe's story is Lady Westkirk told him to meet her in the mews behind the Wallingford mansion. It was dark out there, and he didn't see her until she was right in front of him. Lady Westkirk said she needed his help and led him down into the tunnel. He said he didn't know the tunnel existed.

"He said he was shocked when he found Lady Theo with her neck slit. Lady Westkirk said she found her that way. He wanted to leave her, but Lady Westkirk wanted her moved. She said there would be a hunt for Lady Theo and we, the police, would take his club apart. He couldn't afford that."

That explained why Jeb Marlowe wanted the body found quickly. But why did Lady Westkirk?

"Marlowe said he helped Lady Westkirk undress the body because there was blood all over her clothes. She put the scarf on Lady Theo's neck to hide the cut. And she put the clothes in the hold-all. He doesn't know why there was no blood on the cape Lady Theo was wearing, but there wasn't, so they wrapped her in that to carry her."

"What happened to Roxanne's missing clothes?"

"We found them in Westkirk House, stuffed in a corner of the attic."

"Why did it matter that there was blood on the ball gown? Marlowe shouldn't have cared about that." Their actions were making no sense.

"I suspect he did it because Lady Westkirk told him to, but what I suspect is worthless as testimony. Marlowe admitted he'd become frightened of her, thinking he was next. That's why he said he sold his share of the club and made plans to emigrate."

I shook my head as I looked at James. "That makes no sense. Why did he buy two passages to Australia if he were afraid of her?"

"That's what we asked him." He smiled.

"And?" I couldn't imagine what he said.

"That's when he decided he was tired of talking to us and wouldn't say another word."

"Has he mentioned who his partner is in the club? You said he sold his share."

"Lord Armstrong. And we can't touch him without very good evidence of a crime because his wife is a royal. The higher-ups at the Yard don't want to run afoul of the Palace."

"Then you don't want to question him about what he knows of these murders?"

James shook his head. "So far, neither Marlowe nor Lady Westkirk have implicated him in any crime except for moving a body, and I can't see taking that to my superiors."

"Are your superiors interested in Lord Armstrong's ownership of a club where a murder took place along with being a bawdy house and a gaming den? Lady Westkirk also told me Lord Armstrong was the purveyor of cocaine at the Marlowe Club."

"No one will tell us lowly detectives, but I suspect word will get back to the royals by way of my superiors having a quiet chat with Palace officials. And I wouldn't want to be Lord Armstrong when that happens."

I felt satisfied that Lord Armstrong would face some sort of punishment for his part in this ghastly affair. But the killer? "What did Lady Westkirk tell you?"

"She just kept repeating that Marlowe had threatened her and everything she did, she did by his order. Moving Lady Abbott's body. Moving Lady Theo's body. Hiding her clothes and jewels. And she claimed Willard, the new Lord Westkirk, killed his father in a fit of rage when his father said he was changing his will to favor Lady Westkirk."

"Do you believe her?" I certainly didn't.

"The bruising on the old Lord Westkirk's neck was from much smaller hands than his son has. After we told her that, she refused to say another word."

"It's enough to convict her?" I asked. I hoped it was. There was no way she'd pay for her role in the notorious Lady Roxanne's death.

"It's enough to hang her." A look of suspicion grew in his gray eyes. "Why are you so interested? You never met Lady Abbott or Lady Theo in life."

"From what I heard, someone, perhaps Lady Westkirk, began spreading terrible rumors about Lady Theo. And the Duchess of Wallingford blamed Roxanne for the evil things Lord Theo did. Her life was made a misery through no fault of her own, and then that life was cut short. And Lady Victoria Abbott was barely out of the schoolroom. Her life ended before it began. These murders weren't right. They weren't fair."

I took a deep breath to fight the tears threatening to spill down my cheeks from frustration and added, "Lady Abbott's killer is dead, but Roxanne's killer is still alive to face a judge and the hangman."

I thought again about why Lady Westkirk would face a judge. "I'll never understand why she killed her husband. Unless she thought with him dead, she'd be able to escape to the ship and leave England without being stopped. Perhaps she thought only the old Lord Westkirk would think to have her followed, and the new Lord Westkirk would have the doctors hide his cause of death like Lord Theo Hughes's."

James gave me a skeptical gaze, but he didn't question my words. "She is crazy if she thinks that."

"I think maybe she is crazy. Both her and Lord Theo Hughes." I couldn't hide my shudder.

"Where do you get all these ideas and information about people?" He sounded both amazed and angry.

"I meet all sorts of aristocrats, most of them with disreputable secrets. And they all gossip. Lady Westkirk and I had a long talk at the club last night. At gunpoint." When he continued to look stern, I became serious. "I'm glad this is over, James. I just want to make beautiful hats and spend time with my family and friends. I don't want to do any more investigating. That's your job."

He muttered, "If only you weren't so good at it," before he kissed me again.

This time when we came up for air, I asked, "Will you stay for dinner?"

"I wish I could, but I have a great deal of paperwork to clean up from this case and questions to answer, starting with whose money was in the hold-all. Both Marlowe and Lady Westkirk are claiming it."

"I think most of it is Jeb Marlowe's from when he sold the club. Is he being charged?"

"They're still debating that in the commissioner's office. It is a private club, after all, and a degree of latitude is allowed. Something Lord Armstrong is counting on."

"Dinner tomorrow night?" I asked, making no attempt to keep the hope out of my voice.

"I'd love to. Eight?"

My reply was swallowed in his kiss. We lingered that way for a while before James pulled away. "I have to get back."

"I'll see you tomorrow night."

A few more kisses and he was gone.

I finished straightening the shop, smiling to myself about James's kisses, before I recalled I was due at Lady Kaldaire's for tea. She'd want answers from me, and I was finally in a position to give them to her. Something I couldn't do in my shop. I wouldn't be surprised if the Duchess of Blackford, the former investigator and bookshop owner, was there, too.

As much as I hoped I'd never have to repeat this experience, I suspected the time would come when Lady Kaldaire would insist I solve another crime. And since my father and his family would never give up their illegal careers, I was certain I'd have to cooperate.

If I ever had to carry out another investigation, I

hoped the Duchess of Blackford would assist. Lady Kaldaire had the determination, but the duchess had the experience. And with me now having been involved in two successfully concluded investigations, Lady Kaldaire would no doubt consider us unstoppable.

I wished I had her optimism.

I shouted up the stairs to Noah that I was invited to tea and would be home soon, put on my hat and gloves, and headed out to give the ladies a full report.

I hope you've enjoyed Emily's newest adventure. I'm giving away a short story, **Emily's First Case**, to readers of my enewsletter. This story takes us back to the reign of Queen Victoria as a stubborn tomboy Emily learns about investigating—and the power of family. If you'd like a FREE short story, type https://dl.bookfunnel.com/r8bz6j3vsu in your search engine and sign up for my semiannual newsletter.

In between newsletters, keep up with my latest news at www.kateparkerbooks.com and www.facebook.com/Author.Kate.Parker, or check out www.bookbub.com/authors/kate-parker

Author's Notes

Part of this story was born of the CDC War on Opioid Addiction. At the time of this story, sale, possession, and use of cocaine was legal and totally unregulated in the US and the UK. Twenty years before this tale, doctors were recommending its use as a stimulant similar to caffeine. By 1905, there was a great deal of anecdotal evidence blaming the use of cocaine for insanity and deaths, and many people believed it should be banned. However, regulation and prohibition of the use of cocaine didn't come until more than ten years after the events of this story in both the US and UK. Organized treatment for cocaine addiction was even further into the future.

Of interest to some readers may be the appearance of Georgia and the Duke of Blackford. Seven years has passed since their wedding at the end of **The Detecting Duchess**, and there have been changes to their lives, notably in the form of three children. Changes have come to the lives of John and Emma Sumner as well, but Georgia and Emma remain the closest of friends. I hope you've enjoyed the introduction of some of the Archivist Society members into **Murder at the Marlowe Club** and into Emily's investigation.

I'd like to thank Hannah Meredith, Jen Parker, Eleanor Shelton, Elizabeth Flynn and Jennifer Brown for their help in making **Murder at the Marlowe Club** the best it could be. As always, mistakes are my own.

I hope you've enjoyed Emily's adventures. If you do, tell someone. Word of mouth is still the best way to discover good new reads. Reviews are also a good way to tell others about books that you've enjoyed. And your enjoyment of Emily's adventures is the reason this book is out in the world.

About the Author

Kate Parker caught the reading bug early, and the writing bug soon followed. She's always lived in a home surrounded by books and dust bunnies. After spending twelve years in New Bern, North Carolina, the real-life location for the town in The Mystery at Chadwick House, she packed up and moved to Colorado to be closer to family. Now instead of seeing the rivers and beaches of the Atlantic coast, she has the Rocky Mountains for scenery.

Now that with **Murder at the Marlowe Club** Kate has brought out the second of the Milliner Mysteries, she is hard at work on the fifth in the Deadly Series, **Deadly Travels**. This new story will introduce us to Olivia's life as 1939 brings the world closer to war. Kate reports she is having fun creating new stories to entertain readers and chaos to challenge her characters.

Follow Kate and her deadly examination of history at www.KateParkerbooks.com

and www.Facebook.com/Author.Kate.Parker/

and www.bookbub.com/authors/kate-parker.

Made in the USA
Columbia, SC
16 April 2020